To Laura

Fondly

Norma Carafacci

Crying for Argentina

Crying for Argentina

Norma Caravacci

iUniverse, Inc.
Bloomington

Crying for Argentina

iUniverse books may be ordered through booksellers or by contacting:

iUniverse
1663 Liberty Drive
Bloomington, IN 47403
www.iuniverse.com
1-800-Authors (1-800-288-4677)

ISBN: 978-1-4620-5320-9 (sc)
ISBN: 978-1-4620-5322-3 (hc)
ISBN: 978-1-4620-5321-6 (e)

Printed in the United States of America

iUniverse rev. date: 09/26/2011

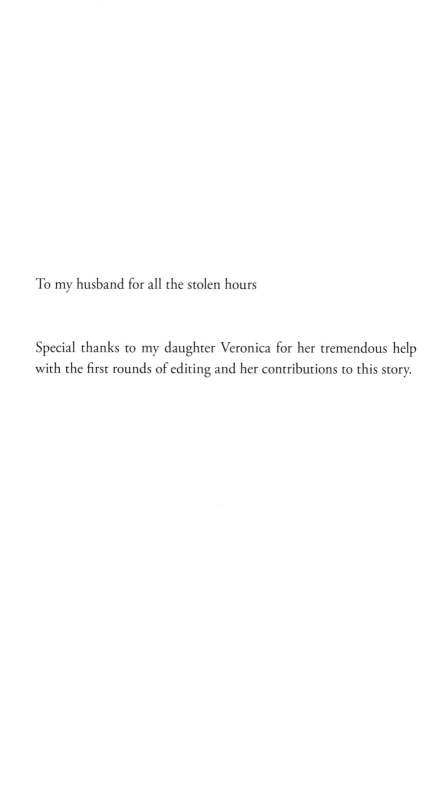

To my husband for all the stolen hours

Special thanks to my daughter Veronica for her tremendous help with the first rounds of editing and her contributions to this story.

"Everything has been figured out, except how to live."
Jean-Paul Sartre

"He who has a why to live can bear almost any how."
Friedrich Nietzsche

"Home is not where you are from, but where you are wanted."
Abraham Verghese

Chapter One

Evita's Gift

~❦~

N ina Salvatti thought she'd never escape the turmoil that had
taken over her life. Ernesto's girlfriend was pregnant, and
David was moving in with his father. At least Buenos Aires looked
beautiful. Tossing the magazine that focused on Argentina's entrance
into the modern age onto her bed, she realized divorce hadn't been
legal there until 1987.

Tears poured down her face. She needed to see her mom.

Pulling out her suitcase, she grabbed a stack of shirts, and dumped
them carelessly in it. *Damn Ernesto and his slut of a girlfriend.* They were
probably laughing at her, probably drinking champagne. She hated
them. She wasn't sure if she'd ever hated anyone before. Well, maybe
Héctor Torres. She hadn't thought of Héctor in years. He had liked to
torment her when she was a little girl growing up in Argentina.

Nina laughed. She tossed her underwear in the suitcase.

She had a lot of memories. People always said passions ran deep
in Argentina. She had been feeling the passion all her life.

~❦~

Nina tried to finish her hot chocolate and toast, but she was too
excited to eat. She'd spent extra time that morning picking out her
prettiest outfit from her closet. She looked down, admiring her white

dress with little pink flowers and matching shoes. Her mother, Estela Salvatti, had taken an extra half hour to curl her long hair and put ribbons in it. Today wasn't an ordinary school day.

As she rode to school, Nina looked out the window. She thought the sun looked brighter. Normally it resembled a pale daffodil. Today it seemed like a bright sunflower. She smiled at her own cleverness.

They pulled up in front of the school.

"What do you do if someone asks you a question?" her mom asked.

"Always keep my hands together neatly in front of me, smile, nod, and say thank you."

"Well, answer the question if needed. Then do all those things. I know some of your classmates tease you, but today is not the time for any of that."

"I know, but it's never my fault, Mom," Nina said, impatient. She heard all the time how she should always be on her best behavior, no matter what anyone else did. There was no telling what her parents would do if they heard that she had misbehaved at the president of Argentina's house.

Nina's teacher, Mrs. Ingleses, was waiting. Estela put her hand in Nina's and squeezed it tight. "Only six, and you're already having a once-in-a-lifetime day. Enjoy yourself."

Her teacher had picked Nina and a few of her classmates to visit the Casa Rosada, the Pink House, the government residency where Juan Perón lived and from where he ruled the country. Part of Perón's policy to improve Argentina was for him and his wife, Evita, to welcome schoolchildren to their home and give them gifts.

Nina waited in the courtyard with the other children for the car that would take them to the Perón residence. She shifted from one foot to the other thinking that Evita was beautiful and glamorous.

"And then Evita gave them a new car," a boy said.

Nina leaned to the side to see who was talking. Everyone had gathered in a tight circle around Franco Escobar.

"She floated down the hall like an angel," Franco said.

He was definitely talking about Evita. Nina felt her blood race. She'd heard about kids in her school receiving bicycles and new cars for their families. She heard that a few had even received new homes. Glamorous Evita, the beautiful, blond woman who attended gala functions in Dior gowns and fur coats and acted like Santa Claus, showering everyone who visited her home with unbelievable gifts.

Nina sighed. That world was far from the simple life her parents provided. Her family belonged to the middle class based purely on their European blood, not on their income. Nina's mom made all her clothes. She didn't mind. Her mom was a whiz with her old Singer sewing machine. It had a wood cabinet and mother of pearl inlays. Her mom would sit at the sewing machine on the weekends and turn out imitations of the latest styles for Nina to wear. She was so good that other women in the neighborhood were always asking Estela for help. Her family might lack money, but Nina felt well loved.

Nina never questioned Evita's status as a heroine. She and her classmates studied the legend of Evita along with math and science. Evita not only gave to the poor, she cared about them. She successfully promoted female suffrage, casting her first vote in the early '50s alongside many other women. Everything Evita did was for the greater good of Argentina. The children admired her to no end.

Giovanna Bertolli skipped up to Nina's side.

"Are you going to daydream all day?" she asked. Giovanna was Nina's best friend in the whole world.

Nina grabbed Giovanna's hand. "Do you remember the time you started crying when that lady said that Evita was a woman of loose morals?" Nina asked.

Giovanna looked close to tears just remembering the incident. "I do," she said. "That woman was a witch."

Nina waited for the special government car to arrive. Her knees trembled. She wondered what the other students in class were learning. She turned to look in the windows. Every eye in the school glared back at her. Her mind fluttered between nervous laughter and joyous expectation for what could be coming.

"You're not going to embarrass yourself in front of Evita today, are you?" Héctor Torres, the biggest bully in her class, whispered behind her.

Nina tried her hardest to ignore him and concentrate on the wonderful possibilities the day held. She imagined he was a tiny rain cloud far in the distance, raining on someone else.

"If you just be yourself, they probably won't even let you in," he continued.

Nina never understood why she was one of Héctor's favorite targets. She didn't come from a poor family; she wasn't clumsy; she didn't dress funny. No one else ever picked on her. She liked school except for the moments of torture he inflicted.

"Not today, Héctor," she said. Then she smiled, adding, "Thank you very much."

He started to say more, but Mrs. Ingleses startled them by jumping up and down, waving at an approaching shiny black car.

The driver, dressed in a black suit, got out of the car and held the door open for their teacher, Nina, Giovanna, Héctor, and two other children. While they were deciding who would take which seat, a second car approached the school, then a third, and a fourth. More black cars continued in a caravan. Nina couldn't see where it ended.

Everyone fit into the cars comfortably. Anyone who dared could have lain flat on the floor of the car and still not touched anyone. Nina remembered how she and Eduardo would fight for the most room in the backseat of their father's car. She also thought about downgrading her father's car to a fort instead of a castle. A man in a black suit began explaining how they would each get five minutes to talk with Evita and thank her for their gift. He repeated how grateful they needed to act, especially if a photographer were near. The children then took turns practicing smiling.

The cars finally stopped. Many hands ushered Nina and the others into the Pink House. Nina could barely see the ceiling of the room where the reception was held. She felt overwhelmed by the large house. She'd never seen anything like it. None of the castles in her picture books compared. There must have been at least five hundred other children, each head turning back and forth, trying to glimpse Evita. Nina had never seen a gathering of this many people. Standing in the giant hall gazing at the rainbows cascading off the chandelier, Nina knew only good things could ever happen in a place like this.

Mrs. Ingleses elbowed her in the ribs, jolting Nina's attention away from the chandelier. Mrs. Ingleses shoved her wired-rimmed glasses up the bridge of her nose. "Eyes front, and stand up straight," she said. "Don't any of you dare ruin this for me!"

Nina nodded and looked forward. Out of the corner of her eye, she saw Héctor trying to get her attention. She wanted to look, but she feared Mrs. Ingleses would then do more than elbow her.

Hundreds of photographers' flashbulbs popped all around them. Nina squinted hard, trying to drive away the specks of light that clouded her vision. Teachers herded their students to the front, where the flashbulbs were concentrated. Nina could make out a fuzzy shape on a raised platform that she assumed was Evita. As she and her classmates inched closer to Evita, Nina started to sweat. She had been holding her hands tightly together like her mother instructed her to do, but they were starting to slide apart. She couldn't tell if it was from the heat in the room or her nerves.

"Don't leave a puddle for people to slip in," Héctor said.

"Go bother someone else."

"Are you going to ask Evita for some manners?"

"The only one around here who needs manners is you," Nina said.

"Smile," Héctor said.

Nina didn't understand Héctor. Her confusion showed clearly on her face.

A tall, lanky photographer took a picture of Nina and her classmates before she could regain her senses. The photographer asked Mrs. Ingleses, "Do you think Evita really cares about the poor?" Nina saw Mrs. Ingleses blush at his forwardness.

"How can you have any doubts? She comes from the poor class. She gives to the poor. She fights for the poor. There is no doubt about that," Mrs. Ingleses said.

Nina liked that Mrs. Ingleses stood up for Evita. It was like watching her teacher defend a fairy princess against a dragon.

"No doubt, huh?" The photographer sounded skeptical. "What about Juan Perón closing the newspapers? That is…" He hesitated. "Well, it's not sending the right message."

Nina looked back and forth between the adults. They looked angry. The reporter's nostrils flared, just like a dragon's. Mrs. Ingleses stood rigid. Nina hoped Mrs. Ingleses had remembered to bring her magic wand.

"He had his reasons," Mrs. Ingleses responded. "The newspapers are a tool of the upper class. Besides, they were telling lies about the Peróns. When the newspapers reform themselves, they will be allowed to reopen." Mrs. Ingleses sounded impatient with the photographer's obvious antagonism. She continued, "Wasn't it Perón who made the farm employers pay their field workers in cash, instead of coupons that could only be used in the employers' own stores?"

There was no forthcoming argument from the photographer on that point. "Yes, he certainly did."

"Has any other leader ever done anything so much in favor of the poor at the expense of the rich?"

The photographer shook his head, conceding another point.

It looked like Mrs. Ingleses had won. She had saved the fairy princess. She had saved Evita. Nina felt like dancing around.

Nina paused, then looked at the floor. Politics seemed complicated. Nina's parents talked about the Peróns' policies at home. It seemed that the Peróns' polices affected all the classes, and no one was entirely happy. Sometimes Nina's parents had to close their shop in the Plaza de Mayo because the workers held a rally. On those occasions, Nina's parents talked about how the Peróns should have educated the poor to make them appreciate hard work instead of expecting handouts.

"I rest my case. The Peróns are truly for the poor. Now, if you don't mind."

Nina felt her teacher's firm hand on her back as she was ushered to see Evita.

When Nina finally arrived in Evita's presence, everything went very fast. It was hard to hear Evita's voice over the flashes of the cameras. Nina was awestruck. Evita was everything the newspapers claimed and more. Every hair was in its perfect place, her skin flawless, her smile worthy of an angel. Nina nodded and smiled at anything anyone told her just to get closer to Evita.

"Congratulations on your school achievements and your good behavior. What would you like as a reward?" Evita asked.

The flashes entranced Nina, and she continued nodding. Absentmindedly she reached out for Evita's sleeve. "Yes," she squeaked out.

Evita laughed and hugged Nina. The flashes melded into a continuous sound. "A nice little girl like you would probably like a doll." Evita waved to a woman who brought over a box as tall as Nina, containing a doll. It was a large walking doll with a lever in its back that moved up and down and actually made the doll walk. The doll looked right and left with every step. The face was made of fine, hand-painted porcelain. Nina stared at the doll's beautiful face. It was clearly not a toy that could be played with carelessly. It needed to be looked after and cared for. She had never received a gift so precious.

"Can I trust you to look after this doll like it's your own child?" Evita asked.

"Oh, yes! I will be just like my mom. Thank you, thank you, thank you!"

Evita smiled and handed her an autographed picture of herself in her traditional black tailored suit, a large white camellia on her lapel. The photo was autographed to Nina with her full name spelled out: "For Nina Graciela Salvatti with affection—Eva Perón."

Nina held the photo against her chest. Parents with lots of money could have bought their little girls similar walking dolls, but not every child could have her name written out on a signed photo of Evita. Nina cherished the photo more than the doll.

All her classmates received gifts ranging from new clothes to a refrigerator. All the gifts were arranged to be delivered later to their houses. They chatted excitedly about the gifts they received. None of the others had received a personally signed photo.

Evita talked with the last of Nina's classmates. Nina turned her attention to the photo. She had a photo signed by Evita. She felt like the luckiest girl on the planet.

Even as she smiled at the photo, Héctor snatched it from her hands.

"Give that back this instant!" Nina said.

"*For Nina Graciela Salvatti,*" he said mockingly, "*with affection.*"

Nina reached for the photo. He put it behind his back.

"Please," she said. She didn't want to think about how far he would go. She had seen Héctor get rough with some of their classmates, but she had never seen him do damage equal to that harming her irreplaceable photo.

"Please," she said again.

"You think you're special?" He took a step backward, away from Nina. From behind his back, she heard a slow, deliberate ripping sound. The sound repeated as little pieces of photo fluttered to the ground behind him. He kept smiling at Nina.

Nina felt the blood rush to her face, and tears flooded her eyes. She tried to hold them back so Héctor wouldn't get any more satisfaction. In an instant, her anticipation of her parents' proud reaction to the photo vanished. Nina thought about running back over to Evita and explaining she needed another signed photo. Maybe there was another girl with the exact same name as Nina who would share her photo. There had to be some way to undo the unthinkable that was happening in front of her.

"You're just a big baby. Your doll will probably have to take care of you."

Mrs. Ingleses came over to them.

"What is going on, you two?" Mrs. Ingleses asked.

Nina fell to the floor and started picking up the photo pieces. She saw Evita's smiling face, her polished clothes, and the black background. She concentrated on the blackness. Even shredded, Evita conveyed hopefulness and assurance. Maybe she could glue them together at home.

Héctor bent down and took all the pieces out of Nina's hands. He shoved them into his pants pocket.

"I was just showing Nina a magic trick," Héctor said. "See?"

Nina felt his hand go under her upper arm and tug until she was standing. Héctor thrust Nina's photo of Evita into her hands. It was exactly as it had been when Evita handed it to her. Nina stared at Héctor, unable to speak. She looked around, expecting people to start clapping. She would bow if they did. Nina remembered that she hadn't seen any signature on the photo pieces she picked off the floor. Héctor had fooled her in the worst way possible.

Mrs. Ingleses stared at them. Nothing appeared to be damaged. Nina worried that Mrs. Ingleses would never see the truth. As far as Mrs. Ingleses was concerned, Héctor had done magic.

"Just get to the car now," Mrs. Ingleses said.

When Mrs. Ingleses was out of earshot, Héctor said, "You should have seen the look on your face!"

He walked away, laughing. Nina recognized that laugh from school, usually after something horrible happened to someone else. She felt sick. Gazing at the photo, she wanted to burn it into her memory and hold it so tightly no one would ever take it away from her again. Evita's smile seemed to say, "Don't worry. It all works out in the end."

—⁓—

Nina flew through the front door of her house. The doll from Evita sat in the entryway. Her mother and father stood on either side of the doll wearing wide smiles.

Nina's mom knelt down to enfold Nina in a warm hug. "Welcome home, little one." Nina peeked up at her father, who nodded and winked. *This is one of the best days,* she thought.

Her parents had already called all her aunts and uncles to share the good news. Her mother seemed equally impressed with the autographed photo and had Nina's father, Miguel Salvatti, put it in a special frame. In Argentina, all a family's possessions belonged to the father. This photo was different. The writing in the corner bestowed it specially to Nina, making it the one item in the house that she truly owned.

She beamed whenever she walked past it hanging on the wall in their living room, never telling anyone what they had both been through. If company visited, the photo became a stop on the home tour. All who visited praised Nina for working so hard that she had earned a photo of Evita.

———∽∾∽———

The Salvatti family didn't have a lot of money, but that never bothered Nina. Her house was filled with love. Her mother cooked good Italian food every day and made sure that Nina had pretty clothes to wear. Even better, Nina's uncle, Antonio, managed the local movie theater and invited the whole family there every Sunday afternoon. Nina loved the movies. She loved to immerse herself in the fantasy of the silver screen, forgetting her simple everyday life and becoming a part of the story shown in the picture.

But she enjoyed the simple, everyday details as well. She liked to sit in the balcony for free. She liked listening to the vendors hawk their wares as they walked up and down the aisles. She always bought the chocolate-covered peanuts, and she always got a stomachache because she ate too many of them.

During the intermission, a local act performed in front of the red curtains. The actors were less than talented, but their missed lines and bumbled acting made her laugh.

Chapter Two

Sad Celebration

Nina heard the gentle patter of rain against her window and snuggled deeper under her covers. Nina appreciated Saturdays during the spring. She wouldn't stay in bed long, but for now, she let herself drift to the sounds of her mom moving around in the kitchen as she prepared breakfast.

Nina's mom sat on the side of her bed. "Wake up, my little one," she whispered. The enticing smell of hot cocoa drifted across Nina's nose. She heard her mom set the cup of hot cocoa on the night table. Estela always came in the mornings to help Nina get up. She would wake Nina up by bringing her hot cocoa, rubbing her back, and singing to her. Nina wanted someday to be a mom just like her.

Nina was pretty sure that every young girl wanted to grow up to be a good mother. The most popular game at her school was playing house. Most girls had younger siblings to practice their skills on. Nina practiced on her little brother Eduardo. She helped her mother any chance she got. She shadowed her mom, watching how her mom took care of the family and made their home a beautiful and comfortable place.

Nina danced around the living room as she dusted the side tables. She liked this job the most because her mom let her use the feather duster. It seemed a most clever device. A variety of feathers covered the handle. Nina liked to imagine that the bird's feathers were jewel-toned and exotic, giving the chore a mysterious air.

Nina stepped over Eduardo in the center of the living room, where he lay on his stomach playing with his toy cars. She squatted down. "It is too nice a day to be inside. Go outside and play," she said, using her best imitation of her mom's voice.

Eduardo pouted, pushing out his lower lip. That was never a good sign, she knew.

"Here, I'll get your tricycle down."

Nina went to the terrace and pulled down Eduardo's tricycle. Eduardo followed her to the terrace. At the sight of his tricycle, his eyes lit up. He climbed on the tricycle and began to circle the terrace.

A job well done. Nina smiled to herself. She liked practicing her mothering skills on her brother.

"Nina, come inside," Nina's mom called from the kitchen.

Nina scurried to the kitchen. She hoped her mom wanted her to help make lunch. It was September. Nina loved that time of the year for a couple of reasons. Nina's mom always prepared special dishes in the spring. Even more importantly, September meant that Nina's birthday was approaching.

Nina slid around the corner into the kitchen. Her mom stood in the middle of the kitchen with a large smile and small package in her hands. Nina's heart thumped.

Her mom held the package out to her. "This is for you, little one."

Nina carefully opened the package. Inside the box lay a tiny version of the apron Nina's mom always wore around the house.

Nina squealed and held out the apron. "This is the best gift ever! Mom, it's perfect."

————

Spring heralded the start of cool afternoons in the southern hemisphere, and the heady aroma of wisteria began to fill the air. Nina treasured the dangling purplish and white blossoms that hung everywhere and danced in the breeze. Together with the vivid green of the sycamore trees, they transformed Buenos Aires into a colorful, fragrant bouquet. The emerging plant life tried in vain to cover the vast number of sidewalk cafes that had sprung up in great numbers during the '30s and '40s. The nickname "Paris of South America" suited Buenos Aires well.

Nina liked to imagine that the streets were transformed roadways within an enchanted kingdom and that the sidewalk cafes and boutiques were magic shops and apothecaries filled with special treasures—just the types of things that she would need to throw the best party. She wanted to outdo her party from the previous year. Actually, she wanted to outdo any of the parties she'd attended during the school year. Nina had a plan. It involved a magician and maybe even a white pony.

Estela and Nina strolled through the streets of Buenos Aires in search of the finishing touches for her birthday party. Nina loved to walk through the streets during the cool afternoons.

They stepped into a chocolatier's shop. Nina heard her mom inhale deeply. She imitated her.

Estela sighed. "Doesn't it smell divine, Nina?"

"It smells good, Mom. You know what would go well with chocolate?" Nina looked down, pausing for effect. But when she looked up to answer her own question, she saw that her mother was not waiting with rapt attention. Instead she'd gone over to the counter and was already chatting with the chocolate seller and sampling truffles.

Nina wandered to the counter. She and her mom needed to get organized. They had limited time to discuss any surprise plans for the party before they met up with Giovanna.

Her mom popped another chocolate into her mouth. "Nina, these would make perfect favors for your party. They come in such beautiful little boxes, tied with such pretty ribbons." She turned back to the man behind the counter. "We'll take sixty."

"They're really pretty," Nina said, "but—"

"But what?" Estela asked. She paid and bustled Nina out of the shop.

"Don't you think my party could use a little magic?" Nina wanted a magician at her party and thought this was a clever way to introduce the idea.

Her mom chuckled. "Whenever my little love turns one year older, it is magic to me."

Nina was about to reply when she caught sight of Giovanna standing outside a curio shop. Giovanna waved madly, and Estela took Nina's hand and started walking briskly across the square toward her.

Giovanna hopped up and down. She and her family had recently moved to Argentina, having received Perónista financial aid to emigrate from Italy. The same was true of many Argentines: the country had no significant native population, so European immigrants comprised the bulk of it, bringing with them their trades, skills, and professions—but often very little money. Giovanna's family was poor as well. Like a number of Argentines, Giovanna had classic Italian looks: dark, dark eyes and thick, dark hair. She stood out in the busy square only because she was so very short and skinny.

Nina liked the idea of her friend coming to help them shop for the standard party favors. It might be harder to drop hints to her mom about the birthday surprises with Giovanna there, but Nina felt up to the task. Giovanna didn't speak Spanish very well, and even though Nina had agreed to teach her Spanish if Giovanna would teach her Italian, Nina was not above taking advantage of Giovanna's limited vocabulary to keep some aspects of her party secret. She felt sure that Giovanna would want it that way, especially if Nina managed to convince her mom to bring in a magician and a pony. Nina almost giggled with glee at the idea of surprising her friend.

"We'll need to pick out some savory meats for your party." Nina's mother headed toward the butcher. "Come along, girls."

Nina hooked her arm through Giovanna's. "I have a plan."

"I love your plans," Giovanna said.

Nina and Giovanna followed Nina's mom. The butcher was terribly boring, but Nina would use the time wisely to talk to Giovanna about ponies. If she could only plant the idea of the white pony in Giovanna's head, Giovanna would mention it to Nina's mom, and Estela, who had a weakness for Giovanna, would be unable to say no. Nina would have a white pony at her party and everything would be fantastic.

Nina remembered when Giovanna's father Lino had gotten sunstroke. It had been a blistering hot day shortly after the Bertolli family had arrived in Argentina. They had no refrigerator to make ice to cool him down and no money to take him to a doctor.

Giovanna's mother went to Nina's mom in great distress. "My Lino!" she cried. "He has no helmet when he rides his scooter to work. The poor man, he has sunstroke. We have no ice. Signora, you help?"

Nina's mom patted Giovanna's mother's hand. "Of course," she said. "You can have all the ice cubes our little refrigerator can make."

The memory made Nina proud. Her mom was a good person, and Argentina was a good place to live. Nina's mom enjoyed helping Giovanna's parents feel welcome. She showed them generous hospitality. The two families had become close. Of course, Nina's mom had invited the whole Bertolli family to Nina's birthday party.

"This will be the best birthday I've ever had," Nina said.

Nina grasped Giovanna's hand. She urged Giovanna to follow her over to a low bench set at an angle in the square. Twining purple blossoms covered the bench.

"I've always wanted to see blossoms woven into the mane of a dancing pony," Nina said. "Haven't you, Giovanna?"

Giovanna picked up a flower and nodded.

Nina twirled a lock of Giovanna's hair and then wove a flower into it. "To have a pony at a party would be even better. The children could pet it and ride it. Wouldn't that be marvelous?"

Giovanna nodded. Her eyes lit up behind her thick glasses. "I have an idea for your party, my friend."

Nina guessed she had Giovanna right where she wanted her. "But I've not told you my plan."

"You must tell me!" Giovanna said.

Nina's mom stepped out of the butcher's shop. "All done, girls."

They set off across the square.

"Mrs. Salvatti, I have an idea about the party," Giovanna said.

Nina's mom blinked.

Nina imagined her mom's surprise. Giovanna was usually hesitant to speak in Spanish; her difficulty with the language made her shy.

Estela smiled at Giovanna. "What is your idea, Giovanna?" she asked in an encouraging tone. She patted the girl on the shoulder. Nina stopped herself from rubbing her hands together. *How can Mom possibly turn Giovanna's request down now after showing her so much support?*

"A pony with flowers in its hair. This would be beautiful for Nina's special day. You think so, too?" Giovanna's face glowed. A ray of sunlight lit the flower Nina had placed in Giovanna's hair. Nina felt like the fates had aligned to help her achieve her dreams.

Nina's mom smoothed down her dress and tightened her bun. "Nina, have you given much thought to what you want for your birthday?"

"I haven't thought much past my party. Giovanna's idea about the pony is neat, isn't it, Mom?"

Estela stopped in the center of the square. Her voice drifted back over her shoulder. "I guess a little girl with a pony at her party does not need many wonderful gifts." She nodded her head sharply and then turned to face the girls. "This is true. A pony is an excellent idea, Giovanna."

Her mom had won.

Giovanna furrowed her brow. "There will be no pony?"

"No," Nina and her mom replied together.

"Okay, Nina. What about your presents?" her mom asked.

Nina didn't hesitate. "I want the same figurines Giovanna has. The ones with the glossy finish and shiny dust."

———

Nina's legs ached. Giovanna and Estela looked worn out. They'd stopped in every shop in the neighborhood, with no luck. Only one shop remained. *I'm sure this one will have the figurines. It just has to.* Nina felt a surge of new energy run through her body.

She turned to Giovanna. "Let's run to the last shop. It'll be lucky." Nina looked at her mom. "Is that okay, Mom?"

Estela laughed. "I don't know where you two find your energy."

Nina jumped up and down until her mother said, "Yes, yes. Run to the next shop."

"Okay, on the count of three…" Nina and Giovanna ran to the last shop, a toyshop with small tea sets in the window and a large tabby cat on the stoop. It looked like just the type of shop that would have the tiny figurines. Nina wanted two pieces: something impressive or exotic, like the Eiffel Tower or a giraffe, and also a pretty piece, like a princess or a fairy.

Curious items sprouted on every available surface of the shop's interior. There were carved nesting dolls and small guitars. Nina found a set of puppets and a miniature stage. The lights on the stage were made of reflecting glass. It looked very clever, but it was not as smart as the figurines.

"Nina, come look at all the dolls!" Giovanna called.

Nina followed the sound of Giovanna's voice around a corner. Giovanna stood in the middle of a small room filled with dolls. Dolls of every shape and size, with every imaginable color of hair and eyes, surrounded her.

"Isn't it wonderful?" Giovanna asked.

"It's okay," Nina replied. None of the dolls could match the perfection of the doll she had received from Evita.

Nina left Giovanna in the room of dolls and went looking for her mom. She hoped her mom had found some of the figurines. Estela stood at the counter. *Maybe Mom already bought my present.* Nina was very fond of surprises, but she also wanted to see which figurines she would get. She crossed the store to stand behind her mom.

Estela and the shopkeeper bent over a mimeograph. She pointed at a picture on the mimeograph. "You're sure you don't have any of these figurines—you won't be able to get any?"

The shopkeeper folded up the mimeograph. "I'm sorry. Those figurines come from Europe, and the government has placed a ban on importing foreign goods. To protect the domestic industry, you know?" the man said conspiratorially. He pulled a miniature tea set out from behind the counter. "I have many equally beautiful items that were made right here in Argentina."

Nina's mom nodded. She talked with the shopkeeper and then bought the tea set. Nina didn't understand exactly what a ban on importing was, but she understood that it somehow meant she wasn't getting the figurines she wanted.

———⟨∿⟩———

Nina sat on the floor of Giovanna's bedroom. Giovanna lay on her stomach on the bed. Nina's birthday party was only two days away. She'd come to Giovanna's house so that they could choose what color hair ribbons to wear for the party.

Nina felt sad about the fact that she wouldn't be getting any coveted figurines for her birthday. *Giovanna is so lucky. I wish I had even a fraction of the figurines Giovanna has.*

Inspiration struck. Nina sprang to her feet. "I have a new game for us to play."

Giovanna flipped over. "What's the game?"

"It's called Figureheads and Tails—it'll be really fun," Nina said.

Giovanna sat up. "How do you play?"

"First one of us tosses a coin in the air, and we both try to catch it," Nina explained. "The one to catch it will be the winner. If you lose, you pay me with one of your figurines. If I lose, I'll pay you with a notebook from my father's shop. Sound good?"

"I guess," Giovanna said. "Let me go find a coin."

Nina gazed up at a shelf hanging above Giovanna's bed holding the beautiful figurines. It held an entire miniature city of animals and buildings, each hand-painted with a story of what must have happened in the fragile life of each written on a small card that hung from the base of each piece. Nina coveted the vast collection and thought that with so many, Giovanna could easily part with a few of them. *They would look so nice in my bedroom.*

"Ready?" Giovanna asked.

Nina glanced at the figurines to locate her favorite one, a ballerina up on her toes in a perfect pose. Someone had painted little roses and ribbons around her legs and skirt and little clapping hands around the base. Nina concentrated on that one as her prize.

"Ready," she said.

The girls stood in the middle of a braided rug at the foot of Giovanna's bed. Giovanna tossed the coin high into the air. Nina admired the way it spun in the light. She noted that Giovanna also watched the coin with rapt attention. Nina quickly leapt into action, expecting an easy win. Giovanna lunged just as quickly after the coin. That startled Nina. She'd underestimated Giovanna's desire for a new notebook.

The coin dropped, falling just beyond Nina's outstretched hand. She sighed with relief when the coin managed to evade Giovanna's hand as well. Nina's hands and arms intertwined with Giovanna's, tying them into a big knot.

Nina concentrated on getting free so that she could resume her pursuit of the coin. Giovanna struggled as well. Apparently she was just as intent on winning as Nina was.

The sound of the coin hitting the wood floor and then rolling under the bed got their attention. Nina dove to the ground. She felt Giovanna at her side. Nina searched frantically under the bed. She figured that her long, slender arms gave her the advantage. She grabbed the coin, and her heart leapt. Nina pulled herself from under the bed.

Giovanna sat on the bed and rubbed her head.

"Are you okay?"

"I hit my head on the bed frame. It's okay," Giovanna said.

Nina jumped to her feet, excited to have won the first round, and ran over to the shelf. Her eyes darting from piece to piece, savoring the anticipation of which one Giovanna would concede to Nina. There was a tiny Ferris wheel with gold lights and happy faces in each car, a horse with waving grass and fences to jump painted all the way around its body, and, of course, the ballerina.

Out of the corner of her eye Nina saw Giovanna, still rubbing her head, go into her closet. Giovanna began shuffling through boxes. It seemed to take forever. *Maybe the closet is where she keeps her first aid supplies,* Nina thought. Anticipation turned to irritation as Giovanna moved more and more boxes and rustled through papers. Finally, Giovanna joined Nina again.

The girl held out the figurine of a sleeping baby. It had no elaborate painting, only broken black eyelashes and a small yellow tuft on the top of its head. It looked similar to the inferior ones Nina had seen in the stores around Buenos Aires. "Here."

Nina pointed to the decorated shelf. "Are you sure you don't want to get rid of any of those?"

Giovanna shook her head.

Discouraged, Nina grabbed the baby and the coin. "Let's have another round."

"This isn't fun. Let's go outside." Giovanna strode to the doorway. Clearly, the game had ended, but Nina's unmet desire for a figurine weighed heavily on her. She tossed the coin on Giovanna's bed and the porcelain baby into the trashcan by the door.

Before she left the room, she stopped to look one last time at the miniature magical city sitting high on the shelf.

—◦◦◦—

The week before Nina's party, her mother wasted no time preparing for the big day. Nina peeked into the kitchen occasionally, and each time more and more of her favorite foods greeted her. Nina saw two kinds of birthday cake, one with lots of whipped cream for the kids and another one with Moscato wine for the adults. She saw tiny sandwiches from the neighborhood bakery, made of paper thin, spongy bread with a variety of fillings, like prosciutto and pineapple, hearts of palm, Roquefort cheese with celery, anchovies with mozzarella and tomatoes, and Nina's favorites, ham and cheese and egg salad.

On her birthday Nina woke up earlier than usual to finish her chores and set up the decorations. She spent more time than she should have trying on several possible outfits and shoe combinations. By the time she finally decided what to wear, some of the guests had arrived.

Nina picked Eduardo up. "You keep the guests in here while I finish getting ready. No one is to go outside. It's not ready," Nina said.

Eduardo gave her a wide smile, nodding vigorously, and Nina set him in the lap of the first guest to arrive. When she checked later to make sure he was following directions, she stifled a laugh. His delaying tactics consisted of letting himself being passed among the guests to be hugged and kissed. After all, he was only a toddler.

"Good!" she said. She hurried out to the patio and placed the final flowers and napkins on tables.

The bulk of the party guests were Nina's aunts, uncles, and cousins, with a few friends and classmates mixed in. Nina was by far the most animated of the bunch, basking in her special day. As the guests entered the patio, she played the perfect hostess and showed them where to find refreshments and where to sit.

Most of her relatives made it to her party, except her favorite aunt, Renata. Renata had given birth to her sixth child two months earlier. Her family lived outside the city and stayed close to her husband's Vincenzo's parents on the Pampas. Nina was disappointed that Renata and the new baby hadn't made it to her party and wanted to know why. She looked around for her mother to find out what had happened. She found her mom working in the kitchen.

"Mom, why didn't Renata come to my party?" she asked.

Estela took her by the hand and led her to the kitchen table. She pulled out a chair and urged Nina into a seat, stroking Nina's hair. Nina always found the gesture comforting.

"We got a letter yesterday saying they couldn't risk the long drive. The baby is having complications. They decided to stay home and wait for a doctor." Tears welled up in Estela's eyes.

Nina knew that whenever a new baby needed to be seen by a doctor, the situation was very serious. Eduardo had been struck with meningitis, and she remembered her parents had feared for his life. Before Eduardo was born, the Salvattis had lost a ten-day-old infant due to inadequate medical care. As shopkeepers, they were not as poor as many, but they couldn't afford a private hospital—only the very rich could do that. Instead, they'd relied on the inefficient public system, which was not equipped with advanced technology or private rooms and not always staffed with well-trained doctors.

Eduardo's meningitis had caused inflammation of his brain and spinal cord and required daily professional care. A private doctor cost the Salvattis a fortune, but they were desperate to prevent tragedy from striking their family again. The doctor visited the boy in the evenings, and the family also hired a nurse to come every six hours to administer injections and antibiotics. Nina and her parents spent long hours caring for Eduardo. He looked so helpless, his frail body ravaged by the disease, and his dark curly hair matted with sweat from the intense fever. He was not the energetic toddler his mother doted on. Everyone always said Eduardo had the face of an angel, but his little face had swollen, and his body shook from the effects of fever. The days stretched on, with little improvement.

One morning, Nina's mom came out of Eduardo's room where she'd spent another long night watching him.

"How is he, Mama?" Nina asked.

"I think he is getting better. The medicine must be working."

"How do you know?"

"He seems less feverish." Estela gave her a sympathetic look. "Don't worry, Nina, your little brother is getting better. I'm sure of it."

Nina had not lost hope. She'd been doing the one thing that

she was sure would help Eduardo pull through. "I've been praying, Mama."

"Good. Tell Him we need His help," her mom said.

"I told God I would be good if he made Eduardo get well." In fact, Nina had offered God a lifetime of good behavior.

"That's good, darling."

"I even told Him I'd stop pretending I was Evita, wearing beautiful dresses and furs." That had been the hardest, but she figured Eduardo was worth it.

"That's not so terrible, Nina. I'm sure God understands. After all, Evita is a generous person. God can't be angry at you for pretending to be someone so good."

Her mom had looked so tired that night, almost defeated. When Eduardo eventually got better Nina forgot her promise to God, and she started to pretend to be Evita again.

Nina thought about her Aunt Renata and her baby cousin. She found great relief in God's understanding. She thought if He could heal her brother and let her keep pretending to be Evita, then He could surely heal her baby cousin.

She scrambled out of her chair and hugged her mother. Estela kept stroking her hair.

"You're a great mom," Nina said.

"Thank you, love. Now go back to your party."

The children had a good time playing traditional birthday games, eating ice cream and cake, and singing silly songs. The adults discussed current politics. Nina paused while playing pin the tail on the donkey to listen to the adults talk. She thought it was amusing, because everyone who lived in Argentina had an opinion on politics.

Most of the guests whispered about their favorite subject—Eva Perón. Nina's ears perked up whenever she caught the faintest echo of Evita's name. At seven years old, Nina didn't understand the politics or the conversations when the adults criticized the methods Perón and Evita used in order to make Argentina better, but she didn't care as long as they were praising her hero.

Nina's aunt Teresa carried a plate of stuffed peppers over to a group of guests. "Did you see how beautiful our Evita looked in the parade?" she asked.

"Stunning. Just stunning."

Nina didn't know the woman who answered, but she decided that she liked her. Nina ran inside the house to retrieve the framed, signed photo of Evita. Whenever anyone mentioned the lengths the Peróns went to in order to protect Argentina, Nina remembered the lengths she'd had to go to just to get that photograph. In some ways she felt like she could relate to a soldier, enduring fatigue and hardships to protect Evita.

She walked outside, hugging the photo, and held it up for all to see. "Look. Evita signed this photograph for me."

"That's nice, dear," Aunt Teresa said.

Nina deflated. The adults seemed more interested in talking to each other than in looking at her most marvelous possession.

Rodolfo, one of the neighbors, walked up to join the group. "Did you hear what she said when she declined the vice presidency?"

Nina wove in and out between the adult's legs. She liked listening to them talk, even though they seemed to forget she was there or that it was her birthday.

"I will never forget," Aunt Teresa said. She looked enraptured. Her eyes sparkled. "'When the history of Juan Perón is written I just want people to know that I, as his wife, tried to bring the hopes and dreams of the people to the President. And that the President would eventually turn those hopes and dreams into glorious reality.'"

Nina recognized those words. Her aunt was quoting Evita. Hugging her picture close to her chest, Nina felt as if Evita was right there with them at the party, bringing them all together.

"I believe in her completely," Giovanna's mother said.

"She was very beautiful in person and kind to everyone, from the first to the last, when I saw her," Nina said. She didn't understand everything the adults were talking about, but she needed to say something about her time with Evita.

Aunt Teresa pulled her close and hugged her. "It's a pity Evita never had children."

"She would have been a good role model for mothers everywhere," Giovanna's mother said.

The adults nodded. They smiled at Nina.

"Happy birthday, Nina!" they shouted. They clapped each other on the shoulders. "Viva Evita," they whispered.

Nina didn't know why they whispered their praise for Evita. She would have shouted it from the rooftops.

Nina ran outside to play with the other children. "Viva Evita!" The joy in her heart swelled.

Her Aunt Rosa rushed to her side. "Nina, no. You must not shout this."

Startled, Nina began to cry.

Aunt Rosa hugged her. "Evita is wonderful, but we cannot shout these things. Politics are complex, and loyalties change. You are young but not too young to learn. Love Evita in your heart. Now, don't cry. Go back to your friends." She kissed Nina and then sent off to play.

It was Nina's most memorable birthday party. She made sure that her photograph never left her side. Only Evita herself showing up could have made the day better. Nina looked around at all the smiling faces of her friends and family. She met her parents' eyes, and they beamed proud smiles at her.

Nina's bliss was interrupted by familiar shouting that started in the house and slowly made its way to the patio. Her parents' faces switched from pride to dismay. Nina had seen that expression on their faces before. It meant their next-door neighbor, Jorge Varela, had stopped by unannounced.

Jorge was a short, coarse man with a heap of black hair that didn't match his stubby, wrinkled body. It was always the same with Jorge; he only needed a "quick" favor—and he needed so many. Whenever he would leave, he would give Nina a piece of warm, stale candy from his pocket and a "goodbye, little girl" that suffocated her with his burnt coffee breath. Nina hated his visits. Miguel tried to block Jorge from coming into the patio, but Jorge's booming voice had the power to move people before he even reached them. He staggered into the patio, his arms flailing and his eyes widening as he saw the table filled with Nina's gifts. No one stopped him as he walked over to it, picked up a brightly colored box, and shook it violently. He grabbed a second package and shook it as well. Several presents fell on the floor.

"That's enough of that!" Miguel said.

Miguel grabbed Jorge's arm and tried to pull him into the house, away from the guests. Jorge swung around to follow Miguel, his arms knocking a few gifts to the ground. His body seemed to be running independently from his mind. He blinked rapidly, constantly rubbed his fingertips together, and jumped at the slightest sounds.

As Miguel crossed the threshold of the kitchen door, Nina heard Jorge say, "I just need some more money again. You know I'm good for it. I'll get it back to you Tuesday."

The only topic of conversation with Jorge was money. Nina noticed he usually came over before the weekend and would promise to bring back whatever he borrowed—plus some—the following Monday or Tuesday. He was true to his word. He always paid her father back. Nina had eavesdropped on some of Jorge's visits to her parents, and she had learned he worked with the government buying old navy ships and reselling their parts. She had heard him mention how stressful it was to "grease the right palms" to get the government's contracts.

"We can talk about this later," Miguel said. "You should head home."

"I need this now. They're going to take my house."

They finally disappeared into the house. A short time later, Nina heard Jorge leave. Nina knew he got the money he wanted. She'd never seen her father say no.

Nina ran back to her gifts, unable to repress her tears. The love she had for Evita was only equaled by her hate for Jorge. He managed to destroy anything that crossed his path. Nina opened the present he had shaken first. Luckily, it was a dress with embroidered pink flowers from one of her aunts. Her heart grew a little lighter. At least Jorge's visit hadn't caused casualties.

Nina opened her presents one by one. Each was undamaged, and she began to hope that all the fallen gifts were salvageable.

But when she lifted one last box, she found another underneath: a small package from Giovanna neatly wrapped in red paper. It felt very light. When Nina picked it up, she heard multiple parts sliding about inside.

It shouldn't have sounded like that. Nina held her breath as she opened the box, then forgot to breathe altogether. Inside the box lay the broken pieces of the Ferris wheel figurine from Giovanna's room. Tiny painted people smiled up at her from amongst the shards of porcelain.

Nina heard a small sound and glanced up. Giovanna stood beside her, staring down at the wreckage of her gift. Then she knelt, putting her arm around Nina, and the two girls cried together.

Nina had always cherished summer, but that year she hated it. Her personal heroine was dying. Evita, the blond saint of Argentina, had terminal cancer. Argentina's national tragedy had become Nina's personal tragedy.

Nina wiped a tear from her face as she heard her parents say that people respected Perón, but they adored Evita. She lit another candle and went back to praying. She would pray for hours, just as she had for her brother when he had been ill as an infant. Maybe the combination of all their prayers could save Evita.

As Nina and Giovanna walked to and from school, they saw little altars adorned with Evita's photograph, the same as in every corner of Buenos Aires. The shrines of the poor covered the altars, and they kept candles lit around the clock. Prayers, poems, and other mementos of their affection heaped so high on the altars that they fell onto the sidewalks, so people had to walk in the street.

Nina and Giovanna didn't say much on those walks. They just held hands to comfort each other.

"Should we get some flowers to put out by our houses?" Nina asked.

Giovanna said nothing as tears flowed down her face. Nina knew they felt the same way and squeezed Giovanna's hand.

"Maybe tomorrow, then."

Summer turned into fall, and Evita's health continue to deteriorate. The press releases coming from the Pink House tried to mask the seriousness of Evita's illness. Instead of the performances of second-rate actors, movie intermissions were filled with carefully edited films of Evita's battle with cancer.

The days were getting shorter and gray. Nina felt sad and depressed and spent many hours sitting at home on a window seat watching the rain hit the streets of Buenos Aires. She was thinking that if Evita was alive when the spring came, perhaps she had a chance of getting better.

Soon Nina was able to get out of her depression. Her teacher had chosen her to carry the Argentine flag during the celebration of 25 de Mayo, the Commemoration of the Revolución de Mayo on

May 25, 1810, the day that the Argentine people had stood up to the oppressive Spanish king, Fernando VII

The celebration was very colorful. The students performed traditional dances dressed in the typical costumes of *gauchos* for the boys and *paisanas* for the girls. *Pastelitos* and *mate cocido* were served at the end of the act.

All of June was cold and rainy. Nina wished she could stay home instead of going to school, where she spent hours in cold classrooms heated with a small electric heater that only warmed a small area around the teacher's desk. She thought that instead of spending money on all those presents for the kids, Perón should improve the schools heating systems. In her naiveté, she did not realize that the distribution of presents was a more powerful propaganda tool than the school's heating, which was something that people expected to work anyway.

June turned into July, and another celebration took place: Independence Day on July 9.

The weather was still very cold, but the sun was showing more often.

On Saturday evening, July 26, Nina and her family were listening to the radio when a special message interrupted the normal transmission. In a voice he could barely keep steady, a reporter announced that at 8:25 pm, Evita had passed into eternity.

A few minutes later, somebody rapped on the door. When Miguel opened it, Giovanna flung herself, crying, into Nina's arms. The girls clung to each other, sobbing together one more time. They begged Estela and Miguel to take them out; people were gathering on the streets, talking about Evita.

"Can you believe Evita was so weak during Perón's reelection parade?" a resonant voice said. Nina tried to match the person to the voice, but the crowd was too big, and it moved too fast.

"They say she was held up by a plaster and wire frame under her fur coat."

Nina wanted to cry. She hoped the plaster and wire hadn't hurt.

"Evita still rode in the motorcade and waved," a tall, slender woman said. "You wouldn't have realized anything was wrong, she seemed so joyous."

Nina waved to her as she passed her on the sidewalk. The woman waved back. There was a feeling of camaraderie in the crowd, which had gathered together for a single purpose. Evita had united them during her lifetime, and now they remained united to commemorate her death.

"She loved us to the end. We will love her longer."

Nina felt overwhelmed. The voices blended together, but all the words spoken were full of love for Evita.

The city overflowed with people. Nina's mom pointed out people from other parts of the country who had come to pay homage to Argentina's first lady.

The lines of people wound all around the city. Nina stood with her parents. As they waited, the children naturally congregated together, and since they were children of Perón supporters, their talk too was full of reverence.

"Do you think she will go to heaven?" Giovanna asked.

Nina felt surprised anyone would even have to ask such a question. "Of course. If anybody would go to heaven, it would be Evita."

"But what if she didn't go to confession last Saturday?" another child asked. Nina recognized Héctor's voice right away. "My dad says Perón and Evita weren't as saintly as everyone thinks."

Nina turned to him. "I'm sure there was a priest with her. Of course she had her confession. No one asked you what you think."

"Besides, what sins could Evita have?" Giovanna asked.

"None, silly," Nina said, realizing that Giovanna was trying to protect the younger children from Héctor's hurtful words.

Héctor sneered. "I thought I'd taught you not to believe everything you see and hear. Didn't you learn your lesson?"

Nina couldn't believe his nerve to say such things about someone who had just died, especially someone who had proved her worthiness, like Evita. She wished they were in school so the teacher could punish his behavior. As Nina's anger rose, so did her voice. "I learned not to lie or spread rumors about people and to always be polite, even to people like you."

Several adults nearby turned to look at the children. Nina caught her mother's eye and knew she was in for a talking-to when she got home.

"Just leave us alone, Héctor," Giovanna said.

"You girls are so sensitive."

Nina glared at him. She could feel anger bubbling under her skin and it took all her willpower not to act on her feelings. She desperately wanted to make Héctor see that he was wrong about the Peróns.

For a moment, Héctor stared back at her silently. Then he glanced away.

"They're going to build a monument to her bigger than the Statue of Liberty in America," a little boy said.

"Is that true?" a girl asked.

"Of course," Nina said. "That's the least our country can do for such a great person."

Héctor looked straight at Nina.

"People are remembered for their actions, not how many statues are built for them," he said. "Shouldn't you be home babysitting Evita's picture?"

Chapter Three

1955 Revolution

"When trouble comes, there is little to go around," Estela said. She carried only two grocery bags. Nina hoped they would be enough. No matter where they went, the store shelves were mostly empty. Everyone prepared for hard times.

The Argentine economy consisted of small, family-owned stores. The merchants, like everyone else, lived a hand-to-mouth existence. From what Nina understood, the merchants did not have enough capital, which she had learned was money, to buy goods to fill their shelves.

"Stay close, Nina," Estela said, a note of warning in her voice.

"I'm right here, Mom." Nina couldn't understand why her mother worried so much. She was ten years old. Surely her mother could trust her not to get herself lost.

"Don't let them see you have groceries," Estela said. She handed Nina the smaller of the two bags she'd been carrying.

Nina and her mother tucked their bags under their coats and stepped into the Plaza de Mayo. The utter stillness struck Nina. Once a bustling center of activity in Buenos Aires, today the Plaza lay silent as a tomb. Nina didn't think it had ever been so empty.

Nina's mother tugged on her hand. They made their way around Plaza, keeping to the outside. Nina jumped over a couple of pieces of rubble lying on the ground. She tried to stop to get a closer look at the pieces, but her mom shook her head and tugged Nina onward.

The rubble looked like large bits of brick and concrete. *Where did the rubble come from?* Nina glanced around. Damaged buildings stood in disarray on all sides of the Plaza. They poked up between undamaged buildings, creating the effect of jagged teeth in a macabre smile. Nina shivered.

She thought the destruction of the buildings perfectly represented the upheaval of the times. Violence had festered in some quarters before sweeping across the country. No household was unaffected. People had talked about war until it had engulfed everything.

It had started with the death of Evita. More than anyone had realized, she'd been a stabilizing force in the country. By 1953, the Perón administration had begun to crumble from within. Then Evita's brother and Perón's private secretary, Juan Duarte, had appeared to commit suicide. The probable murder precipitated the end of Perón's reign. Each dire event strengthened the growing power of the military, and just like that, the Revolution was under way.

Nina hurried on. She turned her eyes away from the buildings around the edges of the square. The sight of them made her too sad to bear. Her gaze came to rest on the sturdy white Cabildo, which had been a government house during the colonial times.

The familiar Cabildo, a monument to the country's colonial legacy, seemed to be intact: its tower and simple arches looked severe and resolute. Nina had heard people say that the navy and air force pilots were careful not to hit it, but after seeing the destruction surrounding the Plaza, she'd expected to find it destroyed as well. Seeing the Cabildo lifted her spirits. Underneath everything else, the Argentines were sentimental people.

Nina saw the doors to the Buenos Aires Metropolitan Cathedral appear ahead. It had been built nearly five hundred years ago; Nina's grandmother had been married there in 1881. Now the cathedral was quiet. It looked completely deserted. If Nina had to describe the

Plaza and its surroundings, she'd say that even the pigeons had fled. The stillness felt eerie, unreal.

"Mom, can we go in to the Cathedral to pray for God to end the revolution?" Nina asked.

"If it makes you feel better, we will do it," her mother said.

Nina could tell her mother didn't want to delay getting home, but they all needed ways to feel more secure. She was glad her mother would let her pray for some peace of mind.

They stopped outside the Cathedral doors. Nina pulled on one of the door handles, but the front doors didn't budge. She shot a questioning look at her mother.

"Evidently the priests aren't confident that their vestments will keep them untouchable."

As they turned around to leave, the side door opened and a sacristan peeked out.

"May I help you, ladies?" His voice trembled.

"We would like to go in and pray," Estela said.

"Please come in," he said. "You're welcome."

Nina felt an overwhelming sense of security as soon as she entered the Cathedral. The building's interior was quiet and dark. It took a few seconds for her eyes to adjust.

The front of the cathedral was dominated by the mausoleum of San Martín, the general who had liberated Argentina from the Spanish in the nineteenth century. Nina's teacher said that the Argentines had possibly copied the mausoleum of Napoleon at Les Invalides in Paris for General San Martín's tomb. Three statues of beautiful women representing Argentina, Peru, and Chile stood around it, gazing protectively across the sanctuary.

Estela knelt in a pew near the back and Nina followed suit. She heard her mom asking God to protect their family. Nina thought praying in such a sacred place would ease her mind. But when she closed her eyes to pray, she suddenly felt as though she were being watched.

These days, everybody watched everybody else. Nina's parents often discussed how they had to guard their words in public. A careless comment or action could be very dangerous.

Nina's sense of security evaporated. "Maybe we should go," she whispered.

———⟋⟋⟍———

When Nina and Estela arrived home, Estela began putting away the meager provisions she'd managed to buy. Nina's dad came in soon after. His hands were bandaged and small cuts covered his arms.

"Miguel!" Estela cried, nearly dropping her groceries.

Nina's father waved Nina and her mom off. Nina gave him a worried look, her heart racing.

"Don't worry. I'm fine," Miguel said. "These are just surface cuts."

"What happened?" Estela asked.

"I boarded up the storefront and brought home what few supplies were left," Miguel said. "We can only pray the demonstrators will spare the store this time." He washed his hands in the kitchen sink. "We can also forget about having a steady income for a while."

Nina settled back into her place at the kitchen table, relieved that her father was all right. It sounded like her parents were going to discuss politics. Nina found their discussions interesting. Plus, there was a serious event coming up that might be affected by the current political atmosphere: Nina's eleventh birthday party.

As far as Nina could tell, the unionists were angry at the military for trying to overthrow Perón. They were using bombs to fight back, and the military was using lethal force to suppress them. In the past, Miguel had had to close the store because of rallies, but there had never before been threats of bombs and death. Her parents sounded afraid and Nina felt a knot form in her stomach.

Miguel began to make coffee. As Nina watched him performing the familiar task, she felt the knot in her stomach begin to ease. She was in her house, safe with her parents.

But Estela paced with a fretful expression lining her face. "Perón, the Congress, the military—they're all going mad!" She wrung her hands. "Perón seizing money from one of the most aristocratic families in Argentina. Congress thumbing its nose at the Church by easing divorce laws and cutting funds to their schools. The Church supporting—well, possibly supporting—the attacks by the army and navy." She shook her head.

Nina's father leaned against the counter top. "Now they've taken the religious holidays off the calendar." He nodded in Nina's direction. "And schools are closed as well."

Nina felt excitement course through her. With school closed, everyone could attend her party.

Her mother must have sensed her excitement. "We'll have to postpone your birthday."

Postpone my birthday? Nothing could be worse.

Nina's father poured cups of coffee for her mother and himself. "I was thinking this would be a good time to visit our family in the country." Her father motioned in her direction with his mug. "It will be nice to go to them for your birthday."

"I couldn't agree more," Estela said.

The prospect lightened Nina's spirits a little, but she still wondered if all her family and friends in the city would remember to celebrate her birthday.

Estela took a pot out of the cupboard. "Did you hear those airplanes this morning? Scared me to death. I was just waiting for the bombs to fall."

"It's just intimidation." Miguel shrugged. "They're flying low to let the government know they're in charge of the situation."

Nina imagined the sound of the planes thundering over the city, then the distant thump and thud of falling bombs coming closer and closer as they hit their targets. She imagined cringing people making desperate attempts to find cover, scurrying down alleys and ducking into doorways. The shadows of the jets would pass overhead.

There would be children too. She'd heard that bombs had already killed some, children just like her or Eduardo or Giovanna. What if Giovanna died? What if she or her brother died? Nina burst into tears.

Nina's mother dropped her vegetable knife and wrapped her arms around her. "What is it, little one?"

"What if the bombs kill children?"

"That is unthinkable. Killing children is sacrilege," Nina's father said.

Her mother rubbed her back. "A sacrilege, yes, but sacrileges have already happened. Even the weather is turning against us now. It's as if God Himself is unhappy with Argentina and her people."

"Then let's pack our bags tonight. We'll leave first thing in the morning," Nina's father said.

—◦◦◦—

Nina and Eduardo were both glad to be leaving the city. Her parents' fears had been contagious, and she and Eduardo sensed that things were terribly wrong.

During the three-hour drive to the country, Nina helped out by distracting Eduardo with games, riddles, and songs. That distracted her as well, an added bonus. Cars packed the road. Nina's family was clearly not alone with the idea to escape the turmoil in the city.

"I feel like we're wartime refugees," Nina's mother said.

The unrest had spread to the outskirts of the city. People in the rain yelled, "Viva Perón!"

Nina watched them as her family drove by in silence.

"Mom? Dad? Will life ever be normal again?" Nina asked.

Her parents exchanged glances. They did not answer her question.

The farther into the country they drove, the quieter it became. They finally had a little peace and contentment, such as it was. The rustling of grass replaced the violent protests. Butterflies flew overhead instead of war planes.

Chapter Four

Life in the Country

⤳❦⤴

Nina looked forward to spending time with her Aunt Renata and Uncle Vincenzo. Their large ranch occupied several hundred acres right in the middle of the Argentine pampas. *If we had to leave Buenos Aires, then I'm thrilled with the choice to come here,* Nina thought as they pulled into the driveway. She saw her cousin Samuel going to the chicken coup to gather fresh eggs, most likely for tasty omelets and soufflés. Before the car completely stopped, Nina opened her door, jumped out, and ran to join him. She had always enjoyed helping Samuel with his chores.

"Mom said you'd be staying with us for a little bit," Samuel said, not even turning or breaking stride.

"The situation was getting serious. That's what Mom and Dad said. So we needed to come here where it's safer," Nina said.

"I'm glad. Mom's made fresh pasta and pastries filled with quince jam for afternoon tea. We don't normally get such fancy treats."

Nina had always valued the carefree nature of the ranch. The people there came and went as they pleased, as long as they did their daily chores.

Nina and Samuel brought the eggs inside the house. The adults sat on the porch drinking mate.

Nina wrinkled her nose when she smelled the mate, a popular concoction in Argentina made of yerba mate leaves steeped in a bowl made from the skin of squash. She didn't like its strong taste. The first time she'd tried it, it had burnt her tongue. Mate could be drunk at any time: before or after lunch, or both. The Salvattis had arrived in time for pre-lunch mate.

A couple of hours later everybody was sitting at a table *al fresco*, enjoying a leisurely lunch that ended with a family discussion of important subjects. The extra time spent after dinner in conversation while still seated at the table was what the Argentines called *sobremesa*. Nina knew from experience that the afternoon siesta that would follow was a welcome tradition. Everybody would take a long nap and get up around four to be ready for five o'clock tea.

Nina was more than happy to fill up on pastries and tea. The buffet included scones, coffee cakes, pies, and even more delicacies.

Card games and other board games took up their time until dinner.

Nina grabbed a plate and closely examined the pastry tray. She paused. All the pastries looked good. She decided to try one of each. She carefully balanced her plate, trying to grab a cup of tea. Her plate started to wobble and the pastries slid toward the edge. Nina squeaked.

"Let me get that for you," Samuel said, reaching around to steady the plate.

Nina laughed. "They all looked so good. I had to try one of each."

"That's perfectly understandable. Here, let's sit on the steps." Samuel took her plate and walked over to the porch steps.

Nina picked up her teacup and followed.

Samuel placed the plate of pastries across Nina's lap after she sat down.

"Nina, Samuel…" Estela called. "We need two more people. Come and play gin rummy with us."

After the game was over, Samuel played the piano while Nina sat enraptured by the music. She particularly enjoyed Chopin sonatas and nocturnes, but she loved Mozart's Piano Concerto No. 20 most of all. It was her favorite.

"There's a rodeo and barbeque in town tonight," Renata said.

Nina had seen policemen and workers riding horses in the city, but she'd never seen anyone ride horses for fun. Attending a rodeo sounded like a great way to spend the evening.

"The men tame wild horses and brand their cattle. I don't know if you can handle that kind of thing, Nina," Samuel said with a laugh.

"I can handle anything you can handle," she said.

"Then I'll race you to the cow barn," he said, and set off.

The pastoral beauty of the pampas enthralled Nina, the city girl. She liked twilight the most, when chirping crickets and croaking frogs serenaded her until darkness set upon the landscape. In the tall grasses, fireflies flickered like occasional pinpricks of light in the darkness. Above, the vast black sky stretched from horizon to horizon, ablaze with twinkling stars, crowded diamonds on inky black velvet.

—⚬⚬⚬—

Nina shifted from foot to foot. Her aunt and uncle had brought her to a rodeo, an actual rodeo. Nina's mom and dad planned to come later for the barbeque and dance. Nina wasn't sure what to see first.

Samuel bumped Nina's shoulder. "Let's watch them ride the horses first, then eat empanadas, and watch them rope and brand cattle. By then it should be time for the barbeque."

"Wow. You have this all planned out," Nina said.

"Follow me, greenhorn. This isn't my first rodeo."

The afternoon flew by in a whirlwind of excitement.

Nina was fascinated by the wild horses and the men who tried to tame them. They were not able to cinch a saddle because the wild horses stood on their hind legs, whinnying and kicking every time somebody approached them. It was a contest to see who would hold out the longest, the horse or the man. Either the horse would buck off the man or the man would cling to the horse till it had bucked itself out. Nina found herself cheering along with the crowd. Sometimes they cheered for the man and sometimes the horse.

As she was gathering her things and preparing to move on, a big roan stallion raced into the arena. The big stallion drew her attention. She tugged on the back of Samuel's shirt. "I want to stay and watch this one. It should be exciting."

"You said that about the last three."

Nina clasped her hand in front of chest. "I promise, this is the last one."

"Okay. Then it's off for empanadas."

—◦◦◦—

Nina felt sure that her parents were going to be frantic. She and Samuel were late because Samuel had insisted on eating five whole empanadas. Waiting for the last one had taken longer than they'd expected.

"They aren't going to be worried. You're with me," he said.

Nina walked faster. Samuel had made them late in the first place.

"Hey, it's okay," Samuel said, touching her shoulder reassuringly. "Nothing bad is going to happen here."

Nina could see the lights of the barn. The barbeque and dance appeared underway. She broke into a run. Samuel ran beside her. They cleared the door at the same time. Nina saw her parents standing with her aunt and uncle inside the barn.

"Mom! Dad!" she cried.

Her parents turned at the sound of her voice and opened their arms. Nina ran to them and her parents embraced her.

"Did something happen?" Aunt Renata asked.

"No," Samuel replied. He shrugged. "We watched them rope and brand the cattle. Then we stopped to get another empanada on the way over here, which made us a few minutes late."

Nina lifted her head and pointed at Samuel. "You. *You* stopped for another empanada."

The adults chuckled.

"My Samuel. He loves empanadas," Renata said.

"I think I know what the problem is." Estela lifted Nina's face and smiled. "It's okay, Nina. We're safe here."

"Unless you're an empanada and Samuel is around," Miguel said.

Nina snickered.

"Told you it was okay," Samuel said, throwing his arm around Nina. "Sorry for making you worry though. Let's eat some barbeque."

Nina felt herself relax for the first time since the violence had started. Politics and taming wild horses were kind of the same, she thought. You had to hold on really tight to see who tired out first. Either way, it was quite a ride.

—⟋⟍⟍—

Nina kicked her feet back and forth under the table. The news was boring, but every night the adults sat clustered around the radio, listening. Every night they listened to the news and then to music and radio plays. Nina and the rest of the children were supposed to listen quietly to the news and learn about current events.

Nina glanced at Eduardo, who crossed his eyes. Nina had to smother her laughter before her parents noticed.

She wished they had a television, but there weren't that many TVs around. One of the kids at school back in Buenos Aires had a TV, but she'd heard that his parents still listened to the radio at night. She didn't get it. If she had a TV, she'd watch it all the time.

Suddenly the words "special announcement" caught Nina's attention.

Juan Perón had resigned as president of Argentina and fled the country in a Paraguayan warship. The revolution was over.

With a whoop of delight, her father jumped to his feet. He danced her mother around the room as she laughed.

Nina jumped up and down. "We can go home now!" she shouted. "We can go home!"

She hugged Eduardo. He looked as excited as she felt. Nina looked around. All the children danced and cheered as if it were Christmas morning.

They'd return to the city. Nina's father would be able to reopen his shop. Nina clapped her hands. Life would return to normal. This really was the best news.

Nina's eyes lit up. She could have a late birthday. Nina spun around to find her parents. She wanted to ask them about having a birthday party as soon as possible.

The adults stood in a tight circle and talked in low voices. They didn't look optimistic.

Miguel wore his serious, political-discussion face. Nina crept up to the edge of the circle, where she could hear the conversation without the adults noticing.

"First, we praise Perón as our savior, our God," Miguel said. "Now he has to flee on a foreign ship. Will this country ever settle down?"

It didn't sound to Nina like she was going to have a party any time soon.

"Now, let's hope the leaders of the revolution—Rojas and… what's the other one's name?" Estela looked around the circle.

"General Aramburu," Nina's uncle said.

"Ah. Another general. Let's hope they don't start fighting each other for the presidency."

"That's already been decided. It's Aramburu," Miguel said.

"Praise God for that," Renata said. "But Aramburu will soon discover that even though he's won, many people still love the Peróns. Especially Evita. Without a doubt, her legacy lives on."

Evita had been an angel of peace for the country. Nina missed her, yet even after Evita's death, her image and name could be seen everywhere in Argentina. They had named train stations and other public places after her. Ciudad Evita was named after her. Even a star in the sky was named after her. Her legend had grown larger than life.

"The opposition fears her legacy," Nina's uncle said. "They've dared to remove her body from her tomb."

Nina stared at him, jolted with outrage.

Her mother looked just as furious and horrified as she felt, clapping her hands to her cheeks.

"My God!" she said. "Where did they take her?"

"I don't know," Uncle Vincenzo said. "Nobody knows."

Nina hoped they were careful with her. Surely they would be careful.

"This is the way they do things," Vincenzo said. "This is how they control the people, control their minds. They use so much fear."

"And ignorance," Nina's dad said.

———

Nina sat on the divan in the front parlor and listened to the radio. The windows were open. She could hear the wind rustling the grass and chickens scratching in the yard. They'd be having afternoon tea soon. *I like the country, I really do, but I want to go home.*

Ever since the end of the revolution, the radio had run almost constantly. Nina listened for news of Evita. All over Argentina, the statues and mementoes of Evita were being removed. However, anything used to disgrace her name remained. Nina didn't want to believe what she heard, but the news was supposed to report the facts.

The new military government displayed Evita's wardrobe publicly to belittle her. Nina didn't really understand how displaying Evita's beautiful clothes could shame her, but the news said it did. They said her wardrobe proved she'd been pompous and phony, enamored with the material trappings of wealth. The government wanted to paint "the saint" as a hypocrite. They wanted to demonstrate that Evita had only talked about helping the poor, while enjoying her own extravagant wealth. The new government tried to make Perón supporters look like naïve children for trusting her words.

Nina heard her parents talk about how the poor felt foolish and betrayed. She vowed on the spot that when she was an adult, she would not trust the political leaders, no matter what they promised or how friendly they appeared.

———

Nina snapped one pea after another. She enjoyed the rhythms involved in helping with dinner preparations. Tonight, it was just her and her mother in the kitchen. Her mom had shooed Aunt Renata out to the parlor with a stern warning to relax. Nina smiled at her aunt's sour expression. It didn't look like her aunt enjoyed the idea of relaxation.

Now that the revolution had ended, Nina wondered when they would go home.

"You're worried about home, aren't you?" her mom asked.

Nina had been pretty sure her mom had telepathy. This

confirmed it. "Yeah. How long do you think we'll stay here? I don't want Giovanna to forget me."

Her mom hugged her. "No one could forget you, dear."

"I love Aunt Renata and everyone here, but I want to go home," Nina said.

"We all do, sweetheart, believe me. Unfortunately, it's not just up to us."

"Who is it up to, the military?" Nina asked.

"It's not safe in the city right now. We must be patient, wait for people to calm down."

"May I go play?" Nina asked.

She left without an answer and went to the bed she'd been given for her family's stay. She needed to be alone. She didn't understand why the government and military couldn't get along for the sake of the people. Estela hurried to pack and get ready to go back home.

"Mom I am so excited about going back."

"Yes, dear. I believe that it's time to get back to our normal life. It's time for all us returning to our own home. It will probably be safe now, we don't really know." Nina stared at her. *Why did we spend all this time here?*

———⟨∾⟩———

Readjusting to life in Buenos Aires kept the family busy. School restarted. Nina was happy to go back to the regular routine.

On the second day of school, Nina heard rumors that Perón's followers were planning a counterrevolution.

Nina and Giovanna stood in the school courtyard.

"Do you think that is going to happen again?" Giovanna's eyes were fixed on Nina's face.

"The contras want Perón back, I'm afraid."

"May I go to the country with you this time?"

"What makes you think that we are going to go to the country again?"

"I overheard your father telling your mother that if things got ugly, you'll all leave for the country."

"We'll see." Nina didn't want to even consider the possibility. They'd just moved home a few days ago.

—–⟋⟍⟍–—

Estela and Miguel decided that Nina, Estela, and Eduardo would go back to the country the first week of December, as soon as school was over. Miguel would join them for Christmas and later for Carnival.

Nina found it hard to stay subdued with the holidays coming. She knew that Christmas in the country would be less extravagant than it was in the city but just as joyous, and February was Carnival month. Carnival marked the beginning of Lent, a most holy season, but there was very little that was holy about Carnival. Its raucous excitement was more about releasing tension than growing in piety.

When Nina and her older cousins weren't helping around house, they would enjoy going to the village to attend social club dances during Carnival. Carnival was an exciting time, full of promise: a time to let inhibitions go. It enabled people to let off steam and enjoy life. Carnival's excitement charged the air.

Nina, her brother, and the rest of the family went into the village for the exciting Carnival parades. Nina marveled at the people dressed up in outlandish costumes who paraded down the village streets, followed by bands of screeching kids and excited dogs. The music stirred her soul.

She laughed at the antics of the village kids and the dogs, but the music itself utterly conquered her. The parade twined through the streets like a snake. People danced with great abandon, driven by the rhythm of the music. Some of them wore masks, and most of them wore costumes inspired by myths and local legends. Bystanders tossed confetti and garlands at parade members and the audience.

Nina elbowed Samuel. "Can anyone march in the parade?" she asked.

"Sure," he replied. "But it gets pretty wild down there."

Dancing was a big part of the Carnival parade, but the tango was left for the evenings. As she stood at the back of the ballroom watching with her cousins, Nina couldn't help but sway her hips. The dancing drew her like an enchantment. Although she wasn't allowed to participate until she was fifteen, when she would be allowed to wear makeup and high heels, she loved to watch the other dancers.

Samuel pointed to the dance floor. "Have you ever tried that?"

"I've only ever pretended in my bedroom."

Nina regarded the whole atmosphere with delight: the band, so formal in tuxedos, their music so dramatic, fitting for the tango, along with the usual violins, piano, and other instruments, like the *bandoneón*, a concertina with a bellows and buttons like an accordion. The bandoneón was essential to the tango; music without its lamenting sound was not tango music. She took great pleasure watching the precise, formal movements, as well as the wild abandon of the dancers with passion in their eyes. Someday she wanted to feel that way too.

Whenever she heard tango music on the radio, she wanted to strut, dramatically, passionately, back and forth across her room like the tango dancers she had seen, her chin thrust forward, a haughty, irreverent look on her face. Nina recognized the same look in the dancers' faces, a look that dared the world to try to control them, and she envied them.

She imagined that the look on the dancers' faces was the same look that she would wear when she found true love.

Chapter Five

Innocence and Education

No longer a girl of seven, Nina had stopped aspiring to motherhood and now focused on planning her career instead. Her years of elementary education had been rigorous, and although a number of their other acquaintances had dropped out, Giovanna and Nina had both done well. Now they planned to take the difficult entrance exam that would secure their place in high school.

Having reached a time of decision, Nina couldn't stop pondering her future. Her mom had found a tutor and arranged for her and Giovanna to attend simultaneous sessions with him and split the cost. The grownups in her life placed an emphasis on the importance of education, and Nina couldn't believe that some of her friends had chosen not to continue their studies, even though high school wasn't mandatory. She loved learning.

After school each day, Nina and Giovanna walked to their tutor's house together. The tutor didn't expect them right away, so they took the time to exchange their news. Somehow the topic of their conversations always veered toward their concerns for the future.

"Have you told your father what you want to do when you graduate?" Giovanna asked.

Nina grimaced. "No. He's not going to like the idea of me being an actress. That's so…"

"So what? *Forbidden?*" Giovanna wiggled her eyebrows.

"Forbidden? No, not really." Nina sighed. "He'll think it's a hopeless fantasy."

"Not so hopeless! Remember Evita," Giovanna said. "She was just fifteen when she came to Buenos Aires to become an actress."

"Maybe not hopeless, then. He'll want me to be more practical."

"Ah," Giovanna said. "Practicality again."

Practicality was something of problem for Nina. Although she excelled in her science classes, she longed to find a dramatic outlet for her energy and passion. Like many other Argentine schoolgirls, Nina's soul had been touched by Evita, and she dreamed of emulating her in her chosen profession.

"My parents are so old-fashioned," Nina said. "They won't think acting sounds like an honorable career, even if Evita did it."

"I guess you're right. How many parents are going to encourage their children to be something as… as…"

Nina grinned. "As thrilling? As romantic?"

"You're right! We all wish we could be as beautiful, as divine as Evita, a goddess of the silver screen." Giovanna flourished her arms around her head and bowed deeply toward the sidewalk.

She straightened, laughing, and Nina laughed as well.

"I'd love to be an actress too," Giovanna said. "I think it would be so much fun. But I too know what my parents would say." With a shrug of hopelessness, Giovanna raised her hand in the uniquely Italian gesture that her father often made. "He'd say, '*Basta*, enough of this nonsense. Learn to be something people will respect.'"

"Speaking of respect, Jorge Varela came over last week begging for money again. Guess what he told my father I should do."

"What?" Giovanna asked with disgust and amusement in her voice.

"He told my father I should consider working for him. As a secretary!"

Giovanna's mouth dropped open. "Unbelievable!"

"He said I wouldn't need to bother with 'this high school nonsense.' I could start right away for him."

"Yuck!" they chimed in unison.

"Even if that were the only job available to me for the rest of my life, I still wouldn't work for him," Nina said.

The girls giggled the rest of the way.

———✲✲✲———

Nina and Giovanna took their exam, then waited for two endless weeks for the test results. When people asked Nina how she thought she had done, she barely knew. The weeks of intense study had prepared her well, but the test itself had blurred in her memory. She kept second-guessing the answers she'd made.

The two girls promised each other that they would open their envelopes together, so Nina's parents invited Giovanna and her family over for dinner on the day they got their results.

Nina barely tasted the meal. She clutched her envelope in her lap, trying to get a sense of the results through the paper. It occurred to her that she didn't have a backup plan if she had failed the exam. Would her only option be working as a secretary for Jorge Varela or someone just as awful? She choked down her food, hoping everyone would soon finish so that she could know the truth at last.

Across from her, Giovanna looked similarly anguished.

Once every plate had been cleared, Estela smiled brightly. "All right. Which of you wants to open your envelope first?"

Nina's panic intensified. She was more nervous now than she had been when the envelope had arrived in the mail. They were in the spotlight now, no escape.

"I guess I will," Giovanna said. She ripped open the envelope, took out the letter, and unfolded it. The envelope fell to the floor.

Sweat trickled down Nina's back. She could barely breathe as she watched in suspense.

Suddenly Giovanna squealed, bouncing excitedly in her seat. "I passed!"

"Great job, Giovanna!" Nina said and the others cheered.

Once they were done congratulating Giovanna, everyone turned to Nina. She slowly tore open her envelope and unfolded the crisp, white paper. The high school's seal and name were written elaborately at the top of the page. When Nina ran her eyes down the letter, she could only make out the word *congratulations.*

"I passed too!" she said.

"Hooray!" Giovanna said. "I knew you would!"

After their parents clapped, Nina's mom brought out the celebratory cake. At first, Giovanna and Nina were too excited to eat it, but after a few minutes, everyone settled down.

"Now that you've passed, it's time for you both to make some serious decisions," Miguel said. "It's not enough just to get into high school. You'll need a focus." He took the letter with Nina's results and read it thoroughly. "You scored highest in science and biology. What do you think of those fields, Nina?"

"I really like them," Nina said. She loved science and found the human body fascinating.

"You've always been so good at helping people," Estela said. "Have you ever thought of going into medicine?"

Nina couldn't help but make a face. The thought of seeing blood or cutting into someone made her feel faint. She liked the idea of helping and healing the sick, but she hated the thought of telling people their loved ones had died.

"Then maybe pharmacy?" Estela asked.

"Yeah, that would be great," Nina said. "I think I would like that."

"Until you go to college, you can always change your focus," Miguel said. "Nothing will be fixed for a while."

"How about you, dear?" Estela asked Giovanna.

"I really want to be a lawyer. I read they encourage you to take acting classes so you'll be prepared for the courtroom," Giovanna said, adding a wink for Nina.

Nina found it strange to imagine Giovanna in a suit, arguing in a courtroom. Then again, she had just as much trouble imagining herself behind the counter of a pharmacy. As she ate her cake, her mind raced with thoughts of the possibilities in store for her.

—◈—

Nina's years in high school passed rapidly, filling all her days with study. Almost before she knew it, Nina faced her fifteenth birthday, her *quinceañera*. This rite of passage celebrated the day when Nina would officially leave her childhood behind and enter the world as a young woman.

In between doing her schoolwork, Nina kept an eye on the details of her birthday party as they fell into place. The amount of planning to be done astonished her.

"Other than your wedding day, this party will be the most lavish one you'll ever have," Estela said. "I want it to be perfect for you."

The only thing to distinguish her fifteenth birthday party from her wedding was the absence of a groom, Nina thought.

As if to prove her suspicions, one of the most important features of the party—a tiered, white cake—looked just like a wedding cake. The cake had charms baked into it, each one attached to beautiful ribbons that spilled down the cake's sides. During the party, the girls would each pull one charm from the cake. According to popular belief, the girl who pulled out a thin brass ring instead of the usual charms would be the first to get married.

A half-hour before the party began, Nina put on her handmade dress of white lace and tulle and a matching pair of lace gloves. She slipped her feet into her first pair of high heels and stood carefully, trying not to wobble as Estela pinned white flowers in her hair. She was quivering with excitement. Every glimpse she caught of herself in the mirror seemed to be of some other person.

"You look like a young Audrey Hepburn. Breathtaking." Estela smiled as she looked Nina up and down. "Your father and I have done our best to turn you into a proper young lady and I think we have succeeded. After tonight, the boys won't see you as a scrawny girl anymore. Pretty soon you'll catch someone's eye."

This topic made Nina squirm. Although she'd sometimes envisioned her wedding day or wondered what it would feel like to have a family, that fantasy had been just as remote as her childhood dreams of becoming a princess.

"I won't be looking at them any differently," Nina said. "I want to stay right here with you and Dad and Eduardo for a while."

"Well, you can't stay with us forever," Estela said. "You know, I was your age when I met your father. We attended the same school."

Nina wondered what it would be like to marry one of her classmates. She pictured the boys in her class one by one and imagined saying, "I love you" to each. She grimaced at the thought—she had no romantic feelings for any of them. It looked like love would have to remain many more years in the future.

Her mom chuckled at her expression. "Just keep an open mind when you meet people."

—◈—

Estela had gone to amazing lengths to make sure Nina's party was memorable, ensuring that the food and entertainment were perfect. She had invited a multitude of Nina's family and friends, and many of the friends brought their brothers and male cousins with them. There would be dance partners for every young lady.

There were no childish games or silly songs at this party. These were the 1960s, the age of rock 'n' roll and Elvis Presley, Nina's all-time favorite singer. Instead of waltzing, everyone danced to "You Ain't Nothing But a Hound Dog" and "Jail House Rock." The enthusiastic dancing style was ideal for young teenagers who felt nervous about holding each other close.

The party marked the start of Nina's social life, and her parents continued to strictly supervise her. Nina had many chances to perfect her ability to converse with young men, especially at school functions. Unlike her friends, however, she never felt the urge to go on dates, which her parents had forbidden anyway.

—⁓—

Two more years passed and senior year arrived. Nina's studies had confirmed her desire to work in pharmacy, and now she spent every spare moment prepping for her admissions tests to pharmacy school. Giovanna frequently joined her, hefting the books she needed to read in order to get into the School of Law.

Despite the stress of preparing for the major exams in store for them, Nina and Giovanna were full of anticipation for their senior trip: a ski vacation to Bariloche, the Switzerland of Argentina. Nina had heard all about its magnificent ski slopes and pristine lakes for years, but had never seen them. She looked forward to spending time with her high school friends before graduation separated them.

"We're going to have so much fun in Bariloche," Giovanna said. She had collapsed across her textbook several minutes before and was now spinning a pencil between her fingers. When Giovanna wanted a study break, she took a study break. She claimed it was how she stayed sane.

Nina smiled as she looked up from her own work. She needed a break too. "It's going to be lovely to get away from the city. Can you imagine what it'll be like to relax and not worry about anything?"

"You can worry about catching Franco's eye! I've seen him staring at you."

"Ugh. He's so dull."

Giovanna grinned. "Nina, you think all boys are dull."

"This one really is! All he does is go to political rallies, and all he talks about is what he did at the political rallies. Boring."

"Oh, dear. You do seem to have such bad luck," Giovanna said.

"Franco criticizes me for not showing more 'passion and involvement.' Oh, and one day he brought me a bag of pastries and proceeded to eat them while he went on and on about President Frondizi's 'plans for the country's development.'" Nina mimicked Franco selecting and devouring a pastry from his bag. Giovanna laughed. "Then he talked about how the Argentine people don't understand President Frondizi's ideas, how Perón spoiled them, and how they now expect socialism. When he finally offered me something to eat, he realized the bag was empty. And he still kept talking!"

"Stop, stop!" Giovanna said. "I'm laughing so hard my stomach hurts."

Nina grinned.

"Okay, so that's a no to Franco," Giovanna said. "But I'm sure you'll find love with someone else."

Nina planned to stay clear of politics and love, and told Giovanna so.

Giovanna nodded, then looked thoughtful. "Speaking of Frondizi…"

"If I didn't want to talk about Frondizi with Franco, I certainly don't want to talk about him with you," Nina said. "The two of us should be able to think of other things to discuss."

"*We* can, certainly, but politics is what all guys talk about, Nina."

"I knew men talked about politics, but I didn't realize that 'romance' meant talking about politics too," Nina said, "possibly while doing romantic things."

"That's what we all want—the country to settle down so no one will have politics to talk about."

Nina and Giovanna laughed, but Nina was distracted by the thought of not having politics to discuss. She couldn't even imagine what that would be like. All through her high school years, myriad national and international events had kept the students buzzing. Political troubles seemed to be constant. They certainly were the single force that governed all other aspects of Nina's life, especially romance.

———

Sadly, but unsurprisingly, politics interfered with the happy events planned to celebrate Nina's high school graduation. President Frondizi's government had been characterized by his economic policy of developmentalism, which sought to build up heavy industry by installing multinational companies. Under his rule, the unions grew unhappy. They were no longer granted the same privileges they had enjoyed under Perón. Frondizi's oil, social, and educational policies also stirred up conflict.

As Nina's graduation approached, the situation worsened. The unions organized several strikes, as well as serious sabotages. Large demonstrations on the part of students and workers, as well as numerous political attacks, resulted in seventeen deaths. The government cracked down hard on the demonstrators, banning strikes and putting protestors under the jurisdiction of military courts.

Given the political climate, school administrators decided to cancel the senior trip to Bariloche. When Nina heard the news, she felt like crying. It would have been her first trip without her parents, and she'd looked forward to gaining more independence while enjoying her friends' company and the beautiful sights. It seemed like politics had managed to ruin something else in her life.

—◦◦◦—

After her high school graduation, Nina started pharmacy school without delay and even took a summer course to get ahead of the game when the real work began. Even compared to her busy schedule during high school, her days of studying were long and arduous. She had no life outside of school, especially during the final exam period.

She lost weight, lost sleep, lost connections with some of her high school friends. The signs of fatigue on her face became obvious to everyone.

Nina noticed that her father would stare at her when she came down from her bedroom for breakfast. Any other father would be pleased that she was studying so hard, but Miguel had old-fashioned opinions. One morning, he actually voiced his disapproval.

"Do you have to spend the whole night studying?" he asked. Nina could hear anger and authority in his voice.

Yes, I do, she thought, but she respected her father too much to snap at him. She had to study. If she didn't, she might do badly on her tests and give her father a whole new reason to be annoyed with her.

"I have final exams in three days," she said. She sounded apologetic and resented it. She shouldn't have to apologize for working hard. "I have to memorize the names of hundreds of chemicals and drugs."

Miguel sipped his coffee. "If you ask my opinion, I think you're wasting your time and sacrificing too much."

"What?"

"Look, you're probably going to get married, have kids, and never practice. Why kill yourself with study?"

Nina gaped at him. Why had he suggested she pursue a scientific education if he hadn't thought she'd ever use it? Many of her classmates had gotten married right after leaving high school, but Nina took great pride in her level of education. For her, finding a husband would be a choice, not a necessity. She would be able to support herself and help others with her work.

"We can't judge the usefulness of Nina's entire education based on one night of sleep deprivation," Estela said, bustling into the room. Before Nina could feel relieved, she added, "But what good is all your studying if you have no friends and no life?"

"I have plenty of friends!" Nina shouted.

"You know that's not what I meant," Estela said. "Good relationships don't just suddenly spring up. You have to talk to people other than your family and girlfriends. Go out for coffee. Go dancing."

Nina felt ambushed. She was too tired to get into the argument she often had with her parents. It always ended the same way: they wanted grandchildren and she wasn't getting any younger. Living in the same house with her parents increased the pressure of their hopes, even as she tried to deal with the pressures of her schoolwork.

"You both know this is important to me," Nina said, tears tugging at her eyes.

Her parents exchanged glances. They seemed to have decided to call a truce, because they said nothing else on the subject.

After that day, Estela always checked on Nina before going to bed, and when necessary, she stayed up to bring her coffee and homemade pastries. Nina knew the disappointment she felt about her father's disapproval wouldn't fade for a long time, but her mother's support meant everything to her as she sought to achieve a science career.

Family Foundations

O n the day of her graduation, Nina got up a little later than normal, relieved that she would never have to study so hard again. She admired her organized desk, with all her textbooks neatly stacked on one side. Soon she would only need to use them as reference books, instead of memorizing every name and chemical for tests.

As she brushed her hair, she practiced for her new job. "You will need to take two of these with every meal until the pain goes away. No, no, it is my pleasure to help you feel better."

She was so proud of herself for what her hard work had achieved. She made herself a promise to continue working very hard in order to give her children the best education possible. It would be worth it.

When she entered the kitchen for breakfast, she found beautiful flowers and a big sign glued to the refrigerator that read, CONGRATULATIONS, NINA—CLASS OF 1967. WE LOVE YOU! WE ARE VERY PROUD OF YOU! Nina's eyes filled with tears, and she hugged each of her family members, thanking them for all the support they had given her.

Nina chose to focus on her outstanding achievement and the happiness of her future career. She never mentioned the conversation she had with her father years earlier, when he told her she was wasting her time. Nina could see the pride in her father's eyes. She

knew he loved her very much; any hurtful remarks he had made, he
had made because he was old-fashioned.

The graduation ceremony was crowded and noisy, but Nina felt
comforted every time she saw her parents watching her and smiling.
After hours of speeches, the ceremony ended, and everyone gathered
in the school courtyard. Nina made sure to stay close to her family so
they wouldn't get lost in the sea of other celebrating families. Estela
talked excitedly with the other mothers and they complimented
each other for the role they had played in their children's successful
lives.

But Nina soon grew tired of the ceremony and congratulations.
The real celebration would come later that night.

"Mom, if you don't mind, I'd like to go home and take a nap
before the party tonight."

"Of course, honey. Anything you want. It's your special day!"

All the Salvattis jumped into Miguel's new car. Nina and
Eduardo sat close together in the backseat. Nina remembered her
father's old car that was always parked in front of their home and
kept them shielded from the cold and rain while they played in
it. Several times Nina and Eduardo would call the man who sold
roasted peanuts and buy one or two cones to eat in the car. When
they shelled the peanuts, the empty shells would fall all over the car's
floor and under the seats.

The party was an exuberant affair. Cigarette smoke filled the air.
People laughed, talked, danced, and drank. Nina wandered through
the crowd, stopping to chat here and there. She felt as light as the

drifting whirls of smoke—she'd finally left school behind her. She stopped for a moment just to listen to the sounds of the party. She savored the tinkling of glasses and burbles of happy laughter. She couldn't remember the last time she'd just stood still.

As the product of a strict Old World upbringing, Nina hadn't had much opportunity to attend parties during her teen years. This was a new beginning, a chance to spread her wings. She planned to get a view of life beyond the mundane routine of school and study. Her self-discipline had seen her through the rigors of higher education, but now that she was finished with school, she planned to have some fun.

"Nina!" Giovanna called out to her.

Nina looked around. Giovanna was weaving her way through the dancing couples, a drink in one hand and a cigarette in the other. Nina pointed at a divan that a couple had just vacated, and Giovanna nodded and headed toward it.

Nina arrived first, jogging the last few steps in order to edge out another couple. She slid onto the cushions, crossing her slim legs and fluffing her short hair, wearing an angelic smile that said, "I've been sitting here the whole time." She pulled out her powder compact to touch up her face. The face that stared back at her in the mirror was familiar; her delicate, regal features didn't seem much affected by years of studying.

Nina looked up from her compact. It seemed to be taking Giovanna an abnormally long time to join her. She scanned the crowd for her friend, finally spotting Giovanna with somebody else in tow.

He was a tall, handsome young man with raven hair, a dark moustache, and a cleft chin that completed his good looks. Nina had spotted him earlier that evening but hadn't even considered approaching him. Her traditional background forbid such assertive behavior.

Giovanna took Nina's hand and tugged her to her feet. When Nina stood, she only came up to the young man's chin.

"Nina, I want you to meet Ernesto Rossi," Giovanna said, giving Nina a grin. She turned to Ernesto. "Ernesto, my dearest friend, Nina."

Then she glided away.

"How do you do, Nina?" Ernesto asked. He took Nina's hand and brought it to his lips. Nina thought she would stop breathing, but she demurely lowered her eyes as Ernesto placed a kiss upon her knuckles. She appreciated the gesture; it had charm, and she admired all things with charm.

Ernesto had charm in spades. He was so handsome that she couldn't meet his eyes directly. Instead she glanced at him through her eyelashes, wading through the typical expected pleasantries without knowing quite what she said. As she did, she noticed that his looks were much more direct than hers, lingering longer on her face.

"A noisy party isn't a good place to get acquainted," Ernesto said. "May we go out to the porch?" He gazed at Nina, waiting for her to make a decision.

"Yes, let's go," she said.

Ernesto took her elbow gently and guided her to the porch, where the glass doors and open air muffled the sound from the party. The autumn night air was quite cool. Nina hugged her arms.

Ernesto quickly slipped out of his jacket and gave it to her. She took his jacket and breathed in his scent, a blend of sweet jasmine and musk. Now that Ernesto wore only his starched white shirt, she could see just how trim and athletic he was.

"Giovanna tells me you like science," Ernesto said.

She nodded. "I just graduated from pharmacy school. I plan to open my own business someday."

"I'm a business major. I still have a few years to go."

Nina wasn't sure quite how to talk to young men, but they

did manage to cover the details of their life and status. Like Nina, Ernesto came from a small family and had grown up in Buenos Aires. His father had encouraged him to go into business school so Ernesto could eventually help with his family's business. Nina was amazed by their similarities.

"I love parties like this," Ernesto said. "You can always meet the smartest girls."

Nina smiled. "I love them too."

It was getting late. "I have to get home now, but I wouldn't mind getting together some other time," Nina said. She wanted to see this suave young man again.

"Definitely. I'll call you."

"Do you want my family's phone number?" Nina asked.

"I'll get it from Giovanna."

Ernesto walked with Nina back into the party. She felt light as a feather as she glided to the door and headed home.

—❧—

"Well?" Giovanna asked.

"Well, what?"

"You silly. Ernesto. Do you like him?"

"Oh, uh… yes. He's a fine young man."

Giovanna rolled her eyes. "'A fine young man.' Is that all you can say? He's one of the best-looking guys around. And he likes you."

Nina blushed, her hand moving absently to her cheek. "How do you know that?"

"I have my sources. Did he make a date yet?"

"He said he'd call." Nina shrugged. "But Margarita tells me they all say that."

"Oh, posh, Giovanna said. "Don't listen to Margarita. When was her last date? This year? Or back in '66?"

"She's a nice girl."

"She'd grab him in a second if she could. Don't worry. He'll call."

Giovanna was right, as per usual. Ernesto called the next day.

—◦◦◦—

Their first date was at the Costanera, an avenue adjacent to the Río de la Plata lined with restaurants and bistros. Customs warehouses stretched along one side of the river, facing tall buildings with nineteenth-century-style brickwork. The river had an industrial feel and a government presence.

It was one of Buenos Aires' most popular nightspots. They could dine al fresco or inside, no matter what time of the year. Nina was very happy with his choice for their first date; she had very happy memories of the Costanera from her childhood.

As they sipped pre-dinner cocktails, Nina gazed across the table, watching the candlelight dance across Ernesto's handsome face as he looked around the restaurant. She cleared her throat to catch his attention. "You like this place?"

"Oh, yes," he said, not hiding his enthusiasm.

"Oh. You come here often?"

"Yes."

"When I was a child," Nina said. "My parents used to take my brother Eduardo and I here during the summer. There was summer theater and inexpensive plays anyone could afford. Back then only pushcart vendors roamed this avenue. These modern restaurants have evolved from the pushcart vendors. They were called *carritos*, little carts."

"And they still are," he said.

"Oh, it was wonderful. We would get the most delicious sausage sandwiches, even though our parents weren't too enthusiastic about them."

"Why?"

"They didn't believe it was healthy. My parents were strict about everything. Believe me, a sausage sandwich was a forbidden treat— but one that Eduardo and I really looked forward to."

Out on the river, the lights of passing boats twinkled in the darkness.

"Hard to believe Montevideo and Uruguay are just across the water," Ernesto said.

"Yes, the river is so wide right here."

"So what was the best thing about the performances here?"

"Oh, they were first-class. Something we never would ordinarily have been able to afford. The Perón government wanted everybody to enjoy the fine arts. If not for them, my class might never have experienced culture."

"Ah," Ernesto said.

Nina detected an undercurrent of knowledge in his voice.

"Giovanna told me that before her family immigrated from Italy, the government of Il Duce used to provide free opera tickets to all classes, even the peasants, so that eventually everyone could go to the opera," she said. "You know how the Italians love their opera."

Ernesto smiled. "Do I! I used to wake up every morning to my father's terrible opera renditions. He thought he was Caruso."

Nina giggled.

"He was terrible. I would put my fingers in my ears, hoping he'd finish soon."

"Oh! They used to serve the best *parrillada.*"

"I'm not much of a cook," Ernesto said. "I'd rather eat dishes that other people prepare."

"The parrillada could have all kinds of meat in it—sausages, sweetbreads, and other delicacies. But the best part was the *chimichurri* sauce they put on it."

"You like hot stuff?" Ernesto asked.

"Not really. But I love the combination of garlic, parsley, red peppers, olive oil, and vinegar in chimichurri. It's so wonderful on the meat."

By the time dinner arrived, they were deep in conversation about tangos and *milongas*, a form of music that preceded the tango. Nina had brought it up because she still felt drawn to the dance. The music and the romance of the dancers moved her, but she'd never been to any of the clubs.

"What do you know about milonga clubs? Not that I object to tango, but you just struck me as…" Ernesto stammered. "Well, the women. They, uh, wear such provocative dresses, with slits up both sides. And stiletto heels. I…"

"Oh!" Nina was surprised. She hadn't thought anything of the women's dresses. She secretly cherished the idea of wearing such dresses and high heels, but her old-fashioned upbringing had always kept her from wearing revealing clothes.

Nina felt a blush heating her cheeks. "I've never actually been."

"Then how…?"

"I get it secondhand from my brother Eduardo," she said. "What's good for the boys is not good for the girls. It's so unfair and so old-fashioned." She shot a glance at him, checking his reaction. He seemed engrossed, not disapproving. "I understand my brother is quite the tango dancer," she said. "I'm told his style is like the Apache, somewhat wild and abandoned, like the legendary Rudolph Valentino."

"Ah, I see." Ernesto looked relieved.

They couldn't seem to stop grinning at each other. They talked and laughed for several hours.

Nina wished the date didn't have to end, but the restaurant finally closed. She stood on the sidewalk with Ernesto outside the Costanera. Nina looked out over the river. The night was perfect. Their conversation had flowed in a steady stream, and they had so much in common.

Ernesto placed a finger under her chin and lifted it. Her breath caught.

"Nina," Ernesto murmured and leaned in for a kiss.

But at the last moment, Nina turned her head, offering him her cheek instead of her lips.

He chuckled, and his lips brushed her cheek.

"You're a wily one," he said. "But worth the wait."

Nina began to fall in love with Ernesto at that moment.

She made him kiss her cheek for four more dates. Each night Ernesto chuckled and brushed his lips against her cheek without complaint.

Nina felt sure she was in love. *To be extra-certain though, I have to kiss Ernesto.*

———✿———

Tonight was the night, she had decided. She was going to kiss Ernesto, or let him kiss her. Nina strolled beside him. The night air felt crisp, and her stomach filled with butterflies. They'd just left the movie theater, but she couldn't remember what had happened in the movie. Tonight she'd find out if the feelings floating inside her were really love.

They stopped outside her door. Nina stared at her feet. The moment she'd been planning and waiting for all evening had arrived. She twisted her hands in front of her. *Do I just kiss him or wait for him to kiss me? How can I guide the topic to kissing?*

Nina noticed that while she stood there worrying, Ernesto carried on both sides of the conversation. *How can he not notice that the anticipation is killing me?* Nina stomped her foot and then looked up.

"Have you made up your mind?" he asked.

Nina felt lost. "What?"

"Are you going to kiss me, or am I going to kiss you? You were muttering under your breath. A trait I find adorable, by the way."

Before the startled Nina could respond, he swooped in and kissed her.

Nothing in her experience had been so uplifting, so wonderful. It was simply thrilling. And she hoped to receive many more kisses from Ernesto in the future.

Nina had her answer. She was in love.

The Horse and Carriage

Nina counted their date at the Costanera as the official beginning of their relationship, but it seemed that the wedding might be the official end. Nina dropped her head on her arms and groaned. The seating arrangements, the flowers, the invitations, her dress… there were so many details. Planning the wedding had turned into a full-time job.

She lifted her head and looked at the two sample menus her mom had provided. Nina valued her mom's help, who had offered to take over finding a location for the reception and planning the menus. All Nina had to do was pick one of the two menus. She smiled. The main course on the second menu was the same dish she had eaten at the restaurant the night Ernesto had proposed.

Their relationship had progressed at a whirlwind pace, and he'd proposed shortly after it had officially started. He'd been very romantic about it. He'd hired a couple of mandolin players, and he'd gotten down on one knee, held out his hand for hers, and offered her a lovely engagement ring as he asked her to marry him.

She'd said, "Yes." Then she'd said, "Yes" again, and a third time. Ernesto had swept her into a passionate embrace.

Ernesto had visited her father to make the traditional request for Nina's hand in marriage. She recalled how Ernesto had sweated before the meeting. Her own palms had been clammy, though it turned out they had no reason to worry. Her parents had been pleased with the match. They'd given it their blessing; just like that, it was arranged and sanctified. The wedding would take place the following July.

Nina felt herself flush. She placed her cool hands over her cheeks. She would choose the second menu. It reminded her of Ernesto's proposal. Another decision finalized.

The days left for planning the wedding were going by too fast. Nina hadn't imagined that there would be so much work involved. She spent day after day taking care of too many details—she often thought if she were still in school she would never have been able to do it. Nina looked at the wedding books and the papers scattered around the table. She liked the idea of using things that reminded her of her courtship with Ernesto for the wedding. She jotted a note about the flowers to make sure to include yellow roses. Ernesto had brought her some on every date. She thought it would be very romantic to include them in each of the bouquets.

Nina felt lighter. Remembering Ernesto's proposal had helped brighten her mood. *Now, if I can only figure out how to arrange the seating at the reception so that Great-uncle Francisco and cousin Marcelo are nowhere near each other.*

The phone rang. She crossed the kitchen to answer it, hoping it was Ernesto. She had a few questions for him about the wedding.

"I found the best apartment for us. Can we go there tomorrow so you can see if you like it?" Ernesto asked. "I'm sure you'll love it because it has a street view and faces east, so there's a lot of light in the morning."

"There's still so much to do. It will have to be early in the morning." Nina recognized the excitement in his voice and knew he would be relentless until she saw the apartment. It would take away a large block of her wedding planning time, but she reasoned their first home together was just as important as the wedding ceremony.

"I'll pick you up at nine," Ernesto said. "If you like it, we can pay the reserve deposit tomorrow and then close escrow in about four weeks."

"What do you mean by 'close escrow'? I thought we agreed we'd rent an apartment. You know we don't have enough money to buy it."

"I know. But I talked with my father, and he's willing to lend us part of the money. If your father will do the same, we can buy it. Instead of paying rent, we can use that money to pay them back."

It irritated Nina that Ernesto would assume she could just ask her parents for a large sum of money after paying for her wedding. But he meant well. He didn't necessarily discuss every decision he made ahead of time, but she knew he made his decisions from a place of love.

"I'll talk to my father," she said, "but I'm not sure if he'll be able to do it. Don't forget he's paying for the wedding reception and my dress, the flowers, music, and everything else."

"See what you can do," Ernesto said.

Nina hated asking her father for even more money, but Ernesto had left her little choice. She decided to tell him about the apartment and go from there.

Nina found her father sitting in the living room reading the newspaper. She sat beside him on the divan. "Dad, I need to talk to you."

He folded the paper. "What is it?"

"Ernesto found an apartment we could buy, but we can't afford it on our own. His father is willing to lend us part of the money, but we will need someone else to lend us the rest. I wish we had a mortgage system in Argentina like they have in America."

Nina's father settled back. He looked thoughtful. "So you would be paying us back instead of paying rent?"

Nina nodded.

"That would be a good investment. Buying is better than

renting," Nina's father said. "I do have some savings set aside that you could use and I'd love to help you buy your first home." He smiled at her.

Nina hadn't expected such a positive reaction. She didn't even know what to say at first. Then she threw her arms around him. "Thanks, Dad! Thank you so much!"

Elated, Nina called Giovanna to share the good news.

"The condo apartment is fantastic. It has two bedrooms, a good-size living room, and a big kitchen. I can't believe we're going to buy it."

"I am so happy for you." Giovanna sounded smug at arranging such a successful introduction.

"Are you bringing a date to the wedding?" Nina asked. "How about the attorney who works in your firm, the one from Cordoba?"

"Him? I've already gone on a couple dates with him, but it didn't work out," Giovanna said. "He thinks that because he's a lawyer, he's a big shot. He forgets that I'm a lawyer too."

"Some men are like that," Nina said, "but I'm sure you will meet somebody nice one of these days. Who knows? Maybe you'll meet someone at my wedding, like I met Ernesto at my graduation party."

"That'd be nice," Giovanna said.

———⌘———

Two months before the wedding Nina became concerned when political unrest, so common in Argentina, again reared its grim head. The trouble was in the northern city of Cordoba, where rioting carried on by students and unionists raged. Often such political upheaval could plunge the country into chaos. Nina had not thought much about politics lately. She was too busy with her work and her upcoming marriage.

Nina stood outside the family church, her father at her side. She had accumulated so many memories of this building, where she had attended Sunday services since childhood. Her wedding promised to be a great day among the other memories. As custom dictated, Nina and her father planned to enter through the church's main entrance and to walk down the aisle to meet Ernesto and his mother, who would be waiting in front of the altar.

Nina felt beautiful. The image she'd sought was a mixture of simplicity and natural elegance. Her auburn hair was held up with a simple satin bow with a tail that hung to the waist of her silk wedding dress. The dress ended in a long, split train. From below the bow, a cloud of tulle covered her. Instead of a bouquet of flowers, she carried a vintage Austrian crystal rosary, a symbol of her devotion to the Church and to her new husband. But the departure from tradition also signified her independence.

Nina blotted tears from her cheeks as she and Ernesto stepped through the church doors after the wedding service, which had been deeply moving. They headed down the stairs toward the car that would ferry them to the reception. The wedding guests poured out of the church after them.

Suddenly the sound of gunfire split the night air. It sounded alarmingly close.

People screamed, scattering in all directions in panic. Ernesto pushed Nina into the car and dove in after her. The driver pulled away from the curb and tore down the street. Up ahead, police cars blocked the street, their lights illuminating the night. The driver slammed on the brakes.

"What's happening?' Nina asked.

"With all these police around, it looks like somebody important got shot," Ernesto said. "Relax—we'll probably be here a while."

The street eventually cleared, and they were allowed to leave.

———❦———

At the reception, Giovanna told Nina that terrorists had attacked the home of a high-ranking military official, wounding the daughter of one of the housekeepers, but harming no one else.

"Can you believe it? We were right there," Nina said.

"It's over now," Giovanna said, "and it's your wedding day. Go dance."

Nina smiled. "You're a very good friend."

"You look so beautiful," Giovanna said, bursting into tears. "I'm so happy for you."

Nina reached out and caressed her hair. "My dear, my dear. Why are you crying?"

"Because I'm so happy for you."

The two friends hugged tightly.

———❦———

Nina thought the guests looked like they were having a good time. After the terrorist scare, some people seemed nervous, but others danced and ate. Giovanna kept moving, talking and laughing, introducing people and encouraging everyone to relax.

When it was time to cut the cake, Nina stood at the front of the room. Her father stood close on one side, Ernesto on the other. The cake had three layers, and yellow fondant icing with delicate sugar flowers covered it. Nina hoped it tasted as good as it looked.

Ernesto's large hand cradled Nina's small one in his. Together they placed the cake knife against the side of the cake.

"Are you two ready?" her father asked.

Nina smiled fondly him. He had appointed himself the task of overseeing the cutting of the cake. He'd said he wanted to make sure everything went well for the rest of the evening. Personally, she thought he wanted to make sure he got an extra-large piece of cake.

"We're ready, Dad" Nina said.

"Okay, folks, on the count of three," her dad said. "One, two—"

Before he could reach three, Miguel collapsed.

With a cry, Nina dropped the cake knife and rushed to his side. Her mother dashed to him with another of the guests right behind her.

"I'm a doctor," he said, grabbing Miguel's wrist to feel for a pulse. Nina watched in horror as the doctor continued to check her father's vital signs.

"An ambulance is on the way," Ernesto said.

Miguel stirred as he began to come around.

"That's it," the doctor said. He helped Miguel sit up. "It looks like you may have fainted due to low blood pressure, but you'll need to go to the hospital to be checked out."

Miguel gave her a sheepish look. "I guess I'm the entertainment for the evening."

"Mr. Salvatti, the paramedics are here," the doctor said.

The paramedics placed Nina's father on a stretcher and whisked him away to the hospital. Nina asked Giovanna to handle the rest of the reception. Many guests were in the process of leaving when Nina and Ernesto headed to the hospital with Nina's mom.

The next morning, Nina called to check on her father's condition. Her mother again told her that he was fine. His blood pressure had dropped at the reception, but he was going to make a full recovery. She told Nina to go and enjoy her honeymoon.

Just before boarding the train for their honeymoon trip to Bariloche in the southern mountains, Nina caught sight of a newscast showing a strangely garbed American astronaut walking on the moon. The crowds surrounding the TV seemed enthralled, but the newlywed Rossis were too wrapped up in their own happiness to pay much attention. They were easily as far away from the world as the men on the moon.

They sat in their private compartment and watched the splendor and majesty of the Patagonian mountains roll past their window, a panorama of color and graceful soaring peaks, snow prairies sparkling in the setting sun high up on the mountainsides. Tiny Alpine-like villages clung to the steep sides of the mountains, and the valleys bathed in the deep purple shadow of late afternoon.

Nina thought the city of Bariloche resembled a Swiss village. Most of the buildings were made of wood logs. There were lots of plazas and parks, and the civic center looked like it should have been on a postcard. Nina and Ernesto stayed at a hotel with the same picturesque style. The cozy room had an enormous fireplace, and the wood floors were covered with colorful woven rugs. Everything seemed perfect, and the newlyweds were very pleased with the choice they'd made.

Nina called her parents to check up on her father. Her mom said he was fine.

"Nina, stop calling and enjoy yourself," her mom said.

Next day they went to the Cerro Catedral, a high mountain perfect for skiing. They took the funicular and slid down on their skis. They exhausted themselves with long days on the ski slopes and in the afternoons came back to the hotel for tea near the fireplace. Every evening at the buffet they stuffed themselves with the most exquisite pastries, hot chocolate, tea, and coffee.

"If I keep eating like this, I'll gain weight," Nina said, looking at herself in the mirror.

"That will be an improvement," Ernesto said. "You lost weight to get into your wedding dress."

"Not on purpose! I was running around so much to plan the

wedding that it just happened," Nina said. "The dressmaker had to take it in twice before the wedding."

"You don't fool me," Ernesto said. "I know that you love it."

"I guess I can't deny that."

The following day they took a tour to Villa la Angostura, a paradise of lakes and mountains unlike anything they had ever seen before.

The first sight of it left them breathless, as did the honeymoon itself.

Chapter Eight

Room for One More

❦

On one of those brilliant summer afternoons that bode well for all, Nina was excited by the news she had just received from her doctor. She was pregnant a year into her marriage.

As she waited for Ernesto to come home, she wondered how she should tell him. *Should I be coy and off-hand? Or should I leap into his arms with the good news?* She couldn't make up her mind, but it was a fun question to contemplate. She was still thinking about it when Ernesto came through the door.

"Ernesto," she said. "It's happened. I am pregnant!"

She watched his face for his reaction, hoping it would be a joyous one. Although they both wanted a baby, she knew the news could sometimes strike a young man hard, typically when he realized the enormous responsibilities he was about to incur.

But a huge smile spread across Ernesto's face and Nina thanked God. Ernesto was taking the news with the inherent pride most macho South American men displayed over conceiving their first child.

"Darling!" he exclaimed. "That's wonderful. Maybe this will be the little Vanessa we hoped for."

He picked her up and twirled her around.

When their excitement subsided a little, Ernesto asked, "Will you keep working?"

"Of course. We are going to need the money more than ever."

"How long do you think? I don't want you to endanger the baby."

She smiled. "Don't worry. I'm a medical professional. I know enough not to overdo it and when to quit work."

"I just don't want to do anything that could accidentally hurt the baby."

"Don't worry. Our baby is in good hands."

He grinned. "I'm sure she is."

The next six months were very special. Nina and Estela strolled the streets of Buenos Aires just as they had in years past. Instead of looking for a dress or a birthday present for Nina, however, they dedicated their efforts to finding clothes and furniture for the baby. Nina treasured the opportunity these trips provided for her to bond with her mom.

They entered a shop displaying more baby accessories than Nina knew a baby could need.

"Do you think I should buy something pink? We're almost sure it will be a girl," Nina asked.

"Yes, a little pink." Estela smiled. "But not too much, just in case it's a boy."

"Mom, look!" Nina pointed to an exquisite crocheted blanket. "It seems to be made of feathers. It's so light."

"That's beautiful, but just look at the price." Estela's eyes widened. "For that much money you could buy a lot of baby clothes. Besides, I'm sure somebody will give you a blanket. Maybe two. Blankets tend to be popular gifts."

Nina put her hand on her belly. "I'm sure no blanket will be as beautiful as this one."

"Nina, try to be practical," Estela said, but she was smiling. "You'll have a lot of new expenses. Actually, that reminds me—have you found a clinic where you're going to have the baby?"

Nina nodded. "I talked to several friends, and they agree I should go to St. Joseph. It's run by nuns, and the care is excellent. It might be more expensive, but it will give us peace of mind."

"Good, good," Estela said. "That's why I want you to be careful with your money. If you need some help, your father and I are more than willing to assist you."

"Thank you, Mom, but I'd prefer Ernesto and I take care of this expense. It's our responsibility as new parents."

"I understand," her mom said. "Still, keep the offer in mind."

———◦◦◦———

Nina's pregnancy went well. True to her word, when she was near full term, she quit her job at the pharmacy. Some days Nina felt like she walked around all day with her hands on her lower back, as if by doing so she could hold up her big belly.

Money soon proved to be a stressful topic. Ernesto had not yet finished his MBA, so they had to juggle their reduced income and Ernesto's schooling with the responsibilities and demands of their upcoming parenthood. Nina found herself worrying about finances more than she had expected.

One afternoon, Nina sat on the couch rubbing her arms to bring warmth to her body; although large with pregnancy, she could never seem to get warm.

Ernesto slammed through the front door, his mood hanging like a dark cloud over his head.

Nina hesitated. She didn't want to ask him what was wrong because she figured he was worried about money, his usual concern.

"We're having your favorite tonight," she said cheerfully. "I think I've mastered it. I've made it exactly like your mother's, I hope."

Ernesto didn't answer. He seemed distracted.

"Ernesto? Your favorite?"

"Oh, yes. Wonderful."

Nina leveled her gaze at him. "Doesn't sound so wonderful. What's wrong? Problems at school?"

"Oh, no. Nothing like that. It's the politics."

"Ah," she said, wishing he showed such passionate concern for family matters before damned politics, the constant concern of every Argentine. Nina knew the Montoneros, an extremely radical group of Perónistas who were rallying for Juan Perón's return, were at the heart of the concern this time. Perón, still venerated by many Argentines, was currently in exile in Spain. Last May, the Montoneros had kidnapped the former president General Aramburu, killing him a few days later. They had claimed that Aramburu had orchestrated the revolution that had swept Juan Perón from power in 1955.

Nina lowered herself into a lounge chair, deciding to put aside their personal situation for a few minutes to hear Ernesto's concerns. "It's hard to understand these political groups. Why murder a man like Aramburu?"

Ernesto sat down opposite her. "Isn't it obvious? They are flexing their muscles, showing they have power and the ability to influence the government—one way or another."

"But how strong are they really?"

"Strong enough, perhaps. Small determined groups can accomplish enormous things," Ernesto said. "Just look at Fidel. His small band of revolutionaries were able to overthrow the president in Cuba."

She became thoughtful. "Hmmm. You're right. What do you think is going to happen here?"

"We're sure of one thing. The Montoneros are determined to bring Perón back."

"If they really want Perón back, why did they overthrow General Onganía and put General Levingston in his place instead?"

Ernesto walked to the window and lit a cigarette, staring out across the city. "We live in a complicated country, darling. There are Machiavellian forces at work here. They ousted Onganía to get popular support. Nobody liked him. He was a bastard and has ruled with an iron hand since '66. We like our freedom, and nobody was sorry to see him go."

"Won't Levingston be just as bad? The only way army generals know how to rule is by force."

Ernesto turned to face her. "The Montoneros are biding their time," he said, speaking as though he were explaining a toy to a child. "They're trying to find a way to bring Perón back, and that means they need the right kind of environment."

"Enough of this. We have our own lives to worry about," Nina said. "All I care about right now is our little Vanessa." She touched her hands to her ample stomach. "Can't we love each other and have happiness in our lives, no matter who is in charge of the government?"

"Of course," Ernesto said. He slipped to her side and wrapped his arms around her.

"Dinner will be ready in a minute."

"Good. Pour me some wine."

—⟨∿⟩—

"Ernesto, do you mind if I go take a nap?" Nina asked. "I'm so tired."

The exhaustion didn't make sense. It was a rainy day in September, and Nina had done nothing but play cards with Ernesto all afternoon. Still, it was no reason to worry. The baby wasn't due for a few more weeks.

"Do you mind making yourself a sandwich for dinner?" she asked.

"Of course not," Ernesto said. "Do you want me to make you a sandwich too?"

"No. I am only thirsty. I'd rather rest."

But only a few minutes after she lay down, Nina felt her first contraction. She stumbled out of bed and went to find Ernesto. He sat in the kitchen, watching the news and eating an enormous sandwich.

"What's wrong, Nina? You look pale."

"I think I am having the baby. Let's get my bag and go to the hospital!"

Nina started rummaging in the closet for her bag as Ernesto tried to shove the rest of his sandwich in his mouth.

"Remember what they taught us in the Lamaze classes?" Nina asked. "Don't panic. There is plenty of time for…" A second contraction interrupted her with more intensity than the first one.

Despite her words, Ernesto looked panicky. "We need to call your parents and mine. We should let them know we're going to the hospital."

"You do it. I'm going to sit down on the sofa."

As soon as she sat down, another contraction came. She could hear Ernesto in the bedroom talking to their parents. Nina clung to a cushion, praying that they would get to the hospital in time. *Please, please let the delivery go smoothly.*

Ernesto came back with the car keys in his hands as Nina was recovering from another contraction. They were coming more and more often.

"It really hurts," Nina said breathlessly.

"Our parents are going to meet us at the hospital."

It took forty minutes to get to the hospital. The streets were slick with rain and riddled with potholes. The visibility was bad. Ernesto drove slowly, trying to avoid gaps and ruts in the road, but Nina felt every bump and rumble of the road anyway.

By the time they reached the clinic, the Rossis and the Salvattis were already there, waiting anxiously. Nina held her stomach and Ernesto held Nina's hand.

"I told you they'd be delayed by the rain," Miguel said.

"Thank God you made it," Estela said. "I was so nervous. I should have brought my crocheting." She turned to Miguel and whispered, "Nina doesn't know, but I'm crocheting a blanket for the baby just like one she admired in a shop. It's almost finished."

Nina was sent to a private room with a regular bed where she could lie down. The doctor encouraged her to walk if possible.

"This is going to take some time. You haven't dilated much, and your contractions aren't getting closer together," the doctor said.

"Isn't there anything you can do?" Nina asked.

"We can give you something for the pain, but we want to give your body a chance to do things naturally before we go into other options."

"How long are you talking about?" Ernesto asked.

"I've known some women who were in labor for thirty-six hours or more."

Nina gaped at him in stunned horror. He smiled apologetically.

"We weren't prepared for this," Ernesto said. "I thought we'd have a couple more weeks."

"Yeah, so did I."

"There are things we still need to get ready," Ernesto said. "I could rush home really quickly and take care of them. Do you mind?"

"It's fine," Nina said. "I'll be fine."

She stared after Ernesto as he left. The reality set in that he might not make it back before she gave birth. Then again, maybe she had a while to wait.

The two mothers tried to comfort Nina, but it wasn't an easy task.

The next ten hours felt like thirty. Nina's parents went to find food for everyone. A nurse came and wheeled Nina into the delivery room, then went away to fetch the doctor. Ernesto's parents rushed away to call him to tell him it was time.

Nina lay on the stretcher, all alone in the empty room. Contractions shook her body and she feared she would give birth at any moment. She started screaming.

The doctor and nurse rushed into the room to calm her down. The doctor was efficient and reassuring. He went to work quickly and delivered the baby. Before any of Nina's family came back, it was all over.

Nina had given birth to a beautiful baby girl. They named her Vanessa.

——∽∽∽——

When the baby and Nina were finally home and the grandparents and well-wishers had left, Nina walked over to gaze at the sleeping infant, sighed, and said, "Did you ever see our parents so excited about anything in your life?"

He smiled. "No, I haven't. If it's possible, they are even happier than us."

She smiled back. "No, that's not possible," she murmured as she looked at the angelic, pink little creature in the bassinette.

Ernesto joined her and ran the backs of his fingers along the infant's cheek. "So soft. So smooth. Nothing like the feel of a baby's skin."

"Ah, for you, the father," Nina said. "But for the mother who has to get her to sleep, not as nice. Please don't wake her. It took me a while to get her to sleep after her last bottle."

"It's my job to shower her with all my love," Ernesto said, unable to resist stroking her cheek again. "Daddy's little girl."

They retired to the living room on tiptoes.

"I know this came sooner than we both expected," Ernesto said, "but have you made your plans for work yet?"

"I'm still planning to work; we'll need the extra money until you graduate," Nina said. "I've already picked a wonderful young woman from the provinces to babysit Vanessa once I go back to work."

"When are you planning to go back?"

"Around Christmas. Vanessa will be old enough by then. And I'll be fit enough."

"You're absolutely certain about this girl?"

Nina nodded. "My mother's planning to be around a lot. She'll see that things go smoothly."

—⁓—

Nina's personal life was going as planned and she was pleased with the progress of events. But nothing went so smoothly in Argentine politics. Whenever she read the paper, something outrageous was happening. The Montoneros and the Ejército Revolucionario del Pueblo—ERP, or People's Revolutionary Army—continued their killing campaign, robbing warehouses to get arms and hospitals to get medical supplies for their fighters wounded in the ongoing struggle. Their tactics included kidnapping foreign executives of big companies and holding them for huge ransoms. Those funds helped to finance their activities.

In March of l971, the ruling military junta, seeing the possible course of events, decided to overthrow General Levingston in favor of General Alejandro Lanusse.

Nina was home from work, playing with six-month-old Vanessa, when Ernesto came home. She could see he was concerned. As he picked up the baby for his evening kisses and playtime, Nina decided not to ask him about any political news.

When the baby was asleep and they were having their evening coffee, Nina finally broached the subject. "What do you think about this new man Lanusse?"

"Well, he's one of their own, but…"

"Yes, but he's an avowed anti-Perónista. How did that come about?"

Looking somber, Ernesto said, "One has to look beyond the obvious with these people. It does seem odd that an anti-Perónista would take power when the prevailing winds call for a shift and Perón to come back to Argentina."

"Have you any ideas?"

"No. Not unless I could get into their devious heads."

In the coming months, new political strategies were revealed. Considering that Lanusse had returned many civil rights back to the people, they were even more bizarre. The hard hand of the military seemed to be lifting, for its own reasons and purposes. Lanusse even rescinded the ban on political parties, and the normal political life of the country seemed to flow once again. Most impressively, Lanusse began a dialogue aimed at national agreement.

In line with this strange turn of events and as the antithesis of the old behavior, Lanusse revealed the location of Evita Perón's body, which had been a closely guarded secret so she wouldn't become a political martyr and a rallying point for her supporters. Evita Perón was, after all, the spiritual leader of the nation.

After sixteen long years, Juan Perón was reunited with the body of his beloved Evita. The gesture warmed the very heart and soul of the Argentine people. The political winds, though, were still uncertain and blowing every which way.

———

The Montoneros became bolder. They engineered the escape of important terrorist leaders from jail and kidnapped airline passengers at airports to hold for ransom. They no longer obscured their objective. They wanted to bring Juan Perón out of exile and back to Argentina at any cost. After the brief openness under Lanusse, politics became a verboten subject among the people, to Nina's relief. Political discussions could be dangerous; people kept their political views to themselves, unwilling to compromise themselves in front of people they didn't know or trust.

After years of military dictatorship, Argentines once again became free to vote for a candidate of their choice in 1973. That didn't mean that shady politics ended. Perón no longer legally qualified for presidency, since he had been exiled from Argentina for too many years. His supporters refused to give up on their dream. Perón himself anointed a candidate of his choosing, Héctor Cámpora, who won the election and was sworn in as president in May of 1973.

When the new administration did not move as far toward the left as the Montoneros had hoped, violence erupted anew.

Nina and Ernesto feared for their country and their new little family.

"This new violence is terrible," Nina said.

"And getting worse," Ernesto said. "They're attacking students and professors who aren't left-leaning enough for them."

Ernesto had recently graduated from business school with his MBA—just in time, perhaps.

"The students are the backbone of our country," Nina said. "They'll be leaders in the future."

"If they live long enough," Ernesto said grimly.

"You mean they're actually killing them?"

"Now and then, people don't show up for class. What do you think happened to them?

Nina hated talking about politics with Ernesto. As the conversations wore on, he would grow more and more impatient until he sounded displeased with any stance Nina took.

"I hear Perón is planning to come back in June," he said.

Nina raised an eyebrow. "Really? That's unbelievable. Juan Perón back in his own country after so many years. What do you think will happen? The Peróns worked hard in the 1950s to appease the next generation of voters, the same people who are now forcing the government to allow Perón back into Argentina after his exile in Spain."

Nina had realized years ago that much that had happened during the Perón era of her youth was designed to turn children into loyal partisans as adults. That was the real reason Nina and countless others had been invited over the years to the Casa Rosada. When the Peróns had congratulated the little girl for academic excellence, they'd actually been bartering for her lifelong support.

Again Ernesto shrugged, a gesture he had been using a lot lately. "I'd feel a lot better about our future if I knew, but I don't. I worry for our little girl's future. Do I want her growing up in such a hot spot? A place where you think you're safe and secure one day, and the next day can't know what will happen?"

On June 20, 1973, Perón's much-heralded rally at the airport drew more violence than anyone had anticipated, forcing his plane to land at another airport. Thirteen people were killed and many more injured by snipers who opened fire on the waiting crowd.

The next day, the people of Argentina heard an old familiar voice on the radio, proclaiming his hopes for a peaceful reconstruction. None of Perón's charisma had faded over the years. His broadcast seemed to regain the confidence of the people.

Nina and Ernesto were hopeful, but knowing the nature of their volatile country, they held their breath. Soon after, the current president of Argentina resigned, and Perón ran for reelection with his new wife, Isabel, on the ballot as vice president. Despite opposition, Perón received 62 percent of the vote, returning him to presidency after eighteen years in exile.

"Do you think Perón is going to be able to restore peace and prosperity?" Nina asked Ernesto a few weeks later.

"You'd think so, but if you're an Argentine, you'd have to think again."

Used to his skepticism, Nina simply nodded. "Things weren't so bad before under Perón. Why can't they be that way again?"

"If we lived anywhere else, I would agree, but, darling, this is Argentina," Ernesto said. "Changes come very fast. From what I understand, the Montoneros are still unhappy with the situation."

"But didn't they themselves want Perón back?"

"Exactly."

"And so?"

"So? The reason why I am not optimistic is it seems the Montoneros' goals, which included the return of Perón, are not being met by Perón."

Nina was perplexed. She tried to hide her confusion so she wouldn't upset Ernesto more than the politics did. "What do you mean?"

"It seems they are further to the left than Perón ever was."

"We should cry for Argentina," Nina said. "It seems she will never be free."

"Or safe either. Never the two, it seems, together."

Replacement

Nina's professional dream was on the horizon: all she had to do was reach for it. She had made a preliminary agreement with three of her coworkers at the pharmacy to open their own pharmacy together. The pooled resources of the four founders would make the initial investment possible.

Nina's excitement and the glow on her face as she arrived home could not be hidden.

"What is it? You're beaming. Are you pregnant again?" Ernesto asked.

"No. Adriana, Susana, Pedro, and I have decided to open a pharmacy. We're all experienced, and I think we can each attract our own customer base. Just think of it. Our own business!" Her smile faded slightly. "Well, almost our own business. What do you think?"

"I think that's fantastic," Ernesto said. "The only way to real success is to work for yourself. Of course," he said, "it's going to be tough at first. It's tough with any new business."

"There's more," Nina said. "Should I tell you now or at dinner?"

"I can only take so much excitement at once. Tell me at dinner. Let me get some time in with my little cherub Vanessa." Ernesto went off to play with their four-year-old, as he always did before dinner.

Both enjoyed the stability of married life, and both adored their child. Their only regret was their inability, so far, to conceive again. Nina saw that it hit Ernesto particularly hard to have no son to carry on his family name. And unlike some children, who wanted all their parents' attention, Vanessa craved a sibling. Nina and Ernesto suspected that if she actually got one, she might enjoy sharing the spotlight less than she thought she would. But her dream of a brother or sister seemed to play a part of her every conversation.

The moment they sat down to dinner, Nina couldn't hold back the rest of her news.

"About the new pharmacy," she said.

"Yes?"

"We've decided our business could use a good business administrator," Nina said. "And since you're the best administrator I know, I suggested you, and they agreed!"

Ernesto cocked his head. He bit his lower lip, something he always did when he had something important to think about.

"I'm flattered, of course," he said. "But it will mean that between us, we'll have to double our investment, and I'm afraid that would put too much strain on our finances."

"Yes, you're right," Nina said quickly. "And we know we have to do everything as inexpensively as possible, at least at first. We've got our eye on a piece of property that should suit our purposes."

"But?" he said, his eyebrow arching.

"But it needs a lot of work. We're figuring out a plan to do the work ourselves. It'll be a community effort. One of us will take care of the kids, another will take care of feeding us, and the rest will turn our little place into the nicest pharmacy in Buenos Aires."

Ernesto smiled. It usually took a while for Nina's enthusiasm to transfer to Ernesto, but it was obvious that she was excited about the new business and their future. They raised their wine glasses. She said, "To the future." They clinked glasses and sipped some wine.

"To the future," he said.

——∿∿∿——

Nina was pleased with how well the new business partners worked together. As she had promised, they turned the new pharmacy into a community project. Each partner brought his or her respective spouse to the project, and they worked together on it every evening. The women cooked dinner, minded the children, and took turns with some of the construction tasks, while the men tackled the building and renovation of the store. The mood was one of cooperation, goodwill, and optimism. Everyone took part without complaint.

One evening when Ernesto, Nina, Pedro, and his wife were putting the finishing touches on the front counter, which needed only the laminated countertop to be complete, Nina noticed the usually cheerful Pedro seemed more quiet than usual.

She nudged Ernesto and gave Pedro a meaningful glance.

Ernesto nodded. Nina realized he too had noticed the change in Pedro's demeanor.

"So, Pedro," Ernesto said. "What do you think of our new president?"

Each person working on the project was an old friend, and the group had little compunction about talking politics—something people didn't do in Argentina unless sure they were among trusted friends. The paranoia wasn't necessarily rational, yet it was always there.

Pedro, who had been sanding a corner of the counter, looked up. "Frankly, my friend, I am worried."

"Because we're going into a new business?" Ernesto asked.

A look of surprise flitted across Pedro's face. "Yes." He paused, carefully sanding some more before continuing. "And because Juan Perón has cancer, and he's not getting any better. When he dies, his wife will become president, and even though Isabel is a Perón, she's not Juan or Evita."

Ernesto frowned. "True. Things aren't going as well under Perón as before. How much worse could his wife be?"

"Certainly she is an unknown at the moment, but one thing we could always count on with Juan was that he's for business and free enterprise."

"Are we so sure of that?"

Pedro shrugged. "Perón is feuding with factions of his own party, but I think when all is shaken out, his pro-business stance, the one he first acquired when he was with Evita, when he achieved all his greatness, will prevail."

Ernesto grinned. "Pedro, I never knew what a romantic you were. You believe everything Perón ever became was the result of his marriage to Evita."

Pedro grinned. "Call me a hopeless romantic," he said, finished with his sanding, running his hand lovingly over the edges he just smoothed. Eyeing the finished counter, he said, "I hope a lot of money comes over this counter."

Ernesto said, "Me, too, my friend. Me too. Now let's all go eat. I see the girls have a feast ready for us."

———

Three months later Nina and the others stood proudly by their labor of love. Every nail they'd driven, every brush of paint they'd applied was a testament to hope and opportunity. The business was soon off to a strong start.

Nina and each of the partners brought a core group of customers to the pharmacy, and they worked diligently at building good customer relations. Soon they were able to finance a new store and hire a crew under Ernesto's management. Business prospered. To celebrate, Nina and Ernesto decided to take Vanessa on their first family vacation.

"You know, my parents keep asking us to come down to their summer place in Mar del Plata," Nina said.

"It's quite a drive, but it would be fun to try out our new car," Ernesto said.

"I'm sure Vanessa will love the beach."

"Let's take them up on that offer then."

Nina got on the phone after dinner and called her parents to ask them if they'd like to come down along on the vacation as well.

It was a convenient and relaxing vacation for the happy little family. Ernesto and Nina had loving grandparents to babysit Vanessa while they visited the myriad restaurants and bistros in the Argentinean seaside resort area. They feasted on the freshest gourmet seafood at night, and during the day, they went to the beach with Vanessa.

Nina loved to watch her family. Ernesto particularly enjoyed playing with Vanessa in the surf. With the sun shimmering and the waves rhythmically crashing on the shore, Ernesto and Vanessa would frolic in the roaring surf like a pair of playful seals. He would toss her into the water like a beach ball while Nina admonished him from the blanket to be careful.

One afternoon, Ernesto and Nina found themselves alone on the beach; Vanessa was off with her grandparents on some excursion. It was a soft summer afternoon, and the seagulls circled lazily, squawking and diving. Nina sat alone on a beach blanket enjoying the last days of their vacation. She watched her husband jog in from the white foamy surf and, panting, drop to his knees before her. She tossed him a towel, and he shook out his hair, spraying her before he dried himself off and took up position beside her.

"The water is wonderful," he said, still panting slightly.

"I'm sure it is, but I like to just lie here and think."

"About what?"

Nina sat up, drawing her knees up to her chest. "I've been thinking… maybe we should send Vanessa to that British school. It's got an excellent reputation and it's also bilingual. It would be great for her to learn English."

"I agree. English is a very valuable asset in this cosmopolitan world."

"There's one potential problem, I guess."

"The cost?" he asked.

Nina nodded. "I've looked into it. It's expensive."

Ernesto smiled slightly. "Like all good things."

"Exactly. It's worth the expense. Anyway, I've worked things out and I think we can afford it."

Ernesto chuckled. "I think you have a secret motive."

"Oh?"

"I mean… you're a bit of a snob."

"A snob?"

"Oh, yes. You'd like to say 'my daughter goes to an exclusive school.' How prestigious that is."

She gave him a playful slap.

"I am not a snob," she said, grinning. "Well… maybe just a little. But it's nice to be able to afford good things and provide for Vanessa. I do want her to have a good education."

"Now that we have money, there are other things we can spend it on," Ernesto said. His eyes contained new eagerness. "I know we went to the clinic before and it didn't work, but we can try again. Maybe a different one."

A few months earlier at Ernesto's insistence, they had visited a fertility clinic in Buenos Aires. Nina remembered the sad, desperate faces of the women in the clinic as they waited to be called. The sight made Nina want to bury her face in a magazine. She could not relate to their pain. Nina didn't mind only having one child. Vanessa took up so much of their time, and she liked focusing on her budding career. She did not feel the same longing as those waiting women and she felt almost ashamed to be near them.

The doctor ran all sorts of tests on Nina. Ernesto wanted the doctor to perform every test he could. He didn't seem understand why Nina wasn't able to have another child.

The doctor asked Ernesto to wait outside, and then he told Nina everything looked fine. She was disappointed that she wouldn't have a concrete reason to give Ernesto about why she couldn't have more children. It would have been easier to blame a physical defect rather than tell him she didn't know why.

"The lab tests might show more, but from what I can see you are perfectly healthy," the doctor said. He went to the door and listened for a moment. "Is everything all right at home?" he asked quietly.

"Of course," Nina said. She didn't know how to answer such a personal question from a near stranger. "Why would you think otherwise?"

"The body can shut down to protect itself," the doctor said. "Occasionally a healthy young woman comes under a great deal of stress from her husband…"

Nina stared at him and he patted her hand. "The mind is a very powerful thing," he said. "It knows when it's a bad time to bring another baby into the world."

The doctor's sympathetic words overwhelmed her. Nina tried to hold back her tears. "It's not that I don't want more children…" she whispered.

"But maybe not with him?"

Nina stumbled to her feet and fled the office. Ernesto hurried to her side when he saw her crying.

"What's wrong?" he asked.

"Nothing," Nina said. "Let's go home."

Ernesto put his arm around her as they left the clinic.

Tears welled in Nina's eyes as she thought about that last visit. She'd told Ernesto that the doctor had said that her body wasn't ready to have another baby.

"I don't want… Ernesto, I can't visit another clinic just yet."

Ernesto nodded, but didn't press the issue. Instead he stood up, brushed off some sand, and headed back into the water.

Ernesto didn't bring up the topic again after their family vacation, but Vanessa did. She constantly reminded Nina of her longing for a sibling. Vanessa would come home from school with questions like, "Mom, how come I don't have brothers and sisters like the other kids at school? I have no one to play with."

"But you have friends, darling."

"It's not the same. Is it?"

Nina didn't answer, and her heart went out to her daughter. When she did respond, she hedged her answers with comments like, "God will give us what He wants to give us when He pleases"; "One does not order little brothers and sisters like they were a gift from the store"; and "One must be patient and accept God's blessings as they come."

After such encounters, Nina would retreat within herself. It didn't matter what she told her child: she'd begun to feel guilty for depriving Ernesto and Vanessa of joy.

She sat at the dinner table and watched her daughter play with her peas. How long could she put Ernesto and Vanessa off? Her guilt over keeping a younger sibling from her daughter increased with each passing day.

Vanessa looked up. "I think I can wait for a little brother or sister. We have to wait for what God gives us."

Vanessa was so accurate at mimicking Nina's thoughts that it felt like they were connected. Nina cocked her head and gazed at her child. "That's a very mature attitude for such a little girl."

"While I'm waiting for God to make up His mind, maybe I

could have a puppy. It will be fun to have one to play with, while we're waiting."

"I see," said Ernesto. "Like a new baby, new puppies require care. You need to bathe them, feed them, clean up after them."

"I'm a big girl," Vanessa said. "I know how to do all that stuff."

Nina liked the idea. Surely a pet would take away some of the pressure for her to have another baby. It would distract Ernesto and Vanessa, at least for a while.

"What kind of puppy do you want?"

"A white one."

"What breed? A spaniel, a terrier—you know. What kind?"

"Any kind. As long as he's little, like a new baby." The delight in her face was irresistible; Nina knew neither she nor Ernesto could deny her.

"Can we look at some different kinds?" Vanessa asked. "Where do you find them, anyway?"

"I know a breeder," Ernesto said. "I can call him right now."

Vanessa hopped onto her father's lap. "Can we, Dad? Can we? Really?"

Nina shared in the happiness. It might have been wishful thinking to assume getting a puppy would take the place of another child for Ernesto and Vanessa, but Nina didn't care, as long as it made them both happy now.

The next day, the whole family looked at one wriggling puppy after another. They finally found a tiny poodle that they fell in love with at once. The little ball of fluffy white fur seemed to especially love Vanessa. She licked Vanessa's face with fervor.

Vanessa screamed with glee. "Yuck. She's so slurpy. Does that mean she loves me, Dad?"

"I think so. She'd bite you if she didn't like you," Ernesto said.

Nina allowed the puppy to sleep with Vanessa that night. She worried that she'd set a dangerous precedent, but what else could she do? They didn't have a place for the puppy to stay, and Vanessa wanted to keep the puppy close at all times.

Vanessa named the puppy Sheila. The adoring Rossis soon found myriad ways to spoil her. Ernesto built her a custom doghouse the very next day. A seamstress made a custom-fitted pillow for the puppy's new bed, which even had a valance around it, like a baby's cradle.

Vanessa cared for Sheila with joy and pride. "Isn't she beautiful?" she said. "Wait until the kids at school hear about her."

Ernesto and Nina shared a smiling glance.

"She's such a proud parent," Ernesto said.

"Yes, such a proud parent."

She could see he was concerned.

As he picked up the child for his evening kisses and playtime, Nina decided not to ask him about any political news.

Chapter Ten

Watchful Eyes

～⟨◊⟩～

A fter Juan Perón's death in 1974, Isabel Perón succeeded him as president of Argentina. Many welcomed her, believing that a woman's hand in government could solve their problems; surely a woman's touch would be kinder and gentler. But politics in Argentina had never been a kind and gentle business. The hands that stirred the political cauldron were anything but kind. It soon became clear that Isabel was not Evita, and her administration was not well regarded. The hardline Perónista leftists, the Montoneros, and the Ejército Revolucionario del Pueblo were killing foreign executives, high-ranking police chiefs, union leaders, politicians, journalists, and foreign tourists. They bombed government buildings and upscale country clubs.

In an attempt to control the chaos, Isabel's government asked her secret police for help with quelling the rebellion involving the small terrorist cells that were forming. Isabel's power had declined to the point where her advisors were actually making the decisions for her; they had no clear strategy for success. The country fell deeper and deeper into political and social chaos, culminating in a coup d'état and a military dictatorship headed by three men. The destitute Isabel was taken prisoner and held in a hotel in the south under military custody.

In its zeal to stop terrorists, the military waged a terror-filled campaign against everyone they considered suspicious. Many innocent people disappeared forever after being taken to secret detention centers. Democratic institutions were dissolved. Parliament became a social club. The military banned political parties from action and forbid workers from striking. All the important government ministries were headed by people handpicked by the dictatorship.

Like many German civilians in the Third Reich, the Argentines knew something was wrong, but never in their wildest imaginations did they realize the extent of the evil at work. Only after decades of secrecy would they learn that illegal detention, torture, and murder had been the order of the day.

———

Ernesto banged through the door with a nervous, worried look on his face. Nina hated it when he wore that expression; it always heralded bad news. He walked over to the kitchen table, but Nina stopped him before he could sit down.

"What is it?" she asked.

"It's just this damn political situation," he said.

As much as Nina disliked hearing about politics all the time, she was secretly relieved that she hadn't done anything to upset him. Ernesto was easily angered lately, especially about politics. But his fuse was growing shorter and shorter on almost all subjects Nina brought up.

"Has something happened?"

"We were talking at work, and somebody said, 'Be careful what books you have around. If the Army finds you in the possession of certain ones, you'll disappear.' Isabel Perón isn't even in charge anymore. The military is killing everyone they don't like."

"What does that have to do with us?"

"Don't you remember that book on Evita's life? The one you love so much?"

Nina's hand went automatically to her neck. Lots of books from Perón's presidency remained on their bookshelves. As they'd moved from house to house, they'd moved the books with them, never thinking that anyone would care what they read, no matter how dire the political turmoil.

"Do you think they'd consider it dangerous?" she asked.

"Who knows? The country's gone crazy." Ernesto hurried to the bookshelf in the living room. "Look, there's my copy of Marx's *Das Kapital*. Imagine if they find that on me!"

"But you had to buy it for your business courses."

"Ah, but books can mark a person and identify their political persuasion," Ernesto said. He pulled *Das Kapital* from the shelf and tossed it on the floor. "Any book with a Perónista or leftist message is being burned. It's just like what happened in Germany in the thirties. These people were uprooted by WWII. Now they're repeating the sins of their fathers, plunging Argentina into fascism."

Ernesto's fear was infectious. Nina scrambled to join him. "We need to get rid of Marx. Get rid of all them."

Nina flung book after book on the floor as she hunted for questionable material. Soon she had gathered a pile of all the remotely political books beside the fireplace. Her hands trembled as she lit the logs and stoked the flames. She couldn't believe the fear growing inside her. *The government wants me to be afraid. It actually wants me to feel this way.* The military and police were supposed to protect their citizens, not treat them like terrorists and wage secret campaigns against everyone they suspected. *How many innocent people will never be heard of again?*

"Parliament's a joke, the political parties are banned from action, workers are forbidden to strike, and all the important government ministries are headed by people handpicked by the dictatorship," Ernesto lamented while Nina stared into the flames.

Nina tore pages out of her books to help them burn faster. Her books meant so much to her. They helped her make sense of the world. As she tossed another book into the fire, she felt a piece of herself drift up in the smoke from the burning papers. Thanks to the government, people were no longer safe to have a heritage. The smoke stung her tear-filled eyes.

After she put every questionable book she found in the fireplace, Nina realized she hadn't come across her copy of Evita's *Reason of My Life*.

"Where's *The Reason of My Life*?" she asked. "If that's the worst thing they could find... where is it?"

"Maybe it's still in your parents' house."

Heart pounding, Nina jumped to her feet and ran to the phone to call her mother. Instead of exchanging pleasantries, she wasted no time. "Mom, do you still have my copy of Evita's book?"

Estela hesitated. "No, we don't have it, dear."

Relief rushed through Nina. Her parents would be all the safer if they didn't have such an incriminating book in their home.

"Actually... we lent your Evita book and your picture of her to Jorge Varela," Estela said. "You remember our old neighbor."

Like many people who never forget their first loves, Nina certainly never forgot her first hate. The thought of Jorge with his fingers all over her framed picture of Evita made her stomach clench.

"Why would you? How could you just give that away? What were you thinking?" Nina's tears turned to tears of rage as she realized what Jorge had stolen from her without her knowledge.

"It was years ago," Estela said. "He said he wanted to impress the government officials he was doing business with. When he saw the picture, he said he would hang it on his office wall. He promised to give them back right away, like always."

"He wouldn't want the picture in this political climate. Has he returned it yet?"

"I'm so sorry, Nina. When your father finally asked him

about it, Jorge said it was stolen from his office. He doesn't have it anymore."

Despite her mom's apologies, all Nina could hear was that her parents had given the picture away and not told her.

Wide-eyed, Nina hung up the phone and turned to Ernesto.

"That was my favorite picture. No one ever knew what I went through to get that," she said. She slumped down on the floor, trying to catch her breath. The picture of her beloved childhood hero was gone forever, thanks to someone else's careless actions. She was devastated by the betrayal.

But she didn't have time to mourn her loss before fear struck her. "Ernesto, what if it comes back to hurt us? My full name is on it."

She almost laughed at the irony of the fear and trouble Héctor Torres would have saved her if he'd really had torn up her photo so long ago.

"Don't be paranoid. It was a while ago. If they haven't found it yet, maybe they won't," Ernesto said comfortingly. "Does the government have the time and resources to look for old pictures of Evita? Or search for lost books? It's insanity, I tell you."

"Insanity," Nina repeated.

Ernesto ran his hands through his hair, a nervous gesture he'd had since childhood. The current government would use anything, no matter how small, to implicate anyone it saw as a threat. Ernesto's words couldn't hide his worry.

"Come on, Nina, cheer up. We'll have fun at the party tonight," he said.

Pedro was having a birthday party, and they'd promised to go. Otherwise Nina would have rather stayed home in bed. A party was the last place she wanted to be. All desire to make contact with the outside world was gone. She was so listless that Ernesto had to help her wrap the present and find clothes to wear.

At the party, Ernesto led her to an empty chair, handed her a drink, and then went off to mingle. The laughter and music seemed muffled to Nina and the lights hazy. Nina's thoughts traveled elsewhere. With so much going on, the party didn't seem important.

Her friend Marta sat down beside her, drawing Nina's attention back to party.

"Aren't young girls terrible these days?" Marta whispered.

Nina scanned the room, automatically looking for girls Marta might be critiquing. She spotted a young couple in the corner getting very well acquainted. Both looked like teenagers. The boy wore khaki pants and a white shirt, mostly unbuttoned. The girl wore a short dress that revealed more legs and cleavage than Nina would ever dare show in public. The boy traced his finger slowly along the dress's neckline and Nina blushed.

Marta was a frequent customer of Nina's pharmacy and would often chat with Nina. Nina enjoyed her company. The two occasionally enjoyed coffee together in their spare time. Nina knew Marta enjoyed disguising her true intentions by first pointing out something humorous.

Her curiosity outweighing her melancholy, Nina matched Marta's whisper. "Come now, Marta, the promiscuity of young girls doesn't bother you."

"But that girl is so obviously innocent, and look what that boy is doing to her. Scandalous!" Marta always seemed to be in light spirits, using anything to achieve a laugh. She was oblivious to Nina's mood, which was the complete opposite of hers, but Nina welcomed her playful manner.

"Tell me what's really on your mind."

Marta sobered. "It involves one promiscuous girl in particular. Her name is Laura. Her mother is a friend of mine."

Nina waited. Marta liked drama just as much as humor and was now playing her information for effect. "She's sixteen, Catholic, and five months pregnant."

"Too late to do anything about it now," Nina said. The poor girl must be going through a terrible time; her pregnancy would be so hard on her whole family. She felt very sorry for any unwed, pregnant teenager in the predominantly Catholic Argentina.

"The family is very religious; they never even considered ending the pregnancy."

"That girl's in for a rough life then." Nina still couldn't see where Marta was heading.

"I know you mentioned how your Vanessa wants a brother or sister—she fantasizes about it."

"That's true."

"And that it made you feel so guilty?"

Nina nodded. "Ernesto and I bought an adorable little poodle hoping it would be a good substitute."

The puppy had been enough for a few months. But little comments and questions about another sibling had started creeping back into Nina's daily life, much sooner than she hoped.

"A dog. How heartwarming," Marta said. "So… do you think you'll consider this baby?"

"What?" Nina suddenly made the connection: Marta thought Nina could adopt the baby. The new possibility stunned Nina. Thought after thought crowded her mind. It would be easier than having a baby herself. She wouldn't have to go through the pain of pregnancy, Ernesto and Vanessa would be satisfied, and it might bring Ernesto and Nina closer together as well.

But it would also mean a new set of worries. Argentina wasn't the safest place to raise a family.

Marta seemed eager. "Well?"

Nina's glance wandered over to Ernesto, who stood among a group of men, drinking and talking excitedly. "Let me talk it over with Ernesto. Then I'll give you my final answer."

Nina waited until they were back at home, getting ready for

bed, to bring up the subject with Ernesto. She couldn't imagine him putting up much resistance against what his heart really wanted.

"Marta found a girl who's putting her baby up for adoption. She's offered it to us."

"What? A baby?"

Nina had expected him to be excited, but Ernesto looked tired instead. He sat on the edge of the bed and ran his hands through his hair. "We just finished burning our books, and you want to bring another life into this climate? It might not be as easy as you think. Often a social worker intervenes in an adoption, and the baby is placed in an orphanage until the paperwork is completed. That could mean many more months before we even get the baby."

"That's true," Nina said. The idea sounded less and less promising.

"Remember how that poor man on TV struggled to get some missing documents from the government bureaucracy?" Ernesto said. "They told him to come back another day. When he returned, they were ready for him, asking for a birth certificate, marriage certificate, vaccine records, and a lot more. You want to go through that?"

Nina sighed. "I thought you might be pleased."

He simply shrugged.

He's bothered me for months about having another baby, and here a baby has fallen into our laps. The thought convinced Nina. She wanted this baby.

"Many people just skip the whole process and get a doctor to sign the birth certificate as if they had the baby themselves," Nina said. Her voice rang with resolve. "When doctors are driving taxis to make enough money, it can't be difficult to get one to do it."

Ernesto looked at her in surprise, but he seemed impressed by her willingness to obtain the baby.

"Let me check around," he said. "I'll see if it can be done. But don't get your hopes up."

———◦◦◦———

Like many other Argentines around this time, Nina became aware of shiny black cars with tinted windows and no license plates. She noticed the black cars for the first time when she was at a bakery with Vanessa and her thirteen-year-old nephew, Gaston.

As the children sat outside and munched happily on their little sandwiches, Nina paid the man behind the counter. When she went out to join the children, she noticed that they were staring across the street instead of eating.

"What are you looking at?" she asked, following their gazes.

She quickly saw for herself. In a small alleyway across the street, two large men in dark suits had pinned another man to the ground. A third man in a dark suit stepped out of a shiny black car, grabbed the helpless man by his collar, and pushed him into the car.

The car could only belong to the government's secret police. Nina felt a wave of fear ripple through the people on the street. In the days to come, whenever people saw the black cars, they would duck into stores or doorways, whether they were guilty of anything or not, hoping they wouldn't catch the attention of the police.

But Gaston pointed at the cars. "Look, no license plates. Daddy says they're looking for bad people. They take them away for good."

It took everything Nina had not to slap down Gaston's hand. Anything she did might draw attention, and attention was the last thing she wanted.

Vanessa took a slow bite from her sandwich. "Why do they do that, Mommy?"

Nina cast a worried look about her, grabbed Vanessa's hand, and motioned for Gaston to follow. "Let's go, children. We have to get home."

She whisked the children away, ignoring their many questions.

She accidentally knocked down a table outside of the bakery, but she kept going. When she looked back at the scene across the street, she locked eyes with one of the secret police. A chill darted up Nina's spine as the man's eyes followed her and the children. He looked like a hawk choosing its next prey.

Nina dropped the children off at her mother's house and drove to the pharmacy. Her heart was pounding, her palms sweaty. She arrived at the pharmacy early, as usual. She asked Ricardo, one of the clerks, if Ernesto or her head pharmacist, Juan, had come in yet.

"Ernesto's already here, in the back," the young man said. "But Juan—I was surprised not to see him this morning. He's usually in early, like you."

"Maybe he's out sick," Nina said. "I'm sure we'll hear from him soon." But she wasn't sure. She was still rattled from what she'd seen that morning. She rushed to the back of the pharmacy to tell Ernesto about the mysterious arrest before she busied herself with the usual tasks of opening the store.

The call from Juan never came. His wife called the pharmacy later in the day wondering if he was there, since he always called her around that time of day.

"I haven't seen him yet, Maria," Nina said. "We were wondering where he was too." Nina tried in earnest to keep her voice calm for Maria, even though her own mind was immediately going to the worst conclusion. "I'll have him call you as soon as he comes in."

Juan didn't come in. *Has he disappeared?* Nina kept picturing Juan being held down by two large men as a third came to toss him in an unmarked car. Nina turned to Ernesto for comfort. "Where do you think he could be?"

"Did Juan have any particular political stance?" Ernesto asked.

"He's one of the least political people I know. He's just trying to make a living; I think the most political thing he ever did was join the union."

Ernesto looked grim. "Today that could be a reason for his disappearance."

"What could?" Nina said.

"I don't know. Anything." Ernesto shrugged. "That's the point. Nobody knows what's in these people's minds. Everyone's a threat. If they have him, only a miracle will bring him back."

———

Five days later, Juan walked into the pharmacy. He looked like his usual self, except for large, dark circles under his eyes and the dirt on his clothes. Everyone's eyes were riveted on him at once, and Nina ran to him and hugged him.

"Juan, where have you been?" she cried. "We, your wife, everyone has been worried sick."

Juan avoided looking her in the eye. He seemed too scared to tell anyone anything, so they pressed into the back room of the pharmacy to put his mind at rest.

"Please, tell us what happened," Nina said. "We were so worried."

When Juan spoke at last, he spoke very softly.

"They picked me up on the street on the way to work," he said. "They blindfolded me and took me on a long ride. No one said anything; I was afraid to ask questions. My heart was beating so loudly I couldn't even hear the sounds of the car. When they finally took off the blindfold, I was in a small room, all alone."

"Did they... did they?" Nina asked, scared of the answer. She couldn't imagine what she would do if one day Ernesto didn't come home and there was no explanation.

"No. They didn't harm me, but they questioned me every day for four straight days. I thought I was going to go mad. The same questions over and over. Never a break."

"What questions? What could they have wanted from you?" Ernesto asked as his hands ran through his hair.

Juan took a deep breath, and someone brought him a cup of coffee. It seemed to comfort him, and he went on. "They kept asking me if we ever supplied drugs to the terrorists. If we had given any medicine to terrorists."

"Us?" Nina asked, flabbergasted. "Supply drugs?" It shouldn't have surprised her so much that the military was working its way into every corner of their lives. First they had to burn their books; now they couldn't even dispense medicine without fear.

"Not recreational drugs, Nina. They meant for medicine. To help their wounded."

Still shaken, Juan related some more minor details about his captivity but was clearly anxious to get home to his family. Nina was amazed he had even bothered to stop in the pharmacy first before telling his wife he was alive.

Before he left, he added, "They warned me to be sure we never deal with the terrorists. If we ever do, the penalty will be severe. They said every pharmacy in town is being warned."

Nina breathed a sigh of relief and heard Ernesto do the same beside her. But her relief was momentary at best: the incident left her more fearful than ever. She realized even the most innocent were suspects, and they were among the most innocent.

Chapter Eleven

A New Joy

N ina felt the sun's rays warm her closed eyelids. She snuggled down into her sheets. Although bleary with sleep, she felt sure that something wonderful was about to happen.

The baby!

Nina jumped out of bed, full of joy. She felt so energized by her excitement that she decided to treat Ernesto to breakfast in bed. However, as she entered the kitchen, the phone rang. Her mother always called at the same time several times a week, but it still caught Nina by surprise.

"Hello, Mom! How are you on this fabulous morning?" Nina couldn't have hidden her excitement even if she'd tried.

"You're awfully chipper," Estela said.

"The best thing in the world has happened. Nothing is finalized. And everything could still fall through but…" Nina paused to find the right words.

"What? What is it? Tell me!" her mom demanded. Nina's excitement was contagious.

"My friend Marta—you remember her? She comes into the pharmacy and buys too much medicine just so she can talk to me behind the counter. She has long, black hair. I think you met her at a birthday party a couple years ago."

"Oh, just tell me your good news!"

"I'm going to have another baby!" Nina cried.

"Nina!"

"Marta knows a teenager who has to give up her baby for adoption, and Marta offered it to us." Nina realized she had picked up a loaf of bread and was cradling it gently in her arms.

Her mom was silent.

"Aren't you happy for us?" Nina asked after the silence had dragged on for what felt like minutes.

"Adoption?" Estela sounded worried. "Have you thought this through? All the paperwork, the waiting period, not to mention the violence right now. The government won't make it easy for you. I thought you were happy with Vanessa."

"Ernesto and I are going to discuss those details today. And yes, I am happy now; I love Vanessa. But I could give this baby all my love and attention." Nina was confused. She'd expected Estela to be happier for her.

"I know you'll give the baby a wonderful childhood. I just want you to realize all the consequences of such a big decision. Do you really want to deal with that right now?" Estela asked.

"It just feels right."

"Do you know the girl? Are you sure she's healthy?"

Estela was asking all the tough questions that Nina hadn't even thought of asking Marta. The only question on Nina's mind was whether or not the baby would be hers in a few months.

"Marta knows the girl and her mother and speaks highly of the family. Ernesto and I will figure out the rest," Nina said, tension rising in her voice.

Estela softened. "All right. You know I would love another grandchild."

Nina finished making breakfast for Ernesto, but her mother's reaction to the news had tarnished her mood considerably.

Ernesto was beginning to stir when she returned. She nudged him awake, then placed the breakfast on a side table nearby.

"Ernesto, what do you think? Should we get this baby?"

He rubbed the sleep from his eyes. "If we still want it, yes. Marta said Laura was going to Catholic school, and you know how they feel about unwed mothers. If she hadn't left the school already on a medical leave of absence, she would have been expelled. Her mother's a teacher at the same school, and would have lost her job. We'll be helping more than just ourselves by adopting this baby."

"Do you think we can get the baby and a birth certificate in our name without any hassles?" Nina asked.

"Yes, I do," Ernesto said.

"Why are you so certain?"

"Because, as I understand it, this is happening all over the country. That's just the way things are done. What do you want to do next?"

"Marta set up a meeting with Laura and her mother. I'm going to sit nearby and listen, but I won't let them know I'm the one who's interested."

Ernesto smiled. "If you think we can do it, then I'm behind you 100 percent."

—⁌⁘⁍—

Nina quickly finished getting ready and said goodbye to Ernesto and Vanessa. She drove the few blocks to the coffee shop, glowing at the thought of a new baby. Vanessa was getting older; Nina missed interacting with an infant or toddler. Her mind filled with the possibilities: new little outfits to buy, a room to decorate, another adorable child to cherish.

She headed into the coffee shop in Buenos Aires. The weather turned rainy just as Nina arrived. It was one of those clammy, cold autumn days in the city when the chill seemed to penetrate to the bone. The hot coffee would be welcome.

Everything was coming together so quickly. A few days before, Nina had thought she'd never have another child. Now she was overjoyed at the thought of being so close to her potential baby. Only a few small hurdles stood in her way. *I'm hardly committed yet and already I can't bear the thought of this deal falling through.*

After Nina ordered her coffee, she spotted Marta at a table with an older woman, presumably Laura's mother, and a very pregnant teen. Nina sat within earshot but stayed out of Laura and her mother's vision, in case her joy or sorrow might give her away. Nina couldn't see their faces, but she could see Marta.

Marta started by looking at Laura, who was squirming and uncomfortable. Nina thought that the strange situation was probably making her feel as awkward as the advanced stages of her pregnancy.

"How's it going?" Marta asked.

Laura glanced at her mother for approval before answering. Her mother obviously still considered her the bad child.

"I'm fine, I guess," she said. "I never had a baby before, and I didn't realize how long and uncomfortable it would be."

The mother opened her mouth to say something, then stopped herself. She still wore her shame and disapproval like a suit of heavy armor over the strain—not to mention the sin—of her child's terrible situation.

Marta spent the next few minutes laying out Nina's terms for the arrangements. Neither Laura nor her mother offered any objections and Marta was soon able to close the negotiation.

"So it's agreed?" she asked. "My friend will pay all the medical expenses from here on out, including the delivery, but nothing more than that. The doctor we found has already agreed to put her name on the birth certificate. If you have any concerns, just come to me."

Laura nodded.

"Yes, it is agreed," her mother said.

"How are you going to handle this final period before the delivery?" Marta asked Laura.

"She'll be living at home toward the end," her mother said. "Nobody will know about it."

———〰———

Weeks later, Marta called Nina with the news that Laura's water had broken.

Nina and Ernesto left Vanessa with her grandparents and rushed to the hospital. They lurked outside in their car, their nerves on edge, waiting for word from Marta, who was inside the hospital. They sipped coffee from paper cups and passed some pastries back and forth, taking a few nibbles here and there. The waiting was the hardest part. Nina knew this should be one of the happiest days of her life, but being cramped in the car with Ernesto for hours on end was wearing her patience.

"It didn't seem to take this long with Vanessa," Ernesto said.

"That's because you went home, and by the time you came back, I'd already had her," Nina said.

"Oh, yeah." Ernesto stared out the window toward the hospital. "I hope it's a little boy."

"I just want it to be healthy and ours without any hassles," Nina said. Oddly enough, she felt more stressed than she had during Vanessa's birth. So much still hung in the balance. She held her happiness back, waiting until the last hurdles were cleared. She reminded herself that anything could still go wrong.

"There was a guy at work who adopted a baby. He and his wife did it by the book and even had the baby wait in an orphanage while everything cleared. Then two years later the birth parents said they wanted the baby back."

"Why would you bring something like that up?" Nina glared at him.

"The situation just reminded me," Ernesto said. "Don't worry. There's no way that could happen to us. From the sound of it, I really don't think Laura and her mother are ever going to want to see this baby again."

The car's interior seemed to shrink as Nina's irritation grew. She opened the door, hoping some airflow would take some of her stress away.

"That doesn't make me feel any better about going around the government for the birth certificate," Nina said.

"Have you looked around lately?" Ernesto asked. "The government has its own problems. It's not going to notice a happy little family that has legitimate-looking paperwork for another baby. It's all going to work out perfectly, you wait and see."

"I wish I could be as optimistic as you."

"If it's a little girl, we could try again for a boy."

Nina didn't respond, and Ernesto didn't seem to notice. She opened the door farther and decided to wait outside the car. Ernesto turned on the radio and seemed to be completely immersed in his own thoughts. Much as she would have liked Vanessa to have a sister, she began to hope Laura would give birth to a boy. They hadn't even secured their second child yet! The thought of trying to have another baby with Ernesto was too much to contemplate.

—∿∿∿—

About nine in the evening, Marta approached the car. She looked exhausted but relieved.

"It's human, and a boy to boot," she said, grinning.

Almost beside themselves with anticipation, Nina and Ernesto clambered out of the car and hurried in to see the baby.

He was breathtaking—pink, with a round, chubby face, deep dimples, and bright eyes that appeared to be looking at them. His hair was a pale brown color and as soft and fine as fresh white flour. Nina's heart hammered in her chest as she worried about some last-minute glitch.

Nina and Ernesto fell in love with him at once, and deeply. Nina could feel their emotional bond already growing permanent. She asked a nurse about Laura's physical and emotional health and also asked Marta if Laura had had any doubts. Even though Marta reassured her, Nina implored her to go to Laura and make certain she hadn't changed her mind. Nina simply could not bear to take this child home if it wasn't going to work. Marta went back into the delivery room and soon came back with reassurance.

"Laura is certain her baby will receive all the love and attention and care she herself can't possibly provide at her young age. Her mom added that last part."

Nina's eyes welled up with joy, and tears were flowing by the time she kissed Marta goodbye. It was all quick and painless. Soon after Ernesto had a doctor sign the birth certificate, they took the newborn home.

Even though it was late when they arrived home, a reception committee was waiting for them in the form of Nina's brother Eduardo and his wife Julia. Eduardo and Julia were the parents of a two-year-old, blue-eyed, blond boy named Julio, and had long empathized with the couple's struggle to have a second child.

Eduardo's eyes filled with tears at the sight of the baby.

Little Vanessa gazed at the newborn as if he were a delicate treasure that could only be touched with the utmost care. When she finally felt comfortable enough to take the baby's hand, she did so as if she were holding delicate porcelain she was afraid to break. She eventually fell asleep with her fingers resting on the baby's small hand.

After Nina put Vanessa to bed, Ernesto made a toast to his new son, "God must have really wanted us to have this baby. Nina couldn't have any more children, the country is killing itself, we live in constant fear, and still this worked out. To my baby boy, David Miguel Rossi."

Nina blushed and quickly raised her glass. "Bravo!"

Everyone else joined in the toast, and Ernesto seemed satisfied.

"And to the godmother Marta and my brother Ricardo, the godfather," Ernesto said.

Eduardo raised his glass again. "And to Argentina for beating the Netherlands three to one for the World Cup gold medal!" he shouted.

Some of the family cheered louder for the soccer victory than for the new baby.

Nina couldn't help but laugh. Amid threats of kidnappings and secret police sightings, Argentina had hosted the 1978 World Cup. The government had thought it would give the rest of the world the illusion Argentina was a normal country so no one on the outside would figure out what was really going on. She didn't know if they had fooled anyone, but at least they had beaten the competition, becoming the fifth country to be both host and ultimate victor.

She snuggled with her new son. At least the World Cup provided a welcome distraction for the people. The whole country was still wild with jubilation at Argentina's victory. It was as if they had proven themselves to the world. Nina suspected the people saw it as an auspicious sign for the future. She prayed they would not be disappointed.

"Everyone at work stopped to watch them win. They were all hugging and celebrating until the news showed a protest by the Madres de Plaza de Mayo," Julia said.

Nina hugged her new son. The Mothers of May Plaza was such a sad group: an organization of women who assembled every week to protest the mysterious disappearance of their children at the hands of the government.

"It was eerie to watch them," Estela said. "No yelling or chanting. They simply marched silently around the Plaza with white scarves covering their heads. They want to remind the world of the price they've paid."

"I can't imagine their suffering, not knowing what happened to their children."

"Can't they let us be happy for just a few minutes without reminding us that the military is torturing people and dumping them alive from planes into the Río de la Plata?" Julia asked.

The news cast a silence over the people at the party. Everyone knew that the government was kidnapping and torturing people, but no one knew about specific acts of violence in much detail. Eduardo nudged his wife, trying to communicate that she'd said too much.

"Where did you hear such a thing?" several people asked at once.

Julia glanced up at Eduardo. He shook his head, almost imperceptibly, but everyone else waited impatiently for an answer.

"My father has a cousin who's a colonel," Julia said softly. "One night after drinking too much at a family party, he said some things he probably regretted the next day."

"Enough of this political talk!" Nina said. "Let's concentrate on this adorable new baby, if you please."

Smiling, the guests returned their attention to the beautiful baby boy.

At the beginning of the New Year in 1979, traditional vacation time for South Americans, Nina and the family prepared to move into a new home. Nina spent all her holiday season packing up their belongings instead of enjoying the usual lavish cooked meals and extended visits to relatives.

Little David would soon need a room of his own. Compared to the homes of their youth, Nina's current Buenos Aires condo was large and lavish, but she wanted a bigger place because the family was growing and she needed help looking after the children.

"It's really the perfect place," Ernesto said. "Eight blocks away and only a half a block from Vanessa's school. And a brand-new building in an upscale area too."

Nina cherished the thought of moving to a nicer neighborhood. Even though she hadn't been raised to put much emphasis on possessions, it felt good to spend freely and not so good to be envied by her friends.

"Ernesto, can you help me bring some of the last boxes over to the new place?" Nina asked.

"Sorry, I can't. I have to go over to the hardware store. We need some wires and paint and stuff for the new house," Ernesto said. "You can handle it. Vanessa will help."

Nina wasn't surprised that something had called Ernesto away at the last minute. "Can't that wait?" she asked, but she knew she was already defeated.

"Have the movers take it over if it's too much work."

"I don't want anything to happen to these things," she said. "It's all my most fragile belongings."

"Then I certainly don't want to be responsible if something breaks," Ernesto said, grabbing his car keys and heading for the door. "You'll be fine by yourself."

Nina had a feeling that he would find a way to be gone all day. His nonchalance upset her. Everything seemed to have the same importance to him. It didn't matter if they were moving into a new home or just needed milk from the grocery store: it was all trivial work for Nina to handle.

—◦◦◦—

The new place, with four bedrooms and a terrace, was a little too big for them. The parents and each child had their own bedroom, and the fourth room was converted into a playroom, because the terrace connected to it, and a bedroom for the new nanny, Fernanda. The terrace was roomy, colorful, and decorated with a variety of plants, which made it feel like a jungle in the summer. New patio furniture and a big barbecue made it an ideal and elegant family area.

Nina was relieved that Fernanda was waiting when she arrived at the new condo.

"Here, here. Can you put this box in the baby's room and then look after David?" Nina asked Fernanda.

She nodded. Fernanda was a quiet girl who kept mainly to herself. Nina felt blessed to have found such a sweet, modest-looking nanny; the children liked her from the start. Everyone seemed to get along with minor complaint.

"Mom, can I go play?" Vanessa asked.

"Stay where Fernanda or I can see you, and no messing with any of the boxes. All right?" Nina said.

"Yes, Mom."

The piles of boxes stretched from living room to kitchen and into each bedroom. Nina didn't know where to begin. She had stopped looking to Ernesto to be there every time she needed him. *But some help would certainly have been nice at this point,* she thought.

Nina jumped at the sound of a terrific crash at the back of the condo. She ran through the house to the baby's room, where she found Fernanda putting David into his crib.

"What is it? What was that sound?" Nina asked.

"I don't know. I was about to go and check," Fernanda said.

"Where's Vanessa?" Nina asked.

"She told me she was going to help you unpack," Fernanda said.

Nina ran to the terrace, then halted midstride in horror at the sight. Smashed boxes blocked the walkway, their contents spilling across the pavement. Vanessa's bike lay on its side with its tires still spinning. Vanessa lay beside it, holding her arm and crying.

"What happened?" Nina asked, rushing to bend over Vanessa.

"My arm hurts."

"I told you to stay where we could see you."

"I hit those boxes." Vanessa pointed to the pile. "They broke my fall."

Nina ran her hand over Vanessa's arm; nothing seemed broken. She told Fernanda, "Take her into the bathroom and wait for me."

Fernanda looked worried as she helped Vanessa off the terrace.

Frustration washed over Nina as she looked at the damage. Not only were boxes strewn everywhere, but some of them had FRAGILE written on them in huge letters. She sifted through the debris and salvaged what she could, but many of her precious possessions were broken beyond repair. *It's useless to yell at a child. Sentimental objects mean nothing to them,* she told herself. But she wanted to scream so loudly that Ernesto would hear her and come rushing home. *Even if he'd been there, he probably wouldn't have been watching Vanessa either.*

Nina went into the kitchen. She poured herself a tall glass of ice water, taking one deep breath after another. Moving was stressful for everyone. Ernesto dealt with the stress by leaving them alone to manage everything; she just hadn't figured out how to deal with the stress herself.

———

One evening, Nina and Ernesto decided to celebrate their good fortune with a night of fun at the Parisian Regina. The famous New York nightclub had opened a branch in Argentina. They dressed in formal clothes and invited another couple along, Lucia and José, who had a child in Vanessa's class. Nina had met Lucia when she dropped Vanessa off at school. Lucia had told Nina how much she admired her clothes and jewelry. Occasionally the two saw each other at school gatherings.

As they returned from the club, Ernesto decided to take a new route. But when he turned down a dark street looking for a shortcut home, they saw a military checkpoint blocking the road. It was too late to do anything about the mistake and they were quickly stopped by one of the unlicensed black government vehicles that roamed the city. Men wearing suits and carrying submachine guns approached the car.

"Turn your headlights off and turn your inside lights on," one of the police ordered.

Nina looked back at Lucia and José in the backseat. She smiled weakly, hoping they would feel safe and not say anything.

Ernesto's hands trembled with nerves. As he reached for the headlight switch, he accidentally knocked against the switch for the fog lights, turning them on. Light flooded the roadblock, gleaming along a number of black police cars and illuminating a number of armed men. They turned to stare at the car and many of them aimed their weapons. Inside the car, the passengers heard the clicking of the police's machine guns.

With a muttered curse, Ernesto quickly turned the headlights and fog lights off and switched on the small interior light.

"Where are you coming from?" one of the policemen asked.

"The Parisian Regina," Ernesto said.

"Please open your trunk."

Ernesto left the car and did as he was asked. Nina heard the policeman at the trunk ask Ernesto how long they had been at the club and other details of the night. They were looking for the smallest evidence they were terrorists.

As the search continued, Lucia began to hyperventilate. No matter how much Nina's eyes pleaded, she wouldn't stop. In fact, her gasps quickly grew louder and more desperate.

An armed man yanked Lucia's door open. As he reached for her, she fainted.

"She needs fresh air," José said and the man nodded. José took Lucia by the waist and pushed her out of the car into the cool night air.

Lucia came around a moment later and started pleading with the armed guard beside her. "They're the ones you want," she said. "They have all the money. We just came along because they pay. Please, we don't have anything."

Nina saw José jab Lucia in the ribs, and she finally stopped talking.

Nina stepped out of the car and went to Ernesto's side. To her relief, the guard took no interest in Lucia's accusations.

After a thorough scrutiny of their IDs and a barrage of questions, the police allowed them to continue. Nina didn't speak to Lucia or José for the rest of the ride. Ernesto nodded goodbye as they dropped the couple off at their home.

Nina was still trembling an hour later. Her greatest fear was that something might happen to her and she would never see her children again. Nina made sure to never invite José and Lucia out to the Parisian Regina again.

Chapter Twelve

No Choice Left

≈⟨⟩≈

O n a beautiful September afternoon, Nina looked around the terrace. The decorations were spectacular. Everyone—the four grandparents, all the aunts, uncles, cousins, schoolmates, and other Rossi family friends, even Lucia and José—had come to David's second birthday party.

Nina had worked hard to pull the party together, but that wasn't so strange. She always worked hard. She glanced around the terrace to make sure everything was running smoothly. Round tables were scattered about, some with lime green tablecloths, some with light blue. In the center of each table was a centerpiece of blue, red, and yellow flowers. Shiny balloons attached to long strings stretched toward the sky. To the delight of the party-going kids, each table offered lots of souvenirs, toys, and party favors. Nothing livened a children's party like gifts for everyone.

Two clowns pranced around, doing all the silly things that delight kids. For those with more fanciful interests, a magician pulled coins from behind the ears of unsuspecting kids and rabbits from a hat and white doves from a child's hair. Laughter filled the air unceasingly. As parties went, David's second was a smashing success.

Ernesto sipped champagne and talked to one of his friends. His voice was low, even with the party noise to cover it. "This situation with the disparity in the dollar can't last. The dollar is being kept low artificially."

His friend agreed. "It's not possible to buy dollars. To do so, you have to show your airplane tickets to prove you are traveling, and you're allowed to buy only one thousand dollars per person."

"Of course, otherwise everyone would be speculating," Ernesto said. "Luckily, I have friends from business school with good contacts. They were able to get black market dollars last year when we took Vanessa and David to Disney World and on a Caribbean cruise. One thousand per person isn't enough for all that, and Argentinean credit cards are only good in Argentina."

Listening to this conversation, Nina remembered the joy of the Disney World trip as though she'd experienced it that very day. She would never forget how Vanessa and David's faces had lit up at their first glimpse of the Magic Kingdom, how Vanessa had gasped at Cinderella's castle, how she had gawked at Mickey, Minnie, and Goofy. Seeing her amazement, they'd come over to give her a big hug from each of them. Her eyes had sparkled as the bands marched down the street playing every Disney tune she had ever heard. It had all been so much fun, so magical.

Nina knew she would never forget the thrill of the Jungle World Safari and Tom Sawyer's Island or the wonder of Pirates of the Caribbean as their little boat plied dark waters while terrible pirates fought for gold and plunder. Nina had often thought that the real joy of Disney World was that it gave parents a chance to watch the sheer delight it gave their children. Nothing could make parents happier than providing that much joy for their children. Disney World had been fun for her and Ernesto, too; it had been a truly magical place that took them all away from their earthly problems.

They had also gone on a trip to Mexico with Lucia and José. Nina had kept her distance from them since the episode with the police outside of the Parisian Regina nightclub. She would have been perfectly happy never seeing them again, but Ernesto encouraged her to remain civil since their children were classmates.

The Mexican trip had been a vacation more geared toward the adults. Nina appreciated the chance to visit places of historic or cultural interest, such as Taxco. The charming old town had once been the colonial capital of Mexico. Ernesto had bought a beautiful silver bracelet and a filigree pendant cross for Nina and several charming trinkets for Vanessa and David; outdoor street-side silversmiths had hammered out their purchases for them on the spot. In Mexico, prices were negotiable and so reasonable they were able to buy presents for all the women of the family. They had also enjoyed the picturesque Lake Xochimilco, where they sailed in a boat adorned with garlands and flowers. The Museum of Anthropology in Mexico City had also fascinated the Rossis. In Chichen Itza, they had viewed the ancient pyramids and ruins of the Mayans, whose science and technology rivaled modernity.

The last stop on that trip had been Acapulco, the beautiful spot on the Mexican Riviera, with its sugar-white beaches and sparkling surf that rolled ashore capped with snow-white froth.

Ernesto had tried to hide his trips to realtors in every place they visited. Nina wondered if he planned to surprise them with a vacation home in one of the wonderful places they had seen.

—◦◦◦—

Nina was jolted from her reminiscing back to the party when Lucia's voice filled the air with tension. "Don't touch that, sweetie!" Lucia cried, snatching a piece of cake from her son, who still had the remnants of his last piece on his shirt.

"Everything's all right," Nina said, hurrying to calm Lucia. "He can have as much cake as he wants. There's plenty."

"Easy for you to say. Both your kids are skinny little things."

Lucia straightened in annoyance. "I saw the way your mother patted my son's stomach. Please inform Telly that I would appreciate her not drawing attention to his condition."

Nina frowned. Only family called Estela Telly, and they only did so because Vanessa had a hard time pronouncing her grandmother's name. 'Telly,' her best attempt, was so cute that the rest of the family had started copying her. They'd been doing it for so long no one seemed to remember her real name anymore. Nina didn't want non-family members to forget as well.

"Not everything has to become a huge drama," Nina said. "He just wants some cake."

"Oh, sure." Lucia huffed. "You can afford a doctor to make your kids pretty if they grow up looking like mine—or you could always just buy another one."

Lucia's shock techniques and constant complaining had tired Nina to no end. She turned away to help David open his presents.

—◦◦◦—

The guests had gone home and Nina was exhausted. Organizing and running a party took a lot of effort and care, but her children had seemed happy, so she counted the party as a success. She hoped it would be a happy memory for them.

After Fernanda had put the kids to bed, Nina and Ernesto sat at the kitchen table drinking tea and relaxing. The more tea he drank, the more serious Ernesto looked. Nina knew the look well. Something had made Ernesto upset and now he was stewing. She tried to savor her satisfaction with the party, not wanting to ask him any questions that might open the floodgates of his annoyance. But eventually she knew she couldn't ignore his mood anymore.

"What's the matter, honey?" she asked. "Aren't you happy with how the party turned out? Or are you as tired as I am?"

"It's not that." Ernesto sighed. "I've been thinking lately. Argentina is no place to bring up children. As much as I love my country, it's much too unstable. There's always unrest, always danger, always some new problem. I'm not worried for myself as much as I worry for the children."

"I know, dear. I worry too."

"Things get so crazy," Ernesto said. "The way the government decides who its enemies are, we might someday be among the disappeared."

"We aren't into politics. We aren't terrorists. We aren't even part of the press or the intellectual elite or professors or anybody who could influence anyone in any way. We are decent, hard-working, simple people." Nina wondered if she was only fooling herself. They'd already had to hide or burn some of their belongings. Her coworkers went missing, and her way of life was under government watch. The government barely even needed a reason anymore. Fear and paranoia touched every facet of Nina's life, but she had done her best to turn a blind eye and focus on her happy family. In some ways, it had been all too easy.

Ernesto's expression remained grim. "You're making my point for me. There is no reason for those kinds of people to disappear, but they do. Nobody deserves to disappear, with some awful fate awaiting them, but they do. And it will go on as long as there are people the government views as terrorists."

"Hush, Ernesto, the nanny is still awake."

"See? See how paranoid we've been forced to become? Now our nanny might turn us in. For what? For simply talking about the state of our lives?" Ernesto jerked his shoulders in an angry shrug. "Everybody's suspicious of everybody else. Frankly, I'm sick of it."

"Fernanda's been spending a lot of time on the phone with who knows who, and she's always scribbling in that journal of hers." Nina bit her lip. "She told Vanessa and David she's keeping a record of their childhoods for them, but I wonder what she overhears. ...I'm just being paranoid. It's probably nothing."

"It's terrible the way you rationalize. If someone is picked up and disappears, people feel they must have done something wrong. It's like bringing a defendant into court in handcuffs. People automatically assume he's guilty."

"But I don't think anything will happen to us," Nina said after a brief pause. She knew horrifying things were happening every day to innocent people. But it had become a way of life to her. Surely violence could touch them no matter where they moved, so why uproot their entire lives? Yes, they might be pulled over by the police and roughly handled, but Nina believed she could live with what was happening.

"That's denial, Nina. Don't you see? It's easier for people to assume the disappeared are guilty. If the victims are innocent, then we're looking at a horror so evil, we can't claim to be part of humanity." Ernesto's voice was taut with emotion, but he spoke quietly. "A person disagrees with someone in power, and he disappears, never to be seen by his family again. Look at those poor women who march in the Plaza. They've decided the worst thing in life that could possibly happen to them already has. What could the government do to them beyond that?

"That's how people are. Like Pontius Pilate, who let the Jews handle the problem of Jesus. He simply washed his hands of the matter. That's the human tendency."

They sat quietly, letting their tea grow cold. Nina knew that once Ernesto got something in his head he didn't let it go. They'd had similar conversations before. In the end, Nina assumed they would sigh and move on with their lives, like they did every time Ernesto started talking like this.

Suddenly Ernesto reached across the table. He took Nina's hands in his own. "Nina, I've made up my mind. I want to emigrate."

"What?" Her voice shook, slightly too loud with desperation and surprise. "Our life is here. Our parents. Our friends. Our family. Our business we worked so hard to build from the ground up. The only way of life we've ever known. We can't leave!"

"We must think of the children. Their futures. It will be hard. It always is. The first generation will suffer, but the next will have a better time of it."

Nina tugged nervously at a strand of hair. "How can a complete unknown be better than at least having family and friends near you?"

"If our grandparents did it in order to have a better life for their children here, why can't we do the same?"

She was hesitant. "But Ernesto, our grandparents did it out of absolute necessity. Is our situation here that bad?"

"No. No, it isn't. Not right now. But that's the whole point. Who knows? Maybe tomorrow they will decide that all pharmacists are dangerous, and we'll go missing."

"But that's ridiculous."

"Of course it is. But in this country, it can happen, no matter how ridiculous it sounds. That's what happens when you live under dictators."

"Is that what you think we're doing?"

"Oh, they don't like to be called dictators, but what else could they be? We certainly aren't living in a democracy anymore."

"But, Ernesto, look what we would be giving up," Nina said desperately. "We have a beautiful home, a country house for weekends. Vanessa goes to a prestigious school. We have good friends, a business, a nanny, and a wonderful social life. We drive brand-new cars. We take great vacations abroad. Have I left anything out?"

"You've left out the most important things: stability and security. We face an uncertain future, and so do our kids. We're living in a country where, for no good reason, we could lose all the good things you've mentioned, as well as our lives."

Nina flinched, and Ernesto continued more quietly. "The world has better technology and communications than it did in the old days; we have many more opportunities than our grandparents ever had. Things might be hard, but not as hard as you think."

When Ernesto got like this, Nina knew hers was the weaker side of the argument. She had good reasons for not wanting to uproot everything and leave the country for an uncertain future, but his logic was relentless.

"I don't know, Ernesto," she said, "but I do know that I should have a say in this matter. And I say no. I must say no. Fleeing this country will bring a lot of sorrow into our lives."

"Why, Nina? Why?" he asked, sitting beside her on the couch. "Our parents can visit."

Nina staggered to her feet. "Stop, Ernesto!" she cried, her face contorted with pain. "You haven't even told me where you want to move."

"Where else? Where else in the world is democracy respected?"

"The United States? Half a world away?"

"Of course. Don't you remember our visit to my cousin Carlos in Los Angeles?"

"You want to move to California?"

"Yes. It has an excellent climate and a lot of opportunity. We can get good money for our property here right now. If we wait any longer, I don't think that will be true."

"So you've already researched it and figured it all out."

"I don't want to have to think about what could happen to the children. And you'd be the one responsible for keeping us here."

Nina felt all emotion drain from her expression. She stared at him. "Can't we talk about this tomorrow? I need to rest. I can't think about this tonight."

"Okay. The longer we stay, the more our lives are at stake." Ernesto shrugged. "Just walk away if you want. Goodnight."

She didn't even mutter "goodnight," but went to bed with her mind in turmoil. She fell into her bed fully clothed and sobbed herself to sleep.

———∞———

In the morning, Nina went to the kitchen and saw Ernesto sitting right where she had left him when she went to bed the night before. *He must have stayed up all night thinking, and now he's waiting for me.* Nina took a deep breath. She wasn't ready to return to their discussion.

"Remember our wedding?"

The question surprised her. "Yes."

"Remember our wedding vows?"

"Yes."

"They made me the head of the family," Ernesto said. "You swore to honor my wishes."

"But didn't you also promise to honor me?" Nina asked.

Ernesto said nothing.

"What? You're going to ambush me with old-fashioned thinking? Why should we remain true to a system where the man is master and the wife obeys without a choice?"

Ernesto gave her no more reasoning beyond that. He was adamant in his decision. He would use his prerogative as head of the household to get his way, and she would have to follow along. It was Old World thinking, but it was strong. It had worked in the past. She knew he had not made a selfish decision, but one for the welfare of the family. Still, it was his decision and his alone. He wouldn't provide any room for discussion.

"All right." Nina knew she couldn't withstand the current of Ernesto's decision forever. "I want you to know I agree to this plan against my will."

"Do you think I would do this unless it was in the best interests of my family?"

"No. But you're completely disregarding me in this."

———✥———

Although she dreaded it, that evening Nina told the kids about their plans. She anticipated that the children wouldn't take the news well. It was hard to give them comforting answers when Nina felt just like they did. She sat both children on her lap and hugged them tight.

"We're going to move to America," Nina said. The words were difficult to voice, since she herself was against the move.

"We're going on vacation again?" David's voice was shrill with excitement. Nina had noticed several times before that he equated the word *America* with Disney World and vacation. Usually the connection would have made her smile.

Vanessa was much less excited. "We're not going for a long time, are we? What about my friends? What about school?"

"Your father has decided it's best if we leave the country for a little while," Nina said, trying to smile as though it were a happy family decision. "I don't think it will be for long."

"Then why go at all?" Vanessa said, nose wrinkling.

Nina kissed them each on the top of the head. "We all love your father, right?"

David and Vanessa nodded in agreement.

"And we always do what he says because we love him, right?" Nina hated using emotional blackmail on the children. She couldn't help but notice that this was essentially the same argument Ernesto had given her earlier in the day.

Nina felt them become resigned to the idea.

"So we have to make all new friends and family in America?" Vanessa asked.

Nina didn't know how to make the children feel like the move was in their best interest when even she didn't think it was.

———✤———

The next day the couple invited the Rossis and the Salvattis over for dinner to inform them of their decision.

When each side of the family realized it was a formal dinner and they had all been invited, they started buzzing excitedly among themselves, as if good news were on the menu. Nina retreated to the kitchen to avoid talking to anyone, afraid she might burst into tears and cut short their happy moods, as she knew her breakdown was inevitable.

Everyone gathered around the table, pouring wine in anticipation of a toast. Nina had put David and Vanessa to bed early so they wouldn't have to see their grandparents upset.

Ernesto tapped the side of his wine glass with a knife to get everyone's attention. Nina stayed close to the kitchen doorway.

"Nina and I have an announcement to make," he said.

Nina's heart sank when she saw her mother take her father's hand and squeeze it. She knew they were sure they were about to hear that a third grandchild was in store. She closed her eyes as Ernesto continued, unable to bear the sight of their disappointment.

"We've decided that Argentina is no longer a safe place to raise our family," Ernesto said. "We're moving to America."

He beckoned to Nina to join him at the head of the table, smiling broadly as everyone else's faces twisted in pain. Nina's mom stared at her in shock. Nina could no longer repress her tears. She sobbed quietly as Ernesto explained their plans.

"First I will visit my cousin in Los Angeles to look for a job and a place of our own. Then I will come back to Argentina, sort our affairs, pack everything up, and move permanently," he said.

Ernesto's parents didn't say anything at all. Nina was surprised they didn't protest more. Perhaps he had already told them the news while she was telling the children. Nina's parents didn't say anything either, but Nina knew she would have to explain everything to them eventually.

"Everyone, raise your glasses," Ernesto said.

Nina had never been more appalled by his inappropriateness. She whirled around and stumbled blindly to the kitchen where she could cry in peace. Estela joined her.

"Do you really think this is a good idea?"

"Of course not." Nina wiped her eyes. "It's like the children and I are being abducted, but we agreed to it."

"Your father and I have lived here our entire lives," Estela said. "Argentina is always changing. They're constantly replacing the people in government with someone they think will do a better job. We lived through more frightening times than this one when we were younger. Undoubtedly there will be more frightening times in the future. But there are also times of peace and quiet. This is your country."

"I tried to tell Ernesto that," Nina said. "I tried to reason with him, but he just wouldn't listen to anything. It's like he's possessed. Everything out of his mouth is America, America, America." Nina was glad that she could be so open with her mother; her sympathy came as a relief. She hoped she was encouraging the same relationship with Vanessa.

"If there's nothing more you can do, then we will just have to make the best of it," her mom said.

After their parents went home, Nina began to ponder the uncertainties facing them. Three days ago, she'd been a happy woman. She'd had a wonderful party for her son, and life was good. Now she was faced with life in a foreign country without friends and family. It frightened her more than she thought possible.

Chapter Thirteen

Better, Except the Same

Nina knew the Christmas of 1980 would be different from any Christmas that had come before. She looked down at the book she'd just finished wrapping: a practical book on moving instead of an entertaining Christmas present. *Yeah. Signs of the times.*

Usually Nina looked forward to Christmas. She went Christmas shopping and then prepared a large meal while she planned the family vacation. At Christmas, she could do special things for her family. She spent a good deal of time getting everything just right, and she found the effort worthwhile when she saw the happiness on her family's faces.

This year, the whole family was preparing to move to Los Angeles. Under other circumstances, Nina would have been thrilled at the prospect of a trip to such a glamorous and well-known destination. But this trip would be no such pleasure.

Nina set down the packing tape and got up from the kitchen table. She poured herself a cup of tea. Nina had tried to convince Ernesto that if the family moved away from Argentina, it would be too traumatic for the children to be separated from their grandparents and their friends. Her arguments had fallen on deaf ears.

Ernesto was convinced that the family's future lay in America. He insisted that Argentina was too unstable; even if things seemed to be going well at the moment, it wouldn't last. Of course, in Argentina, *going well* simply meant longer gaps between demonstrations in the streets, casualty-free clashes between unions and soldiers, or fewer military aircraft buzzing over neighborhoods to intimidate the populace.

Ernesto wanted to get out of Argentina by the beginning of the new year.

———

Nina stood outside the den. She knew that her final attempt to dissuade Ernesto from the move would probably fail, but she had to try. She knocked before stepping into the room.

"Ernesto, isn't family the most important thing in the world? Not money?"

"Yes, of course."

"Then why are we moving away from our families?"

Ernesto sighed, but met her eyes with a steady gaze. "When we talk about family, we mean two different things. You're talking about your parents. I'm thinking about my children. Nina, you have to be forward-thinking. Your children are your family. Your parents have already had a lifetime. We need a future for us and our kids. We're talking about different things."

Nina had no response. Ernesto might have seemed open to discussion, but Nina knew her views didn't matter to him. He never had room for anyone else's opinion.

"Just make sure all the boxes are packed and ready to go when the time comes," Ernesto said.

———

The day before the family left, the condo manager threw the Rossis a surprise going-away party. He invited Nina and Ernesto's families, their friends, and most of the neighbors in the surrounding condos. The manager set up decorated tables and made enough barbeque for the whole city.

Nina was touched by his kind gesture. Her eyes grew teary when she thought about the amount of work that must have gone into throwing the party for them. She was shocked to see some of her distant relatives there, even though she didn't normally talk to them.

One of her cousins and his wife came up to her with a gift.

"Here you go. You'll need this in America," her cousin said.

Nina opened the gift and recognized a common can opener. "Um, thank you," she said, a little confused.

"My son has a friend in America," the wife said. "He told us that all the food there comes in cans. You have to scrape the pots and save all the leftovers you can."

"I've never actually lived there, but I've visited several times, and I've never seen that," Nina said. "It's actually the opposite. Food is very plentiful in America."

The cousin's wife gave Nina a sour look. "We heard it's not a great place to live."

As she looked down at the can opener, Nina realized that her cousin and his wife were doing what children do when they see another child with a toy they want. They were making America sound bad because they wanted to move there too.

Her cousin was also venting the usual hatred for America, a common opinion amongst Argentines. They insisted that the imperialistic Americans were always meddling in other countries' politics. Nina thought that many Argentines had forgotten that America was always ready to help during natural disasters or unstable political situations. Just like kids, Argentines wanted the help and support that parents give, but didn't want any advice from them.

She chuckled to herself after the two had walked away.

They were the only people to say anything negative about America. Everyone else focused on positives and told Nina what a great opportunity this would be for her. She knew she should be happy to move to such a wonderful place, but she couldn't repress her sorrow. All the stories of America's greatness were just stories. She knew for a fact that Argentina was beautiful, Argentina was home. Her whole life was here: her family and her friends.

Ernesto and the children basked in the joy of the party and what lay before them. Nina felt empty inside. She was being separated from her family, a part of her. The day of departure loomed like a trip to the guillotine.

———

Ordinarily the family would have been too tired after the long flight to America to take in Tinseltown, the "glamour capital" of the world. But the new air of the United States had filled Ernesto, Vanessa, and David with fresh energy.

Nina found nothing joyful about their new surroundings.

"Mom, Mom, look at that!" Vanessa said over and over at every building they drove past on the way to their new home.

"Yes, honey, that's nice," Nina said. She was too depressed to truly enjoy either the tall royal palms that lined every important thoroughfare or the warm, sunny weather, too depressed to be dazzled by Hollywood or to marvel at the opulence of Beverly Hills.

"Hey, look—I think that man was in a movie I saw," Ernesto said to Nina. She did not respond. He whispered so the children couldn't hear, "Don't ruin this for everyone else. At least try to have a good time."

Nina stared out the window. Being uprooted from her life was hard, and, worse, she felt like Ernesto was insensitive to her feelings.

"I don't feel like it right now, okay?" Nina said.

"You might as well feel like it," Ernesto said. "It's not like this is a temporary move."

The rolling hills and enormous houses symbolized her forced exile from Argentina. *I didn't choose to be here, and I won't be forced into liking it,* Nina told herself.

They soon reached Carlos and Elisa Panetta's house. The Panettas lived in Glendale, a community located in the northern part of LA County. Carlos had suggested the Rossis settle there because he would be close by in case they needed help. Ernesto had agreed.

Nina's family piled out of the taxi after a long drive. As far as Nina could tell, they were nowhere near the beach: she couldn't smell the sea or see any sand. A husky man in his thirties with dark hair and a mustache walked down the driveway toward them. He looked a little like Ernesto, and Nina assumed he was Carlos. An attractive woman with raven black hair accompanied him, her expensive clothes swept by a cool breeze.

"Welcome, welcome!" Carlos boomed.

The others hugged and kissed, but Nina looked around. She noticed nothing but hills and trees. She heard the strange howling of a wild animal nearby.

"It's certainly not the beach," Nina said. She knew she was being ridiculous, but she was too tired to care. Ernesto glared at her.

"The beach is only fifteen miles away, about an hour's drive in traffic," Elisa said. "We try to go a few times each summer. We can take you when it warms up in May."

Nina had wanted to live near the beach, but Ernesto had said no. He'd had reasons too: homes near the ocean were not only pricey but subject to maintenance problems due to the salty air. They also had higher insurance costs and a lot of beach traffic.

It seemed to Nina that Ernesto brushed aside anything she wanted to make her time in America more enjoyable, considering them silly fantasies or outlandish requests. She'd argued for her choices, but been voted down every time. Every opinion she'd voiced had fallen on deaf ears. Ernesto had made up his mind. They would live in Glendale.

———∽∾∽———

Nina dreaded looking for a house for the family. As long as they lived with Carlos and Elisa, she could hope that their situation might be reversed. But once they bought their own property, there would be no going back to Argentina.

On the other hand, Nina desperately wanted to get out of the Panettas' house. Elisa had an odd personality that bewildered and intimidated Nina. She struggled to gauge Elisa's thoughts with little success. Clearly Elisa had an attitude. She acted as if the Rossis annoyed her, so Nina felt guilty for staying at their house. Nina had little choice. She had to find a new house.

———∽∾∽———

Nina trailed after Ernesto and the realtor.

"What do you think?" Ernesto said. "This is a beautiful ranch house. It's got four bedrooms, a den paneled in cherry wood, a big swimming pool, and a nice backyard."

It did. It was beautiful.

"And through the sliding glass doors is a panoramic view of the mountains and their purple majesty," Ernesto said, waxing poetical. "If all that rustic charm isn't enough, the house has every woman's dream: a large formal dining room."

While Nina liked the house, her enthusiasm did not match Ernesto's, who sounded like a realtor himself. He and the kids were swept up in the idea. The swimming pool and yard, year-round features in Southern California, were enough for Ernesto and the kids.

Vanessa and David shared their father's enthusiasm.

"Now we can have a big dog!" Vanessa squealed as she ran around the empty house. David chased after her, laughing.

Her family kept finding new reasons to stay. With each new reason, Nina found it harder and harder to deny them happiness. But she felt like she was signing her life away with every decision they made.

After they chose a house, the next important step, key to remaining in America, was locating a suitable business to buy. An immigration attorney advised them to buy a business in the United States and to employ at least fifteen people. With an E-2 visa, they would be free to visit back home whenever they wished, coming and going as they pleased. The visa was renewable after five years. While it wasn't the ultimate solution, it thrilled Ernesto and numbed Nina.

"What do you think of a cosmetics factory in San Fernando?" Nina asked while looking through the classified ads in the newspaper. She liked the idea of an unlimited supply of beauty products and the chance to tell her friends she was in the glamour business.

"The price is too high," Ernesto said.

"What about real estate development?"

"The people who would actually be working for us would be independent contractors and not on the payroll. Payroll and payroll taxes are part and parcel of the E-2 visa," Ernesto said.

"Oh, yeah," Nina said. She went back to the paper, but didn't mention any more ideas she came across.

When they looked into a hair salon on Rodeo Drive in Beverly Hills, Nina finally began to cheer up. She liked the idea of owning a Hollywood hotspot where the really big celebrities went to get their hair cut; she could be passionate about a business like that. They would be serving a very exclusive clientele.

"I'd love to run a salon," Nina said. The possibility had pierced through her gloom. "It's a great opportunity. I'd like to work in the beauty industry. And Rodeo Drive is the most exclusive address in the country. I would love working there. Imagine the people I could meet and mingle with."

"But look. The landlord wants a percentage of the gross sales," Ernesto said. "I don't think it's right to reveal our books to strangers."

"Why not?" Nina was surprised. How come he was so willing to leave everything behind in Argentina but had a problem showing people how well they were doing in America?

"For one thing, the landlord wants a cut of our gross sales."

Nina thought a moment. "If it's part of the rent, it won't cost us any more."

Ernesto let the statement hang in the air. "I'm just not sure I want some stranger looking at our business."

"You're being paranoid. What are we hiding?" There seemed to be only one reason for Ernesto to pick this small issue as the sticking point: he didn't want to agree to her idea. *Maybe I'm getting paranoid too.*

"I just don't like the idea." Before Nina could retort, Ernesto added, "Besides, if the business has a lot of expenses, he will still have his same percentage, and we'll be the ones losing money."

They might have been in America, but the Rossis were still a traditional South American family: the man made the decisions. Nina couldn't answer his objections. She had the sinking feeling a glamorous hair salon on Rodeo Drive was not to be.

They also considered the possibility of Nina going back into the pharmacy business. Ernesto asked, "Have you looked into requirements in California?"

"Yes, I have. I need to pass the exam to get a California license. That's not likely. My English isn't good enough for that; the technical vocabulary alone is like another language."

"Too bad. It would have been the perfect solution."

"Yes, too bad."

They finally settled on a printing plant about twenty minutes from their home in Glendale. It was small but had a steady clientele and a payroll of twenty-two people. Best of all, most of the employees spoke Spanish. Since Ernesto still struggled with English, this arrangement would be ideal for him.

Ernesto wasn't the only one who had to catch up with doing business in America. The paper plant had modern equipment that Nina had never seen before. Every component in the plant was mechanized. When the previous owner asked Nina to fax him the finalized paperwork, Nina had no idea what he was talking about. The factory secretary showed her the fax machine. Nina was impressed.

Nina's new routine in Glendale kept her busy, but that made her happy. She liked routines and quickly adjusted to them. She'd drop the kids off at school and then drive to the business to help Ernesto with any managerial issues that came along. Because she no longer had a nanny's help, she quit work early enough to pick the kids up from school.

Nina liked the way numerous tasks made the days go by faster; she liked having less downtime to think about things.

———✥———

Eventually they hired a nanny from El Salvador. She was a sweet girl but unfamiliar with Argentine culture, and she and Nina spoke different forms of Spanish. With their newly acquired English, the kids were using Spanish words differently, too, further confusing Nina and alienating her in her own home.

The language barrier affected Nina in other ways. She couldn't seem to have a good conversation with anybody other than Ernesto, and she missed it. She craved stimulating conversations and the challenge of a good intellectual debate, but she didn't want to assimilate. Trying to be at home in America would be a sign of defeat.

Nina still desperately needed to communicate with her parents in Argentina. Telephone calls to South America were very expensive, so she lived for letters from home. They arrived regularly, full of her mom's recipes, local and family news, and inquiries about their new life in America. The letters were always upbeat and helpful, although they tended to deepen Nina's homesickness. She still felt like an alien in a foreign land and was bitter with her husband for not being able to put up with the rigors of their homeland in favor of stability in America. The letters became her lifeline.

Nina's mom called to announce they would be coming to Los Angeles for Christmas that year. Nina felt her world finally coming back to life. When she picked the kids up from school, she was very excited to share the good news with them. Her mood was contagious, and the children couldn't help but smile as well.

"I have great news!" Nina said. "Guess what it is!"

Vanessa squealed. "We got a pony!"

"No, no, that's not it," Nina said.

"You made all my favorite desserts!" David said.

"It's way better than that."

"Oh, my God!" Vanessa shrieked. "You're having another baby!"

Vanessa and David looked at each other with wide smiles.

"Well, I guess it's not quite that great," Nina said. Everyone seemed to be waiting for her to have another baby. For Nina, having two children and one husband was more than enough. "Your grandparents are coming up to visit us for the holidays."

Far from being disappointed, the children beamed with excitement and started bouncing up and down. Nina had expected just such a reaction. She smiled.

"They can stay in my room with me," David said.

"There's plenty of room for everyone," Nina said.

———•••———

The big day finally arrived. Nina shifted from foot to foot. Her whole family stood with her at the airport arrival gate. She felt expectant, nervous, and overjoyed. As she watched the sea of heads bobbing down the ramp, she looked for her parents. There were so many tall heads that at first she couldn't find her parents. Then they burst out of the crowd of passengers.

Nina leapt into their arms, desperate for the familiar happiness of their embrace. They hugged her eagerly, tears and laughter marking Nina's first truly joyous moment since she had arrived in America.

Now it was time for the newly Americanized Rossis to show the old folks a bit of America and a good time. Nina wanted to spend as much time with her parents as possible. She'd planned several day trips that included lots of time in the car so they could talk. She just hoped the kids could handle the car rides without getting too cranky.

Their first stop: Palm Springs in the California desert. It was impressive, with its palms and swimming pools and glitz. They rode the cable cars to the top of Mount San Jacinto for a magnificent view of the desert city below. For lunch, Nina and Ernesto took the Salvattis out for their first taste of Mexican food. They had never eaten anything like that before, and her father was mesmerized. He kept asking the waitress for the recipes of each entree they ordered and repeated the words *burrito, guacamole,* and *salsa* so he could commit them to memory.

Her father loved everything about America and was eager to share his love of the country with almost everyone they encountered. Nina overheard her father talk about how people in America could pay their bills by mail instead of standing in long lines, how sunny and warm it was in the winter in California, and how the banks in America gave people thirty-year mortgages to pay off their homes. Her father marveled at how Americans accepted people from all parts of the world and made them feel welcome. He thanked everyone who talked to him for being patient with his broken English.

As Nina reached the car, she realized they had forgotten to lock it when they went into the Mexican restaurant for lunch. Nina recalled overhearing her parents discussing break-ins to her father's car many times. Her heart sank when she thought they would experience the same thing in America.

Estela began searching frantically through their belongings to see if anything was missing. They had left some expensive belongings in the car, such as cameras and coats. Some of it had been sitting in plain view.

"Why didn't you check to make sure the doors were locked?" Ernesto hissed to Nina.

"You told me to go into the restaurant to get seats. I wasn't even out here to lock it." Nina moved away from the car in hopes that Ernesto would follow so her parents wouldn't hear them arguing.

"They're your parents," Ernesto said. "You should be looking out for them."

Nina stared at him in disbelief.

"Nothing's missing!" her mother cried. She looked at Nina with an expression of wonder and confusion. Nina was relieved, not only because their belongings were safe, but now there was less reason for Ernesto to continue fighting.

Ernesto crossed his arms and continued to stare at Nina. She ignored him, deciding to attribute his behavior to the long drive ahead.

"I told you America is the greatest place in the world," Miguel said. "They don't even steal when it would be so easy."

Nina joined her parents near the car. They swept her up in their wonder and amazement, their love of the country. She smiled broadly as she shared in their hugs.

"Everything's fine. Let's get back on the road!" Miguel shouted with glee still clear in his voice. He made Ernesto drive to a nearby bookstore, where he bought almost every available book and cassette on learning English. As they headed for their second destination, Las Vegas, they listened to cassettes on learning English the whole way.

When they first arrived in Las Vegas, it amazed and overwhelmed them with its array of glitzy hotels, tall neon signs, throngs of excited tourists, the lure of big-time gambling, and the world-class entertainment available everywhere. The Salvattis walked around in awe at the wonders of America.

Estela appeared to be most enchanted by the casinos.

"I love the noise, the lights, and the excitement as people win money," she said. She sat down in front of a slot machine. "I want to stay as long as I can."

———

Later that night, Nina jolted from her sleep at the sound of loud pounding on her door. Heart thudding with adrenaline, she untangled herself from her sheets, rushed to the door, and threw it open.

Her father stood on the other side, looking frantic. The fear on his face sent Nina into a panic.

"What's wrong? Where's Mom?" Estela wasn't with her husband. In Nina's sleepy mind, this meant that something awful had happened to her, maybe a heart attack.

"Nina, Nina, they robbed me and kidnapped your mother!" Miguel shouted.

"What happened?"

"I woke up just now, and your mother's gone, and my wallet's missing. Call the police!"

Stunned, Nina ran to the phone in her room to call security. Before she dialed, she asked, "Was the door forced open?"

Her father paused to think for a minute. "No."

Nina's fright became confusion, and then amusement. Perhaps no crime had actually been committed.

"So no one broke into the room, but Mom and your money are missing," Nina said. "And we are in Las Vegas...." She put her hand over her mouth to conceal her sudden laughter. "Give me a minute and we'll go downstairs."

After she got dressed, they ventured down to the slot machines.

There, amid a sea of half-empty machines, Estela sat, smiling and pulling the arm of a slot machine. Miguel nearly danced her around the room in his relief, and when they told Estela the story, they all laughed until their sides hurt.

It feels good to laugh so hard. Nina couldn't remember the last time she had felt such joy. Mixed in with her pleasure was the knowledge that her parents were the ones making her laugh. They were the reason she'd never wanted to leave Argentina.

"I was too excited," Estela said. "I couldn't sleep."

"Come on, Mom," Nina said. "We have a long drive ahead of us tomorrow. Go to bed."

Everyone returned to their rooms, but Nina knew Miguel would be sleeping with one eye open. And she would be sleeping with a smile on her face.

—◦◦◦—

They drove across the desert to the Hoover Dam and the Grand Canyon; all the passengers in the car were asleep except Nina and

Estela. It was the longest trip they would take during their visit. Nina planned to keep them entertained outside of the house so they wouldn't discover how lonely she was.

"Nina, dear, I love visiting all these new and exciting places, but why can't we just stay home for one day?" Estela said. "It's exhausting."

"I just want to show you how great America is." Nina smiled at her own words.

"We didn't come here to see America. We came here to see how you are doing."

"We're all fine. Everything has settled into place; it's wonderful here." Nina tried to seem upbeat, but she felt like a child caught holding the baseball that broke the window. *Nothing ever gets past my mom.*

"So America is an improvement on everything that was wrong in Argentina?" Estela asked.

Nina's smile faded. Tears gathered in her eyes and ran down her cheeks.

"It's the same, except I'm all alone now." Nina whispered quietly, almost mouthing the words. "I can barely understand the kids. Ernesto has awful mood swings. No matter how hard I try, nothing ever pleases him. He's constantly complaining about the food—it has too much salt or too little, something's always wrong with it. If I discipline the children, he says I'm too hard, and if I don't, he says I'm not doing my part as a mother."

Looking at her mother's expression, she regretted letting her defenses down. She tried to smile again. "But that's married life. It's no big deal."

Estela reached for Nina's free hand and held it the rest of the way to the Grand Canyon.

———⁂———

On the ride home after driving her parents to the airport, Nina tried to hold back her tears but couldn't keep from sobbing. All the reasons for staying in Argentina that she had suppressed after moving to America come to the front of her mind. If it meant feeling this way every time her parents or family from Argentina visited, she didn't know if she could handle it. It brought great joy to see them, but the pain she was feeling in the car was almost unbearable.

Ernesto rolled his eyes. "When are you going to get over this? We've been here a year already. Don't you think you should be getting used to it by now?"

Sniffling, Nina tried to compose herself. She dabbed at her eyes, unable to believe his callousness. He should comfort her when she felt this way, not contribute to her pain.

"I'm trying. I promise, I'm trying."

"How hard?" he asked coldly.

"You don't understand," Nina said. How could he not miss their homeland? How could he not care that his parents and siblings now lived thousands of miles away?

"I don't understand what? That we're making a better, more secure life for our children?" Ernesto scowled. "All you do is complain how much you miss home. It's time to grow up."

"I suppose you think I'm childish."

"Yes, I do. We just saw your parents. We'll be visiting Argentina again before the year is out."

They drove in silence for a while. Nina wanted to scream at him—for taking away her family, using their own children as leverage against her to move to America, for not even trying to make her life any easier. Bitterness swept over her. For him, America was new and filled with possibilities. But she was trapped in the same life she'd led in Argentina, only worse.

Eventually he said, "But I get the feeling it's not good enough."

"I didn't say that."

"You don't have to. Your attitude says it all. The kids shouldn't have to live with your constant complaining."

"I told you I was trying. I wish you wouldn't take it so personally."

He swung his head toward her, a look of incredulity on his face. "Not take it personally? How else can I take it? My life and the kids' lives are all affected here."

"I just miss my family and friends. I want to be around them. All the time. Not just on a holiday when I have to be sad all over again. Because when they leave, the cycle begins again."

Talking to him was useless. Always the same argument, repeating forever. Nina found relief in imagining never having to talk to him again.

Ernesto said nothing, his eyes straight ahead on the road.

The More, the Merrier

N ina missed her parents the moment they left. She knew couldn't
do anything that day until she was sure they had arrived safely
in Argentina. All the next morning, she sat by the telephone, ignoring
her plans for the day as she waited for her mother to call. By the time
the phone finally rang, Ernesto had left for work, the kids had gone
to school, and Nina was all alone in the too-quiet house.

"How are you?" she asked. "How was your flight?"

"It was fine. We're glad to be home." But Nina's mom didn't
sound entirely glad. She sounded tired, distant, even worried. "We
loved seeing you and your family, Nina. It was a wonderful visit."

"I loved your visit too," Nina said, "but don't worry about me
now that you're gone. I'll be all right."

"Good. That's good."

Nina hesitated. This wasn't the cheerful, reassuring conversation
she'd expected. "Mom… is everything okay?"

"It's just your father. There was a pile of mail waiting for us
when we got back. The bank statements—aren't good." Her mom's
voice shook. "We leave for a little while and the country gets even
worse."

"How bad is it?"

"So bad I can hardly believe it. Bad even for Argentina."

"Mom, please just tell me." Nina could feel herself growing

impatient, but beyond her impatience lurked the beginnings of fear. She'd expected an ordinary conversation, nothing more than a routine phone call about being home again, about the flight, about how tired her parents were at the end of it. Now she feared her parents might be in real trouble.

Nina heard a brief clatter as her mom passed the phone to her dad.

"Dad, will you please tell me what's wrong?"

"It seems that all the money in our CDs has shrunk by more than 70 percent." Her father, at least, spoke to the point.

"Are you sure it's really that bad?" Nina sounded calm and reasonable, even to herself. "Those things are always so hard to believe."

"You're right. It's hard to believe, but it's clearly down by more than 70 percent." She heard the frown in his voice so clearly that she could almost see it. "That's not the worst part, actually. It looks like our house here in Buenos Aires and the summer place in Mar del Plata have devalued by at least 50 percent."

Nina's eyes widened and her hand moved to her neck. The slight pressure at her throat stopped up all the words she might have said, but her father kept talking, not noticing her sudden silence.

"The Galtieri government is looking for a scapegoat," he said. "I should have known we'd come back to chaos. The newspapers at the airport were full of talk about war with Great Britain."

"Going to war? Why?"

"Over the islands off our coast, the Malvinas. The ones the British call the Falklands."

"But what is there to fight over? Some sheep? There can't be more than a couple thousand English living there."

"That's right," he said.

They were both silent, just for a moment. Nina heard paper rustling.

"I've got the newspaper here. God help us. They've invaded. Right on the front page it says they've captured the small British garrison on the island."

"And that means war?"

"No doubt. You moved to America at the right time."

Nina hated to hear him say that. Because she'd moved to America, she was thousands of miles away. Now Argentina was at war, and she couldn't be with her parents to help them. There was no worse feeling. Already she was full of worry, sure that something terrible would happen. She didn't trust her relatives to look after her parents as well as she would have if she were there.

She felt tears gather in her eyes as she spoke again. "I'm so sorry I'm not with you right now."

"Nonsense. You live where you can invest money and know it will grow and be safe. I worked my whole life at the store so I could invest in real estate, and now it's worth less than I first paid for it. If I did the same work in America, I'd already be rich and retired!"

"Dad, I'm so sorry."

"We'll be all right," he said. "Your mother and I have been through worse."

———

Despite her usual distaste for politics, Nina began to follow the news every day. Margaret Thatcher, the iron-willed prime minister of Great Britain, refused to let General Galtieri's dictatorship drive her people from the Falklands. To do so would be to lose national prestige, something she was unwilling to risk. Even American newspapers tracked the events now that outright war threatened Argentina.

Eager to resolve the situation in a manner favorable to themselves, the British assembled a major task force and sent it to the islands, negotiating all the while. They seemed to hope for a peaceful resolution; Nina hoped too. But the Galtieri government responded merely by strengthening its defenses on the islands. By the time the British arrived three weeks later, no political settlement was in place. Fighting ensued.

The professional Argentine Air Force did well against the elite British forces. However, the Argentine Army fared badly. Unlike the Air Force, it was mostly composed of eighteen-year-old conscripts performing their military obligation. Hundreds were killed.

On May 2, 1982, a British submarine sank the *General Belgrano*, an Argentine Navy cruiser, costing the nation three hundred lives. By the time the brief war ended in June, the British had killed more than six hundred Argentines and reclaimed the Falklands.

———

One Sunday evening, Nina was preparing the children's lunch for school the next day when the telephone rang. She hurried to answer it, hoping her mother had called with news. When they had last talked, Estela had told Nina that the people of Argentina were demanding the return of democracy following the poor performance of the Argentine military. She hoped that the situation would continue to improve. Perhaps the war could bring good changes instead of bad.

When she answered the phone, however, a man's voice replied. "Hi, sis. It's me."

"Eduardo!" Nina cried, and burst into tears. She hadn't heard from her brother in ages. "How are you? How's your wife and son?"

"We're fine. All doing well," Eduardo said.

"Good, good," Nina said. "And your work, how is that?"

Eduardo sighed. Like Nina, he had followed his interests to shape his career, but instead of working in a pharmacy, he had become a chef in a fine restaurant. A year ago, he had seized his opportunity to buy a large portion of the restaurant's stock and a partnership. Nina remembered how proud he had been.

"I guess I'm a bad businessman," Eduardo said. "When I bought the stock, I took out a loan at high interest. Now the restaurant is facing bankruptcy. We're having some trouble at the moment, but I think things are going to get even worse."

It was Nina's turn to sigh. She wished she could hear good news when her family called, just for once. It seemed like everyone was having money troubles.

"I'm just not sure what to do now," Eduardo said. "I've been looking for a new job, but so far I haven't had any luck."

Ernesto had been lurking nearby, listening to her conversation. Now he slipped into the other room. Nina heard a click on the line as he joined in from the other phone. "You're looking for work?"

"Yeah."

"You and your family should immigrate to America," Ernesto said. "We could give you a job in the business here."

Nina blinked. Eduardo and Ernesto had met before on occasion and were friendly when they saw one another at family gatherings in Argentina. Still, they weren't close enough for Ernesto to give such unsolicited advice.

Eduardo also seemed taken aback by Ernesto's forwardness. Nina heard him clear his throat.

"That's not exactly a decision I can make over the phone," he said.

"Nina? Go ahead and put some tea on," Ernesto said. "I'm going to talk to your brother for a little bit longer."

Nina hesitated. How could Ernesto just barge into her conversation like this? She would love to have her brother in America with her, but there would be other costs that Ernesto hadn't considered.

"Go on," Ernesto said. "Hang up the phone."

Nina didn't want to protest in front of her brother, so she complied.

Nina didn't know what to do. She stood in the middle of the kitchen, imaging what it would be like to see her brother again. She would be thrilled. At the same time, her parents would be sad to give Eduardo up: she would be gaining, but they would be losing. And she was already worried about them, growing older and older in an unstable political situation.

Nina looked through the cupboard for a teakettle and filled it with water. Even going through the motions of brewing tea made her miss home.

Eduardo is a bit of home, she thought. She put the kettle on the stove.

Eduardo was a grown man. He could, and would, make his own choices. His choices might bring Nina greater happiness, but that didn't mean she was responsible for her parents' ultimate sadness. Was she?

Nina fetched a box of tea down from the cabinet. At this very moment, Ernesto was talking Eduardo into moving to Los Angeles. Nina got teacups out of the cabinet and placed a bag in each cup. If she did nothing, she would finally have some family close to her.

The water started to boil. Nina poured the water over the tea.

———

Two months later, Eduardo, his wife Julia, and their five-year-old son, Julio, arrived in Los Angeles, exhausted by their journey, but excited to start the next stage of their lives. The very next day, Eduardo began his job at Ernesto's printing plant. The day after, little Julio began school with his cousins.

Although they plunged into American life with optimism, Eduardo and Julia encountered some problems in their transition.

Not only was Eduardo working in Ernesto's printing plant, but he
and his family had moved into the Rossis' house. Although friendly
and pleasant, Julia was shy and didn't want to interfere with Nina's
way of running the house. Meanwhile, tensions ensued as Eduardo
adjusted to accepting Ernesto's authority both at work and home.

Every time Eduardo and Ernesto quarreled over financial or
work-related problems, Nina felt caught in the middle. She owed a
certain amount of loyalty to her brother. On the other hand, she was
not about to challenge her husband on any subject. Their marriage
was already going through a rough patch without her defying him
in front of others.

Fortunately, Eduardo never held any of the tensions against
Nina. Eager to find an outlet for his cooking abilities, he relieved
her burden of preparing meals by making many delicious dishes for
both families. His specialty was Nina's favorite: barbecued chicken
marinated in a lemon dressing.

"Nina, I can make dinner for everyone tonight," Eduardo would
say before he left for work.

"Thank you," Nina said each time. "That's a great idea."

She wasn't about to turn down any help—no one else was
offering.

—*∾∾*—

Eduardo and Ernesto's struggle for dominance wasn't the only of its
kind in the Rossi house. Julio and David got along most of the time,
but they managed to find reasons to quarrel almost every day.

"This is your house," Julia said. "My son will follow your rules
here."

Nina appreciated Julia's thoughtfulness, but her decision left
Nina to appease the boys without showing any partiality between
the two.

Every afternoon after school, the boys went outside to play in the swimming pool. The first half-hour generally went well, then they'd start to bicker. Inevitably, after a few minutes of this they would look over to Nina for a decision. She hated it. She didn't want to look like she showed favoritism to David, but she didn't want to always side with Julio either. She didn't want her son to feel betrayed by his mother.

Her stomach hurt every afternoon.

"I want to play with the inflatable alligator," Julio said.

David pulled the toy closer. "I had it first."

"I want to play with it!"

"It's mine!"

Two pairs of eyes turned in Nina's direction. She forced a smile. "How about we go get some ice cream?"

The boys clambered out of the pool with whoops of delight.

Nina rubbed her stomach. One more afternoon down, an unlimited number to go. She felt as though she were carrying an enormous weight on her shoulders. She wished something would ease her burden.

———

Each month stretched on forever. Watching her brother and sister-in-law adjust to American life, Nina began to make a greater attempt to understand it herself. She noticed how much of the culture seemed to center around shopping at the mall. She tried a shopping expedition, then tried another. Before she knew it, she'd found that she enjoyed her mall trips, which gave her an acceptable reason to get out of the house by herself.

"Can I help you find something, ma'am?" a Nordstrom's clerk asked.

Nina started in surprise, glancing up from the burgundy dress she held in one hand. "No, thank you," she said. "Just looking."

The clerk smiled as she turned away. "That dress is definitely your color."

Nina liked it when salespeople started conversations with her. Even though part of their job was to pay attention to her, she liked feeling as though she were interesting to someone. At home, she felt like a bulletin board where people dumped their requests and walked away.

"Actually, can you tell me about these socks?" Nina asked, pointing to a display in the accessories department.

"Of course," the clerk said. "Are you going camping?"

Nina shook her head absently, picking up a thick pair of brown socks.

"Whether you're camping or not, those are great with boots," the clerk said, "and they're wonderful in any cold weather. I love camping in the Angeles National Forest. Have you been up there? It's freezing at night!"

As the clerk described the many advantages of having a nice pair of thick socks, Nina wished she had the time to ask about an item from every department.

"I'll take them," Nina said.

But as she gave the clerk the money, she regretted buying something so foolish. This wasn't even a luxury item like bubble bath or jewelry—those things were expensive, but at least she had a reason for buying them. Hiking socks were completely useless. She would never wear them in Glendale. She'd spent money just so she could talk to someone.

Well, maybe it had been worth it. She needed a way to escape.

After that first purchase, Nina often came home from the mall with things she didn't need. She always made sure to throw the receipts away and hide the items so it wouldn't upset Ernesto. She knew he wouldn't understand. He might even be angry that she'd spent his money on ridiculous trinkets.

As winter approached, the Rossis and Salvattis stayed home more and more often. David and Julio charged around the house with their toys. Vanessa complained about the noise. Julia, Eduardo, and Ernesto complained as well. No one knew what to do in the evenings.

Nina wanted to run somewhere far away, somewhere where she could escape the noise and frustration of the crowded house. Instead, she set up board games and baked cookies almost every night; even though Eduardo was a great chef, he didn't like to bake. The more she worked to make everyone happy, the more demanding everyone became.

During one of her weekly phone conversations with her mother, Nina finally confided her problems.

"Everyone is constantly asking me to make this, fix that, clean this, or help with that," she said. "At this point, I don't think they even consider doing anything themselves."

Nina imagined what would happen if she went on strike. If she insisted that everyone do his or her own housework, chaos would ensue and piles of garbage would rapidly accumulate. Nina chuckled, but she quickly sobered at the realization she would be the one to clean it up eventually.

"I feel so trapped right now," she said.

"This situation is only temporary," Estela said. "Don't let it overwhelm you."

"Easy for you to say," Nina said. "If I don't do everything everyone wants, suddenly everyone's unhappy. It's crazy."

"You need to make whatever sacrifices are necessary to keep the peace," Estela said.

"I'm making so many sacrifices already."

"You're the peacemaker in the family. If you won't make an effort to keep the peace, you won't have any peace."

"So I'm suddenly the caretaker of the whole family?" Nina asked.

It didn't seem fair. It was certainly a responsibility she didn't want. How could she be the source of her family's happiness when she could barely find happiness for herself each day?

"That's just the way a mother feels sometimes," her mom said. "Don't despair. Everything will get better before you know it."

—◆◆◆—

Estela was right; the situation did begin to improve. A couple months later, Eduardo left the printing plant to start work as a chef in a high-profile restaurant. Soon after, he and Julia finally found their own home. Nina had a feeling that everyone would be better friends now that the other family had its own place to live. The new house was certainly closer than any house in Argentina.

A few weeks later, Vanessa graduated from elementary school. Full of new energy, Nina arranged a big party for her and invited the Salvattis. As she had suspected, everyone was in better spirits at the party. Even though Nina had counted down the days until the Salvattis' move, the house had seemed strangely big and empty after they left. She welcomed the opportunity to see her brother and his family again in a fun setting.

"Thank you again—so much—for letting us stay with you," Julia told Nina as she helped set out cupcakes in the kitchen.

"Don't mention it," Nina said. "I know you and Eduardo would have done the same thing if we needed help."

Julia smiled. "Of course. Isn't it funny, though, the way Argentina works? Soon as we left, things started to settle down there. That's why you and Ernesto moved over here, right? Because of all the unrest?"

"What do you mean?" Nina paused in the act of placing a final cupcake on the tray. She didn't want to get her hopes up, but news of Argentina stabilizing made her heart sing.

"Haven't you heard?" Julia asked. "After the war, international human rights organizations kept pressuring the military until it actually gave up its power."

"Really?" That was incredible. The Argentinian military had always fought hard to keep its power, one way or another.

"Mm-hmm. They've announced that general elections will be in October and the full transition to democracy in November," Julia said. She picked up the tray and prepared to sweep it out of the kitchen. "But you and Ernesto look like you're doing really well for yourselves here in America."

As Nina reentered the party, she felt dazed. A few words from her sister-in-law had opened up a new world of possibilities for her. Democracy in Argentina! With the new political landscape in place, it might be possible for Nina's family to move back home.

They'd have to do it soon, she thought. If Vanessa started high school in America, it would make it more difficult for her to get into a high school in Argentina. *No time like the present.* Nina decided to move quickly to plant the seeds for going home. Suddenly she couldn't wait for the party to end.

Two hours later, as she and Ernesto tidied away the remains of the birthday streamers, giftwrap, and leftover cake, Nina made her move.

"I guess you've probably heard all about what's going on in Argentina."

"Yeah, of course."

"Isn't it wonderful? Can you believe that they're going back to democracy at last? The economy is really beginning to stabilize."

"It's great." Ernesto picked up and threw away half-eaten pieces of cake.

He wasn't paying attention, so Nina decided to stop hinting.

"I want us to go back," she said.

Ernesto said nothing, but his shoulders slumped and he sighed.

"I've been thinking about it," Nina said. "This is the perfect time."

Ernesto still didn't reply, so Nina plowed on ahead. "If we go now, Vanessa can start high school. David will be starting first grade. The military's no longer in power, the government's going to make people pay for their crimes, and everything's stable and secure."

"Do you honestly think they just fixed all their problems overnight?"

"It's our homeland. It deserves another chance," Nina said. "Anyway, it's not like everything in America has been perfect."

Ernesto put down the slice of cake he'd been holding, a scowl on his face. "We've talked about this before," he said. "We've talked about this too much."

"I know," Nina said softly. The tensions between them were as bad as they had been when they'd first came to America. Their frequent arguments had done nothing to solve their problems; they'd only exhausted them both.

"You keep putting this country down," Ernesto said, "but it's given us a good home, a good chance at business. In Argentina, nothing really changes. You might think it's better now, but I promise you, it won't stay that way."

Nina shook her head, refusing to let him make her angry. "You don't have to leave right away, but I think the rest of us should. I'll take the kids back to Argentina to start school. You can stay here for as long as you need to sell the business and the house. Then come and join us."

"It is not a seller's market," Ernesto said. "It doesn't matter how long I wait; the market can go nowhere but up. We'd be trading money for time. Time is easier."

"You should know by now that money isn't everything," she said.

He ran his hands through his hair in frustration. "That's easy to say—until you have obligations to meet."

"I've thought about this," Nina said again. She knew they had more than enough money in the bank for her and the children to return to Argentina. "Ernesto," she said, "I'm really looking forward to going back home. I've missed it so much."

Eduardo and Julia's presence had kept her and Ernesto stiflingly close for too long. At the same time, it had put more distance between them than ever. A geographic change might make things better between the two; certainly it would make arguments more difficult. *Maybe my absence will make Ernesto's heart grow fonder.*

Anyway, nothing Ernesto could say would change her mind, especially when she used words like "back home." Ernesto knew America could never be home to her.

"Fine," he said. "Go ahead. Move. See for yourself that nothing has changed. Nothing ever changes there."

———

A month and a half later, the couple sat at their kitchen table sipping coffee. Cardboard packing boxes littered the rooms, but they had decided to take a breather. Nina and the children were leaving the next day, but they didn't have much more to organize.

After his initial objections, Ernesto had been surprisingly compliant. He had reluctantly decided to sell all the furniture and the house; he would live in a one-bedroom apartment until he sold the business, keeping an E-2 visa until the whole family could get their green cards.

"You still don't look very happy about this," Nina said. She hoped her tone wouldn't betray how little she cared if he were happy or not.

Ernesto toyed with the coffee spoon in his saucer. "I guess I just don't trust Argentina," he said. "We've seen so many ups and downs over the years. How can one be confident this new democracy, this new age of human rights will last? How do we know that tomorrow, next month, next year, some general won't seize power and put us all back thirty years? That's happened before."

"You need to stop taking such a pessimistic view of things," Nina said. "We need to be hopeful for our country."

As she looked at his frowning face, Nina had to suppress a smile. Now it was Ernesto's turn to be upset about a move; well, she was glad. This was his chance to feel what she had felt: frustration at having no say in the matter. She hoped he would suffer as much as she had.

"Hopeful?" he asked. "Argentina's history backs my feelings. It's been a mess for decades."

"The past doesn't control the future, not as much as you think." Nina took another sip of her coffee.

"Anyway," Ernesto said suddenly, "you've been complaining the whole time we've lived here. And now that you get your way, you're calling me the pessimist. That's not quite fair, is it?"

"Does this change any of our plans?"

He shook his head. "I'll sell the business when the price is good, whenever that is. You and the kids can visit during winter, spring, and summer vacations."

Nina gazed out the window. She knew the separation of a husband and wife normally wasn't a good thing, and this was, at best, a compromise—one she hoped would work out.

———

The next day, they drove to the airport in silence. Even Vanessa and David sat silently in the backseat of the car. Nina was glad Ernesto didn't stage any last-minute fights or suddenly impose his will on the rest of their decisions. To her, the silence made a welcome change.

At the airport, tears glistened in Ernesto's eyes as he said goodbye to the children. Nina thought the future must seem tenuous at best—at least to him. But she had hope.

She got on the airplane and didn't look back.

Chapter Fifteen

Too Good to be True

Nina's confidence wavered for the first time during takeoff. As the ground fell away from underneath the airplane, she noticed how beautiful the City of Angels looked from above and she began to wonder if she might miss it. Cars shrank to tiny toy miniatures; buildings dwindled into buttons on a grid. She was finally going home, but at what price?

Nina glanced across the aisle at her children, who were already getting out the coloring books that would serve as their in-flight entertainment. She loved them so much. She wanted them to have the best lives possible. *Is this move truly the right thing for them?*

For the past few months, she'd been so sure that it was. Vanessa remembered her years in Argentina and seemed eager and willing to go back. She understood that the move was mostly due to Nina's nostalgia and determination. But David didn't understand the enormity of the move they were making. He'd only been two when they'd first moved to America. At the age of five, he was moving again. Argentina may have been his home country, but America had become all the world he knew.

The move had split their family apart. For the first time, Nina became aware of the implications and consequences for her family, but she still couldn't let herself face them. She'd told Ernesto that hope was important; she couldn't start drowning in anxiety now.

She turned back to the window and concentrated on her joy at going home.

—⁓—

Even the air in Argentina is different, Nina thought as she walked through the airport. Vanessa and David trotted after her. She could see that they were beginning to be excited despite their weariness. They beamed when they saw their grandparents waiting for them at the exit.

Their happiness could not rival Nina's. She had left the tension in Glendale far behind; her doubts had faded during the long flight. Laughing, she ran to hug her parents.

She did not notice Jorge Varela standing beside them until, rude as ever, he pounced and engulfed her in a surprise bear hug.

"Welcome back!" he bellowed, not seeming to notice how Nina kept her arms limp at her sides, refusing to return the hug. She looked past Jorge to her mother, searching her face for answers. *Why is Jorge here?*

"Jorge came along in case you had a lot of luggage," Estela said. "He has a big truck."

"That was very thoughtful," Nina said.

She noticed Jorge starting to hug Vanessa and David, who looked confused and wary. Neither of them remembered Jorge; there was no way she was going to let him touch them. She ushered the children into her mom's arms, diverting Jorge by pointing him in the direction of their luggage cart.

"All our things are over there," she said. "Thanks for your help."

The moment he was out of earshot, she turned to her mother, frowning. "What on earth is he doing here?"

"Honestly, I don't really know," Estela said. "He saw us leaving the house and asked where we were going. Your father said the airport, and he said he'd follow in his truck."

Nina didn't like the sound of that, but her mother just shrugged. "At least this way we can all ride comfortably in our car together and you won't have to say anything more to him," she said.

"I hope he's not expecting a tip when we get home," Nina said and they laughed as they left the airport together.

The next few days brought Nina all the joy she had anticipated. While her children stayed with her parents, she set out to find them a perfect house to live in, immersing herself in the happy task of providing a home for her family. The search gave her the perfect opportunity to soak up all the beauties and familiar sights of Buenos Aires, the one city she loved and called home.

When she found a suitable house, the cost was—as she had expected—a little higher than her budget allowed. She phoned Ernesto to discuss the situation, already knowing what he was going to say. She wasn't wrong.

"It's a bit more than we initially allowed for, but it will meet all our needs," she said. "I especially wanted somewhere where the kids will get a good education. This place is perfect: David will be close to St. Cyrano, which provides a bilingual education, and Vanessa will be near an ideal high school. Not only that, but it's a very nice place to live."

"So what happened to *money isn't everything*?" Ernesto asked after a brief silence. "Seems like you're realizing it's something after all. You're going to need it to live the way you want."

Nina sighed. "Ernesto, please don't lecture me. I already understand the issues involved. I know we'll have to make compromises. But remember, you'll be selling the business soon, so we'll have more money to work with in the near future."

Ernesto couldn't refuse; like Nina, he wanted a good education for his children and was in no position to deny Nina's wishes.

After they purchased the house, Nina set about furnishing it. At first, she thought this would be even more fun than house-shopping, but trying to keep a balance between the family's needs and the budget quickly became exhausting. When she remembered all the beautiful furnishings she'd had to give up in order to move to LA, she felt very angry. She still believed that the drastic change in their lives had not been necessary. She had lost more than she had gained.

A couple weeks after her return to Argentina, Nina stopped by Lucia and José's home to pick up some of the old furniture she'd put in storage. To Nina's surprise, Fernanda, her former nanny, opened the door. She wondered how Lucia had gotten hold of Fernanda after she'd left, but her happiness at seeing a familiar face outweighed her curiosity.

After a few minutes, Lucia came to the door. She gasped theatrically at the sight of Nina, but her smile seemed genuine.

"Nina!" she cried, hugging her tightly. "I'm so glad to see you after all this time! How wonderful!"

"Hello, Lucia," Nina said, stepping back to get a breath.

"It's so good to see you!" Lucia said. "Where's Ernesto?"

"He stayed in LA to get the best price for our printing business," Nina said. "He'll be back here shortly."

"You picked the perfect time to return," Lucia said. "All that military stuff is done with and they can punish them all. It's been all over the TV."

Nina remembered that Lucia had a way of making horrific national tragedies sound like school gossip she'd overheard. As for Nina, she never watched much TV. On the political front at least, the news was always dominated by nerve-wracking and graphic stories filled with tragedy. She had always preferred books.

"My hope is that we can get back to living a peaceful life as soon as possible," Nina said, but she had to admit to herself that she was curious.

"Come in," Lucia said. "Come and sit down."

As she led Nina to her sitting room, Lucia kept chattering about the news.

"There were the mass graves, for one thing," she said. "Can you believe anyone would be so inhumane? They forced prisoners to dig their own graves, then slaughtered them and tossed them in. The images they show on TV—well, it's difficult for any compassionate person to understand."

Her words stunned Nina into silence. She could barely believe the extent of the bloodshed that had gone on shortly before she had left and during the time she had lived in America.

"There are sickening accounts of prisoners tied together and bound to explosives," Lucia said. "And they took nuns in helicopters and dropped them into the Río de la Plata, claiming their skirts would serve as parachutes! Even for a country that does not have strong ties to the Church, that is horrifying. For Argentina, it is so much worse."

"Yes, truly horrible." Nina shook her head, trying to make sense of it all. She felt a small twinge in her stomach; maybe Ernesto had been right to demand that they leave when they did.

"But the most revolting story of all is about the poor pregnant mothers who were murdered after delivery. Those poor families not only lost their children but their grandchildren too."

The very thought of someone trying to take little David away brought tears to Nina's eyes. It was so surreal that something that terrible had happened without the people knowing anything about it.

"David was born about that time, wasn't he?" Lucia asked.

Nina nodded. "We adopted him from a teenager in our neighborhood. Her mother didn't approve of her pregnancy and they wanted to get him to another home."

"That's good," Lucia said. "You certainly don't want to be mixed up in the military's business when names start coming to light and punishments are handed out."

"No, I wouldn't." Nina couldn't stop imagining the suffering of the young mothers who had just given birth, moving straight from the ultimate joy to terror before they died.

Lucia brought out the furniture. Nina thanked her for storing it for so long, and in exchange, Lucia made Nina promise they'd get together again soon.

—*ww*—

As she began to feel more settled again, Nina went to see her friends Susana, Adriana, and Pedro at the pharmacy they had started together years before. She wanted to reassemble the pieces of her old life that she had been forced to divide when she'd moved to America. She could hardly wait to go back to work again.

All her friends were happy to see her, and each asked many different questions about her life in America. Nina was happy to see her old friends too, but she soon made it clear that she had come to them on business.

"Is there room for me to take my old job back?" she asked.

Pedro rubbed his face, looking away. "You've been gone for several years now."

"It doesn't matter: I've kept current on all the terminology and medicines," Nina said. "Go ahead. Test me. I love this job just as much as I did when I worked here all those years ago."

"You and Ernesto sold your shares in the business when you moved to America," Susana said.

"Nina... we hired someone to take over your workload," Adriana said. "I'm sorry."

Nina felt her face go red as she stared at them. She hadn't anticipated this.

"We're making barely enough money to pay the people we have now," Pedro said. "I'm sorry, but there's no room for you, even as an employee."

The news took Nina completely aback. She was so flustered that she could hardly form a response. She wanted to point out that she was a large reason why they had done so well in the first place. With her business-sense and passion for the pharmacy, she had no doubt that she could easily make them successful again.

Instead of making her case, Nina hurried out of the pharmacy as quickly as she could, still reeling from the unexpected rejection. Adriana stopped her before she reached her car.

"Nina, I'm so sorry," she said. "I wish we could make this better for you."

"Yeah, I'm sure," Nina said, swinging the car door open.

Adriana touched her arm. "Did you really think you could move back to Argentina and just pick up your life where you left it?"

"I didn't expect absolutely *everything* to be different," Nina said, flushing. She had hoped that life would be the same. She hadn't wanted to admit to herself that her detour in America might have changed things past all mending.

"How are your kids?" Adriana asked. "Will you bring David by so we can see how he's grown?"

Nina let her aggravation die a little. "They're fine," she said. "We all need to make adjustments. Vanessa has to be tutored all summer so she can get into high school."

"Well, take care of yourself and keep in touch," Adriana said. "Something will open up eventually."

Nina drove back home, completely defeated. Before they had moved, Ernesto had pushed her to sell her share of the business for a much lower price than it was worth. The pharmacy had always been her dream, and after she'd finally achieved it, she'd been forced to sacrifice it for Ernesto's dream instead. Now her old business partners resorted to treating her like just another customer, worthy only of small talk. She wasn't sure whom to be angry with anymore.

—◦◦◦—

During one of their telephone conversations, Ernesto mentioned an encouraging development. He didn't go into any details, only saying he'd found an opportunity he didn't want to miss and that he'd fill Nina in when they talked next.

Even his hints sounded promising. *He must have sold the printing business for more than it's worth*, Nina thought. Perhaps he would soon be able to join the rest of the family—and with more money than they'd planned. Nina began to have greater hope for their future.

The next time the phone rang, she demanded to hear his good news.

"Eduardo found it and I couldn't pass it up," Ernesto said, his voice full of enthusiasm. "I've just made the down payment on a brand-new townhouse!"

"A townhouse?" Nina asked faintly. "In America?"

"Eduardo and his family are about to move, and I bought the townhouse right next to theirs," Ernesto said. He sounded breathless with excitement. "There are lots of advantages to buying this particular property. The biggest is that I'm able to buy it with a mortgage payment no higher than my current monthly rent."

This wasn't the good news Nina had expected to hear. She was so astonished, and Ernesto was so pleased, that she couldn't think of a way to question his decision.

"It's really a fantastic deal," Ernesto said.

"How exactly?"

"For new construction, we can get a mortgage payment no higher than what I am paying now for rent. The thing is, renters don't build equity. That's why this is such a great deal."

"I guess so."

"You guess so? I'm telling you it's fantastic. The unit has two bedrooms and two levels, perfect for our family."

Nina froze. She'd feared this. Not only was Ernesto blatantly defying the plan they'd made, but he hadn't given her any hint of warning in advance.

"So," Ernesto said, "what's your problem with it?"

"A townhouse seems so permanent," Nina said hesitantly. "When we decided that you'd stay in the States, I thought that was just a temporary arrangement."

"I know." She could almost hear him shrugging her objections away. "Still, this is a better situation, no matter how long I stay. Besides, the escrow is ready to close and the new construction is almost finished."

"It is?"

"Yes. I thought I told you that."

"Somehow you neglected to mention that," Nina said.

She wasn't about to let her dreams die. They could still sell everything in America and live in Argentina permanently. She clung to that hope.

"What if you take a lower price than is right for the business? Will you consider that?"

"No! I don't want to lose any more money," Ernesto said. "It's important. One can't be frivolous about money."

Nina frowned. "That kind of thinking can keep us apart for a long time."

"Maybe so," he said.

Nina was furious. *If that is how he wants it, that's fine with me. I'll show him.*

In the next few weeks, she forged ahead with settling into her new life in Argentina.

—◦◦◦—

Ernesto's birthday fell at the end of February. In America, the whole family would have gone out for dinner to celebrate, and the children would have sung "Happy Birthday" as loudly as they could. This year, however, Ernesto was in America and the children were in Argentina. They had not felt his absence as strongly as they did then.

"When will Dad be moving to Argentina?" David asked.

"Soon," Nina said. "Very soon."

David smiled, but Vanessa didn't look convinced. She was a second-year high school student and had begun to see through Nina's stalling techniques.

"Will he be moving back this year?" she asked.

"He'll be here soon, Vanessa," Nina said. "We're just trying to get things straightened out."

She didn't even know which things needed straightening anymore: everything about their relationship seemed crooked. These days, she mostly wished she could go to LA to spend time with Ernesto. She knew they needed to work through the issues raised by their separation, but she didn't know if she could say anything that would help.

Eventually Ernesto promised that he'd visit around Easter. But the week before Easter, he called to cancel.

The children had gone to bed and the house was quiet. Nina could read the morning paper at long last; she didn't have the time or space in the morning, when seeing the children off to school consumed the early hours. Later, breakfast and last-minute schoolwork covered the table, and Nina spent her time planning the day and going on a daily shopping expedition for meat and produce.

But in the evening, when the children were in bed, she could sit at the kitchen table and spread the whole newspaper out before her. She loved to puzzle over the crossword after dinner, alone in the kitchen, and after that, she read her way through the various sections of the paper. These days, as per usual, the news was hardly cheering. The newspaper was filled with stories about the many people who had disappeared in the '70s and the atrocities the military government had committed against the citizens of Argentina.

Nina was reading an article about an upcoming cultural event when the telephone rang. *That's probably Ernesto. Nobody else calls at this time of the night.*

"Hello?"

"Hello, dear, it's me," Ernesto said.

"How are you doing, darling?" Nina thought he sounded depressed.

"Not so good," Ernesto said. "I have business problems."

Nina's heart skipped a beat. "What kind of problems?"

"I forgot an important lesson from business school: if you run a business, you need to be around all the time. Every single day. Otherwise, even the best employees take advantage," Ernesto said. "I was naïve. I thought it wouldn't happen to me, but it did."

"You knew better." Nina's voice trembled with anger.

"Don't forget that I did it for you and the children," Ernesto said. "You insisted that I visit for a week."

Here we go again. Nina felt dizzy. "I understand that. Nevertheless, if your absence caused problems, the problems will translate into diminished income."

"I'll have to cancel my Easter visit," Ernesto said. "I can't afford to be away from the business at the moment."

"This is all very vague, Ernesto… Can you at least tell me what's going on?"

"The last time I visited Argentina, my employees charged cash for some projects and pocketed the money." Ernesto's voice was almost a whisper.

"You know you can't let your employees get away with something like that!"

"Believe me, I don't want to hear any lectures from you."

"Oh, you have everything figured out, haven't you?" Her eyes filled with tears.

"I am juggling family, business, and international trips at the same time," Ernesto said tautly. "All this stress might very well give me a heart attack."

Nina had no answer for that. This conversation was only a different take on the conversations they'd been having for the past year. Every time he called, Ernesto talked about why he couldn't sell the business. He thought of one problem after another.

If it hadn't been their only source of income, Nina would gladly have given the business away so that Ernesto could join them. She wanted her family to be whole again.

She also realized that the business problems were partly her responsibility. She had enough business savvy to notice any problems big enough to bring down the whole enterprise. Two pairs of eyes were better than one, after all. But she'd ignored the problems she'd noticed because they would be a reason to stay in America.

If she had to do it all over again, she would do the same thing, she decided. She felt relieved as she realized the truth. America was not the land of opportunity that Ernesto made it out to be. Nothing about America had helped her marriage or provided her family with a stable, secure life.

—⁓—

Ernesto didn't return to Argentina until the next May. He didn't bring good news with him. After greeting the children and giving them gifts, he stood with his hands in his pockets and broached the subject to Nina.

"Business is worse than ever."

"I'm tired of hearing about business," Nina said. "Can't we just enjoy your visit?"

"You need to hear about this. Business is bad, Nina. It's getting worse and worse."

"What better reason to sell it and get out?" Nina loved the thought of wiping away every trace of their life in America and starting fresh in Argentina. She tried not to sound too cheerful about his business catastrophe.

"I wish that were possible."

For once, Ernesto's gloomy remarks about his business sounded truly serious. "What?" Nina asked. "You can't sell at a lower price and just be done with it?"

"I can't sell out at any price," Ernesto said. "The damage has been done."

Nina glared at him. "I thought money was so important. Now, all a sudden, it isn't? That business is our only source of income. How could you let it fall to pieces?"

"I've been doing my best to keep it afloat," Ernesto said.

"Fine. So what will we do now?"

"I need your help to fix it," Ernesto said.

Nina stared at him. "You need me? Aren't you the one with the business degree?"

"You did such a good job with your pharmacy," Ernesto said. "You have the experience you need to turn things around for us. A fresh pair of eyes would be useful."

He glanced across the room at her, giving her a shadow of the charming smile she had once found so endearing. Nina frowned. She was surprised that he would turn to her for help, but she wasn't all that surprised. He had found a convenient excuse for keeping a foothold in America. He would go to any length to keep her connected to that country.

"Look," Ernesto said. "I miss the children. I barely know them anymore! I suggest that I stay here with them while you go back to LA. Take a few weeks to assess the condition of the business for yourself. Then *you* see if it's worth selling."

Nina regarded him in wary silence.

"As you said, it's our only source of income," Ernesto said. "I know you miss the pharmacy. In fact, I'm pretty sure you miss business in general. Why not give it a shot again?"

—◦◦◦—

A few days later, Nina flew to LA. She soon saw that conditions at the plant were exactly as Ernesto had described. His laxity had seriously damaged the business.

Nina could barely remember feeling so conflicted. She believed that the business could be saved, but not without a lot of hard work. She didn't want to give Ernesto an excuse to cling to the business, but she liked the challenge of righting its problems. As she considered new strategies, Nina began to suspect that she had hated America because Ernesto had never given her a say in their business. Now he had actually asked for her help. Perhaps they had needed to unite behind a single project in order to come closer together.

Perhaps this could be the project, Nina thought. But she dreaded remaining in America, and thus she phoned her husband with a heavy heart.

"The situation here is just like you said, Ernesto. It's a mess."

"Do you think anything can be done?"

"Yes."

"Well... what?"

"It's going to take a complete reconstruction." Nina glanced at the notepad where she'd scribbled some ideas. "Since we started business, we've wandered from the practices that made us successful in the first place. We'll need to go back to the basics. That will take a while, but it's possible."

"And the employees?"

"Back to the basics with them as well," Nina said. "Those who work, stay. Those who don't, go."

"So what do you want to do?" Ernesto asked.

This had been his plan all along and Nina resented it. There was no way they could stay in Argentina *and* save the business. He knew that. She knew it too.

She toyed with the pencil in front of her. "We need to move the family back here," she said reluctantly. Every word disgusted her. "We'll rebuild the business from the ground up."

"Are you serious?" Ernesto asked. Nina could hear the triumph in his voice. After all, he had won without putting up a fight. He'd done nothing but wait for the situation to play out.

"Do you know another way?" Nina asked coldly.

"I'm with you," Ernesto said, his voice full of joy. "Let's do it."

Out with the Old

Absence had not made the heart grow fonder. If anything, it had made the long-awaited reunion of the Rossi family all the more painful. Looking back at the past six months, Nina saw that the tensions between her and Ernesto had only escalated since she and the children had returned from Argentina. Lately it seemed like both Ernesto and Vanessa were ignoring Nina's feelings more and more. They rarely did what she asked unless she offered them a whole list of reasons. Interacting with them both had grown even more stressful.

Now her parents were coming to LA to celebrate Christmas with her. Nina had made the house ready for their arrival and told her family that she wanted them to come with her to the airport to pick them up. But when she reminded them that morning at breakfast, Ernesto and Vanessa frowned.

"Can't come," Ernesto said. "They need me at work today."

"I told you they were coming today," Nina said. "I thought you could make time."

Ernesto grabbed the last piece of toast and pushed his chair back from the table. "I'll have plenty of time to talk to your parents while they're here."

When Ernesto hurried out of the kitchen, Vanessa jumped up to follow him.

"Vanessa, where are you going?"

"I have to get some research done at the library," Vanessa said. "There's a big paper due for school. If I get it done now, I won't have to worry about it while Grandma and Grandpa are here."

She didn't even grab a jacket before heading out the door.

Nina didn't feel like arguing. She felt like she'd done nothing but argue for the past six months, and she was tired of it. She found it easier to just let Ernesto and Vanessa do what they wanted, even though this simple request was important to her.

David still sat at the table, eating his bread and jam.

"You want to come to see Grandma and Grandpa, don't you?"

"Yes!" he said.

Nina was just glad to get out of the house, which had become more and more confining. Every letter that needed mailing she personally took to the post office. Every morning, she drove the children to school. She handled all the paperwork at the consulate in person on multiple trips. Getting out of the house helped her feel like she was escaping the tension there.

Nina drove to the airport with David beside her. She was concentrating on the hum of the road when he asked, "Mom, where do babies come from?"

Nina chuckled. *Ah, the classic question.* She hoped she was ready for this one.

"Well," she said, "most of the time, a baby grows inside a mommy's tummy, and she gets bigger and bigger."

David giggled.

"In your case, you grew inside a different mommy's tummy, and when you were born, she gave you to me."

"I'm glad she gave me to you," David said.

"Me too." Nina smiled. David always brought her joy when everyone else seemed intent on making her gloomy.

Nina arrived at the airport full of anticipation. She could hardly wait to see her parents again; after visiting them frequently while she lived in Argentina, she'd had a hard time adjusting to the distance between them while she was in America. But now she would see them very soon. She'd made plans for fun activities and trips they would enjoy during their stay.

Nina and David wandered through the airport until they spotted an information screen with her parents' flight information. A quick glance showed that the flight had been delayed.

"Excuse me," Nina asked an airline employee. "When can we expect the flight from Argentina to arrive?"

"It won't be here for several more hours, ma'am," the man said. "I'm sorry."

Nina's heart sank, especially when she saw David's disappointed expression. "Don't worry," she told him. "They'll be here soon. Why don't we get lunch somewhere while we wait?"

As she'd hoped, David brightened at the thought of lunch in a restaurant. Once they had found a place and ordered their meals, he returned to his earlier line of questioning.

"Is Vanessa from another mommy?"

"No, dear, she grew in me."

"Oh." David frowned, perplexed. "Did you grow other babies that you gave away?"

"No, I only ever grew Vanessa," Nina said, smiling. Vanessa was beginning to sound like a plant. "Sometimes mommies can't have other babies themselves. When that happens, sometimes really loving mommies offer to help."

"She had me because you couldn't grow more babies?"

"Not... exactly." Nina paused, gathering her thoughts. How could she explain—to a six-year-old, no less—something as life-altering as giving up a child?

"Your mom loved you," she said. "She would have loved to keep you. Unfortunately, sometimes, in hard circumstances, a mommy can't keep her baby. Just like I couldn't have more babies, sometimes some mommies can't keep babies they have."

"So the mommies help each other." David seemed content with the conclusion he'd reached. His meal arrived and he tucked in. He didn't ask any more questions.

Nina was relieved. She doubted she could think fast enough to explain Laura's unwelcome pregnancy to David.

Returning to the gate after lunch, Nina soon saw her parents waiting. She scooped David up and rushed to greet and hug them. She was overjoyed that her parents could visit for an extended stay and her parents were more than delighted to see her.

—◈—

In the days leading up to Christmas, Nina took Estela shopping while Ernesto worked and Miguel stayed home with the children. Everyone was happiest this way.

Estela had always loved to shop for gifts, but she especially loved shopping for her grandchildren. Consulting Nina about her purchases, she soon filled the car with presents. For David, she bought a remote controlled ship that could be floated on a lake; he seemed very interested in navigation and often said that he wanted to be a ship's captain when he grew up. She bought a beautiful vanity set for Vanessa and an expensive leather schedule book for Ernesto. She bought presents for Eduardo and his family as well as some custom jewelry for herself.

"Aren't you going to get something for yourself, Nina?" Estela asked abruptly.

Nina blinked. Her mind had been wandering as she watched her mother look at a necklace display. "What are you talking about?"

"You should think about yourself a little more," Estela said. "Remember when you were younger? You took the time to make yourself feel good. You might be older now, but you're still too young to lose interest in your looks."

"I suppose."

"Just look at yourself, Nina," Estela said.

Nina caught a glimpse of her reflection in a store mirror. She saw herself in the mirror every morning, but today she actually looked. Her clothes were comfortable, yes, but now she saw how unflattering they were. Gray hairs stuck out amongst her longish dark hair and dark rings around her eyes made her face look gaunt and sickly. The change startled her. She'd been a beauty-conscious young woman once. Between supporting Ernesto and dividing her attention between her two children, she'd stopped taking care of herself.

Estela's words chafed and saddened her, but they touched upon a core truth. Her mother was right. Nina couldn't handle her situation all by herself, but she didn't have any other options.

"I can't spend money on frivolous things," Nina said. "We need to put everything in the business to get it going again."

"Ernesto didn't seem to have any remorse in letting the business run down to the point that you had to move back with the children again."

Her mother's criticism stunned Nina. Embarrassment swept over her in a tidal wave. How had the situation gotten so out of hand that her mother had noticed her husband's lack of maturity? Nina had tried to hide what was going on, but her mom's eyes were sharp—and now she'd actually brought the topic up in public. Nina was angry; her loyalty lay with her husband and her family and her mom's criticism intruded on their privacy. At the same time, her mother normally never voiced negative opinions. *How did it get so bad?*

"Some new dresses and a haircut never broke the bank," Estela said, her calm voice cutting through Nina's flurried thoughts.

They stood outside an upscale clothing store. Nina paused for a split second. Her mom was trying to help, and Nina wasn't used to that. No one had tried to help her for months. Why drive off the first person to offer?

"You're right," she said. "Retail therapy is just what I need."

Nina felt herself growing lighter as she entered the shop. With her mom's help, she picked out several new outfits: shirts with trim, distinctive cuts and skirts made with soft, well-stitched fabric. Estela bought Miguel a cashmere sweater and Nina a beautiful blue dress for Christmas.

Nina finished her shopping by buying a few toys for David and a makeup set for Vanessa. On their way home, Nina and Estela stopped at a salon for haircuts. With every purchase, Nina could feel herself becoming a new person.

——✦——

The whole family reunited in Los Angeles for Christmas. The festivities began with a feast on Christmas Eve. The table would soon be heaped with delectable foods: chicken salad with potatoes, peas, carrots, and red bell peppers; rolls filled with ham; empanadas; prosciutto and melon. Many of the Argentine favorites were served cold; December was a summer month in Argentina and usually very hot.

Nina and Estela did most of the work in the kitchen, and David tagged along to help. He pulled out several kitchen drawers, climbed up them like stairs, and then sat cross-legged on the counter. Nina watched him closely. David could be quite a character, and he looked very intent as he regarded his grandmother with more interest than usual.

A few minutes later, while Estela cut up meat for the dinner, David wandered over and hugged her. "Telly, is there a baby inside you?" he asked. "Mom says when tummies get big, there's a baby in there."

Estela paused, knife in hand, and glanced at Nina with her eyebrows raised. They burst out laughing.

"Telly?" David asked, waiting for an answer. His questioning face just made them laugh harder.

"Hey, keep it down," Ernesto said, sticking his head into the kitchen. "We're trying to watch TV out here."

Nina felt as though his insulting demand had sucked all the good cheer straight out of the kitchen. She wanted to clobber Ernesto, but Estela was still laughing.

"No, David, not every large tummy has a baby," she said.

David didn't ask any more questions, and Estela continued preparing dinner, chuckling occasionally.

At midnight on Christmas Eve, the whole family gathered around the Christmas tree to open presents. Most of the gifts were for the children, but the adults were also pleased with their presents. The spirit of Christmas kept everyone celebrating until the early hours of the morning.

The familiar happiness of the holidays couldn't mask the tense awkwardness among the Rossis. Nina found the simplest communication with Ernesto difficult. After seventeen years of marriage, they were virtual strangers living under the same roof.

———

Early Christmas morning, Nina lay in bed and stared at the ceiling. She'd once heard that people could lull themselves back to sleep by counting sheep. She doubted the method could help her; she had too many concerns spinning around and around in her head. Her life had gotten completely out of her control, yet she still felt guilty. No matter what she told herself, she kept wondering what she'd done wrong. *How can I find a bridge to cross over to the way things used to be?* She feared that she would not find an answer; she could barely remember the way things had been anyway.

She knew she wouldn't be able to handle much more of this. Her fears, her guilt, were wearing her down into nothing. She wondered, deep down, if someone else had come into Ernesto's life.

One, two, three… For now, it seemed that her only hope lay in counting sheep.

———

The tense domestic situation continued all the way through the New Year's celebrations to Ernesto's February birthday. Since 1986 was the first year the whole family had been together for Ernesto's birthday in many years, Nina went out of her way to recreate the fun atmosphere of the parties they'd attended early in their marriage. She let the children choose a fancy restaurant, making the reservations weeks in advance. She told her parents, Eduardo and his family, and a few friends to meet there at seven o'clock. To her great pleasure, Vanessa and David both enjoyed teaming up with her to surprise Ernesto.

After doing her usual work as Ernesto's right hand at the plant, Nina left early on the day of his party to take the children shopping and to make the last preparations. Before she left, she told Ernesto to meet her at seven o'clock at the restaurant. Since they went out to dinner on that day every week, she doubted he'd suspect the surprise awaiting him.

By seven o'clock that evening, everyone was in place—except Ernesto. The guests fidgeted. By the time eight o'clock rolled around, they were all beginning to get nervous.

"If something happened to him, the police won't know we're here. They'll be calling the house," Eduardo said.

Nina's sharp glance stopped him in his tracks, but the damage had been done. David started crying and Nina slapped Eduardo on the arm. "Go calm him down," she said.

She left the others to find a telephone. She dialed home first. *Maybe he just forgot.* No one answered. She tried the plant, then every other phone number she could remember, but Ernesto was nowhere to be found. Panic began to rise up within her.

Nina tried to compose herself, but she caught sight of her reflection in a mirror before she went back to her family. Her face was flushed and tense; her forehead lined with sweat. Hands trembling, she searched through her purse for a tissue. She couldn't look her reflection in the eye. If she did, she wouldn't be able to stop crying.

When she returned to her guests, she told them that Ernesto's car had broken down and that he was stuck at work. She told them they should go home.

Eduardo offered to take their parents back to Nina's house.

"Are you sure you want us to leave?" Estela asked.

"This is a stressful time because of rebuilding the business, right?" Miguel asked, trying to calm the tension that had filled the room.

Nina could no longer fake domestic tranquility. Ordinarily she would have attempted to save face in front of her parents and her brother, but things were too far gone.

"Please go home," she said. "The kids and I will stay."

The seriousness in her voice silenced any possible objection. The guests reluctantly left the restaurant, casting worried glances back at Nina and the children. Nina ordered food, but David just pushed his spaghetti around on his plate and Vanessa didn't even pick up her fork. *All this money wasted. I was trying to put things back to normal. I just wanted us to have fun together.*

Nina didn't know whether to leave or not. She didn't know what she would do when or if Ernesto finally showed up. She looked at her watch. It was a quarter to nine.

"Let's go home," she said.

The children looked relieved as they gathered their things to go. But just as they were about to walk out, Ernesto sauntered through the front door. He strode over to them with a big smile plastered on his face.

"You're still here," he said. "Good. I'm hungry."

Nina stared at him in disbelief. *Two hours' delay, and he's pretending nothing's wrong. This is going to get ugly.*

"Vanessa, David," Nina said. "Go to the car, please."

She watched the children hurry out to the car, parked near the entrance. As soon as they had climbed inside and closed the doors, she whipped around to face Ernesto.

"Well?"

"Well what?" he asked.

Okay, he wants to play dumb. Nina could feel herself quivering with rage. She stepped up to him and poked him in his chest.

"Really?" Her voice shook. "You're that clueless? I told you to come at seven o'clock. It's two hours later."

"I'm sorry," he said. "I was working late. I guess I lost track of the time."

"The *whole family* was here to surprise you for your birthday!"

"I was at the office working," he said.

Nina thought her head might explode; her blood pounded in her head. *That's the best lie he can come up with?*

"I called the office three or four times. You didn't answer. Try again."

Ernesto's eyes flickered. "I've not been feeling well. I had to use the bathroom several times. You must have called while I was away from the desk."

"And when you got back to your desk, you didn't check the messages I left?"

"The light on the answering machine wasn't blinking. I'm sorry.

Did you guys already eat?" Ernesto seemed oddly unfazed at missing his own birthday party. He even seemed upbeat about it.

"I'm going home," Nina said. "Think of a better story for the rest of the family."

———⁓———

The emotional turmoil continued into the spring. The household never settled down.

Nina's parents returned to Argentina in March. By April, Nina knew Ernesto was having an affair—maybe several.

The first clue was the ride-share program that he seemed to run all on his own. Its sole clientele were lovely young ladies; Ernesto was the only driver. Every time Nina insisted that Ernesto stay in on certain nights to be with his family, he had notify one of the female workers at the plant. Lupe was a particular problem. She hung around Ernesto all the time; when he told her that he had to stay home with Nina, she would become agitated and storm out of the room. Nothing made it hard for Nina to figure out what was going on.

April showers did not bring May flowers. Instead, Nina filed for divorce. When she told the children, David didn't really understand, but Vanessa was terribly upset. She would suffer as much—if not more—than her parents. She knew that she faced not only a new home life situation, but would also have to explain the new family circumstances to her friends.

Ernesto swore to the whole family that he was faithful and loving to the end. When he left, he took one suitcase full of clothes and toiletries. He left everything else behind.

———⁓———

Nina had to know if Ernesto had moved in with Lupe or not. She'd suspected for a while that he might end up living with her, but she'd wanted to pretend that Ernesto hadn't been romancing Lupe the same way he'd romanced Nina all those years ago.

A week after Ernesto moved out, Nina stopped to talk to the plant's receptionist. She knew Judy was the biggest gossip at the factory; if anyone knew Ernesto's business, Judy would.

When Judy saw Nina coming, she widened her eyes, looking very innocent. "Hey, how ya doing, hon?"

Nina normally found Judy's accent endearing. Today it grated.

"Did he do it, Judy? Is he living with her?" Nina struggled to keep from breaking down. She had her pride and she wasn't going to give Judy any more gossip than she could help.

Judy shot her a look filled with pity. "Yeah, hon. He did."

Nina didn't want Judy's pity. She didn't want anyone's pity. She spun on her heel and walked out of the building with her head held high.

———

It took several months for Nina to decide what to do next with her life. Her nomadic lifestyle had turned out to be a disadvantage. Because she'd been traveling between Argentina and LA for a couple years at a time, she'd not developed any close friends in America. When Nina looked back, she realized that she shouldn't have focused exclusively on her friends and family in Argentina. She wished she'd tried to befriend David and Vanessa's classmates' mothers. If only she'd done that, she would have had someone to talk with over coffee once in a while.

Nina soon learned that she always seemed to be the odd person out at social functions. Many potential women friends stayed aloof; apparently the newly divorced Nina was seen as a predator, and they kept close watch on their husbands.

Still, Nina's situation in America was very different from how things would have worked in Argentina. Back home, it was common for young people to live with their parents until—and often even after—marriage, since housing was expensive in Buenos Aires. It was not uncommon for an entire large family to live under one roof along with the matriarch and patriarch of the family. These heads of the extended family were not only leaders but also solved disputes and problems. Even if they were not well liked, they were always respected.

Had Nina been divorced in Argentina, her parents would undoubtedly have had a say in how she composed herself and lived her life. But she probably wouldn't have gotten divorced in Argentina in the first place. Under Argentina's medieval family system, her parents would have encouraged her to endure anything rather than break up her family. Society would have pressured her to live with her husband's philandering for the sake of the family. Nina was grateful for the enlightened American attitudes toward women and divorce.

With that in mind, she accepted the challenge of finding a friend. Eventually, one woman in Nina's neighborhood introduced her to her single sister, Lydia. Lydia was cheerful and good-natured, but lonely, and she and Nina quickly became fast friends. They went to movies and often ate out together. As Nina prepared to see a movie with Lydia one night, she realized that it was easier to be single with someone else than to be single alone.

Nina tried to get the kids involved in her new social life, but Vanessa was completely involved with her teenage friends. Even when she was available, she seemed embarrassed by her parents' situation and didn't want to acknowledge it, let alone be a part of it. Even though David was younger, it was much the same for him.

Ernesto's life had radically changed as well. He saw the kids on appointed weekends and tried to be civilized with Nina in front of them. Nina wondered if she should be grateful, but wasn't.

The first Christmas without a husband or father at home was sad for the little family, and since the Salvattis remained in Argentina, it was especially lonely.

The year is ending as sadly as it began, Nina thought.

She often counted sheep at night.

Chapter Seventeen

Beginning Again

After her divorce, every morning began the same way. Nina pulled out of a grey and listless sleep, pausing before she opened her eyes. She knew what was coming. She wondered why she bothered.

Sunlight hit her closed eyelids. *It must be later than I thought.*

She could get up. It would be all right. She just needed to think about her children. She kept going for their sake.

She opened her eyes. The fog of sleep dissipated, and the familiar rush of pain and anguish swept through her—pain so acute she could hardly breathe. Sweat covered her body. Her stomach lurched.

Nina rolled on her side.

Yep, still the same. She'd have to stay in bed till the pain and nausea passed and she could breathe with some ease. She wouldn't even be able to stand up otherwise. She figured the pain had its roots in her frustration, loneliness, and failure. Of these, she felt failure the most. She endlessly pondered her life with Ernesto, trying to figure out where she'd gone wrong. She still didn't know.

She wondered if Ernesto felt like a failure too.

Nina heard David and Vanessa talking in muted voices in the kitchen. They were probably trying to let her sleep. *All I have left from my marriage are my children, and if things go wrong with them, then my life is over,* she thought, not for the first time.

I need to get up. Nina wrenched herself to a sitting position. She tried to keep an optimistic attitude, but it wasn't easy. It seemed that if she stayed in bed analyzing all the facts, she'd eventually find a solution. She was becoming obsessed.

Nina climbed to her feet. She wasn't sure what solution she could find. The damage done wasn't going to go away, and even if a magic spell would allow her to start again from the beginning, she would have done things exactly the same.

She put on her robe and headed to the kitchen for breakfast. She stopped in the kitchen doorway to watch her children for a moment. Vanessa and David sat at the kitchen table squabbling over the funnies in the morning paper.

At least it was Friday and she could spend the weekend with her children. But the consolation was a small one: she probably wouldn't be able to spend as much time with Vanessa as she'd like. Vanessa always seemed to have plans with her friends. She'd want to go out and do things like see a movie or go to a party. Hanging with her mom just didn't rate.

David was a different story. He was still too young to mind spending time with his mom. Nina always tried to take him to places he'd enjoy. She didn't know how many times they'd gone to the video games store or to some Disney movie. She'd like to take him to a baseball game someday. Nina thought Paulette Bouvier, her French Canadian friend, had mentioned at some point that her son had season tickets that he didn't always use.

—◦◦◦—

Nina called Paulette that afternoon. Paulette answered before the second ring, which meant she was screening her calls.

"Are you waiting for a call from a handsome man?" Nina asked.

Paulette laughed. "No. I'm avoiding Marcelle's fiancée. She wants me to go shopping. She has endless energy."

Nina knew that Paulette adored her son's fiancée. Paulette had talked Nina's ear off about how wonderful she found Nicolette Mourad. After all, like Paulette, Nicolette was a doctor.

"Don't be such a baby. You'll have fun," Nina said.

"Why did you call? Other than to call me names…" Paulette asked. Nina could hear the smile in her voice.

"I wondered if Marcelle still has season tickets. Though I don't remember which team is in this area," Nina said. She laughed.

"It's the Dodgers. He does. I'm sure he'd be happy let you use the tickets. He's too busy to use them. I'll ask him the next time I see him. Drat, I hear the doorbell. Maybe that's Nicolette."

Nina laughed. "Have fun shopping."

—◦◦◦—

David was easily pleased, but Nina had difficulty finding outings for Vanessa to enjoy. Season tickets for baseball just wouldn't cut it. With Vanessa's sixteenth birthday approaching in April, Nina thought she'd found the perfect treat: a family trip to Paris. Vanessa spoke French well and Nina thought she'd enjoy getting a chance to use what she'd learned in school with native speakers. Also, what better country to practice? Every teenage girl longs to go to France.

Yet somehow the trip fell flat. It should have brought them closer together, but it didn't. They'd missed the magic. Both David and Vanessa were growing up and wanted to be independent. Nina understood all that; she even sympathized. But they were taking it too far, trying to abandon her completely.

The first sign of trouble came when Vanessa wouldn't sit next to Nina in the airport.

It was supposed to be a spectacular birthday present—Nina's big gift to Vanessa. Vanessa seemed willing to accept the gift as long as she didn't have to be seen with her mom.

"Jeez, Mom it's so uncool to have to do things together all the time."

Nina had felt that comment like a knife in the back, but she'd hidden her pain.

Vanessa relented once they reached Paris and agreed to a limited number of family activities.

Nina had chosen a hotel close to L'Etoile. As soon as they were unpacked, the three of them took a stroll to enjoy the spring weather and the *patisseries.*

Against Nina's wishes, Ernesto had given Vanessa money to spend on the trip. This was typical: Ernesto never paid attention to Nina's desires or requests. His disregard caused a number of problems with the children and often made Nina end up looking like the bad guy. So when Nina warned the kids to not eat too many pastries because it was close to lunchtime, Vanessa ignored her and bought several pastries.

While they enjoyed visiting the famous sights in Paris, the City of Light and Love, something essential was missing. They all knew what it was. Nina suspected the celebration would have been more celebratory if the whole family were together. Ernesto's presence would have perfectly completed visits to the Arc de Triomphe, the Eiffel Tower, the Louvre, and the Notre Dame Cathedral. It would have brightened their shopping and dining excursions.

As the three ate lunch in a quaint little restaurant in the St. Germaine district on the colorful Left Bank, Nina noticed Vanessa picking at her food. She assumed it was because she'd eaten so many pastries earlier.

"Don't you like your cordon bleu?" she asked, discovering even as she spoke that she almost feared the answer. "I think it's delicious."

"No, it's okay. I guess I'm not too hungry."

Nina accepted that explanation. "What do you both think of Paris so far?"

"I think it's the most wonderful city in the world. Except maybe..."

Nina smiled. "Buenos Aires?"

"Yes. Paris is everything everyone told me. I just..." Vanessa paused and looked to David.

"What?" Nina asked.

"I guess I just was thinking how really wonderful it would be if..."

"If Dad were here." David finished her sentence.

Vanessa nodded.

Nina felt a wave of sadness sweep over her. *Here we are in Paris, and all the children talk about is their father and their broken home.* No matter how hard she tried, it seemed she always failed. Soon she would weary of trying.

Nina thought a trip to Versailles would cheer everyone up. She bought train tickets the next day and looked forward to the train ride and talking more with the kids. As they boarded the train, Vanessa sat several seats in front of Nina and David and soon struck up a conversation with a teen girl near her. Nina couldn't understand the rapid French she spoke as she conversed with her new friend.

As she took in the scenery, Nina held David in her lap. She enjoyed the transition from Paris to the countryside. Every mile or so the train stopped and let people on and off in the middle of the country. Nina assumed they must live close by and traveled by train. She envied their simple existence.

Vanessa interrupted Nina's daydreaming. "Mom, I think our stop is coming up."

"Sit down. We still have a few more miles."

"But my friend said we are really close. I think we should get off the next time the train stops," Vanessa said.

Nina looked out the window and noticed they weren't near any stops. The train slowed and stopped to let more country people off. "It will be obvious when we are at the former palace of the French kings." Nina pointed to the countryside. "This doesn't look like it. Versailles has its own train station. Now sit back down."

"This is definitely the stop for Versailles!" Vanessa turned toward the train doors and sprang off the train.

Nina felt her jaw drop as she stared after her. She couldn't believe that Vanessa had completely disobeyed her and jumped off the train. She couldn't possibly leave her in the countryside by herself. Nina snatched up David's hand and hurried out of the train to join Vanessa.

Before they could reach Vanessa, the train stirred and pulled away again. Nina looked at the vast pastoral beauty surrounding them and her blood began to boil. *How can Vanessa do this to us?* Nina knew she'd gain nothing by indulging in any righteous anger now; if she lost her temper, she'd sacrifice any remaining pretense of maternal authority she still possessed.

Nina sniffed. She was the adult in this situation, no matter what. She needed to make her children feel safe and protected, even if she wanted to throttle one of them.

She called to a French woman walking away from the tracks. The woman responded in French, which Nina didn't understand.

"What did she say, Vanessa? Ask her how far it is to Versailles."

Vanessa talked with the French woman briefly before relaying the conversation to Nina. "Apparently if we follow the train tracks we'll get there."

"No kidding. Did she say how far it was?"

Vanessa kicked the dirt, glaring at the ground. "About three miles."

"Three miles! That's almost an hour's walk."

"You don't have to freak out, Mom."

"What on earth possessed you to jump off a train in the middle of nowhere when I told you not to? What were you thinking?"

Vanessa shrugged and started walking along the train tracks toward Versailles. "There's nothing we can do about it now."

Nina almost choked. What creature had possessed her dear, sweet daughter?

"Don't worry, Mom," David said confidentially, taking her hand. "She's like that with everyone."

Nina had never seen anything as beautiful as the countryside surrounding them: the green grass, the flowers, the trees and shade. They reminded her of the vacations she had taken with her family when she was a little girl. The countryside around them seemed like an older version. Nina smiled.

They started walking. Nina pointed out the brick houses with ivy-covered walls. She laughed when she saw chickens and geese running free on the road. David picked her a bouquet of wild flowers. Accepting it, Nina felt transported. They could have been walking the same road two hundred years earlier, and it would have looked the same.

Her delight was infectious. Even Vanessa began to whistle.

To Nina's surprise, a rash mistake had eased into exactly the type of moment she had wished for on this trip. She was with her beloved children and they were having fun together, happy for a little while.

———✿———

Once she returned to LA and all the troubles of home, Nina clung to those happy memories of her time in France. In the mornings, she would lie in bed and remember the best parts of the trip, how carefree they all had been together. Her anguish would slowly begin to melt.

Those were not happy days for Nina. The divorce settlement had included half the printing business, but she was struggling to manage it. Although she could strategize business plans, she found it hard to implement them. Her employees knew she wasn't hardnosed, so they exploited every situation to their own advantage. They did not fear her in any way. Instead they gave her excuses for everything: excessive sick days, jobs not completed on time, sloppy work, mishandled customer complaints, missing deadlines on job orders, missing the filing of important tax documents. Their problems ran the spectrum of possibilities.

With no one else to turn to, Nina had no choice but to ask Ernesto for advice.

"What can I do to make them respect me?" she asked. "I don't necessarily want them to fear me, but I at least want them to worry that they might get fired for negligence. They don't have any respect for me at all."

"I've told you this before. You need to not only threaten them but to act on your threats as well. Fire someone. That'll make your point better than a hundred threats."

She hesitated and said, "I—I—I don't think…"

He interrupted. "You don't think you are capable of firing anybody. Is that it?"

"Yes, I guess that is it."

"You fired me all right," Ernesto said.

Nina scowled.

"I don't think there's much hope for you as a business manager," Ernesto said. "If you don't want to lose everything, I'm going to have to take over."

"That's fine with me. I'd welcome it."

They decided Ernesto would manage the business for Nina. He would pay her a monthly stipend, on which she would be able to live well. The arrangement seemed perfectly harmless, even good.

Vanessa's grades dropped drastically as her behavior deteriorated. Her high school counselor informed Nina that Vanessa had been skipping school for weeks and hanging out with other kids at a fast food place when she was supposed to be in class.

Nina was furious. She warned Vanessa that if her truancy continued, Nina would send her to a strict boarding school.

Nina felt her life spiral into a living nightmare. She couldn't control anything anymore: she could manage neither her children nor her business, and her parents were living thousands of miles away. Her friends' support helped, but their ability to help was limited by Nina's circumstances.

Vanessa continued to skip school. True to her promise, Nina contacted a boarding school in Santa Barbara. It was a very respectable one, with numerous extracurricular activities, like tennis and horseback riding. In some ways, it hardly seemed like punishment. Horseback riding had been Vanessa's favorite activity since she was a little girl. She used to spend a lot of time at the Salvattis' country house with her grandparents.

One afternoon, Nina received an invitation to a Rossi family caucus. It didn't sound like an invitation, more like a command, and the topic—to her dismay—was Vanessa's exile to boarding school. If the ensuing drama hadn't been so ridiculous, Nina would have laughed. Unfortunately, this was reality, and that reality was her life.

Nina went. She wished she hadn't. As the meeting progressed, she had to struggle not to jump across the table and pull out Lupe's hair. It soon became clear that Nina wasn't going to be able to follow through with her threat; Ernesto and Lupe had intervened on Vanessa's behalf. At the farce—the family caucus—everything Nina wanted was relentlessly overridden by Ernesto and Lupe. They told Nina that they had decided that Vanessa should move in with them.

Nina had lost the company of one of her children. Again she experienced the bitterness of utter defeat.

—◦◊◦—

Freed from the burden of overseeing a business and an unruly teenager, Nina used her free time to study English and make further friends. As her efforts paid off, she noticed that her command of the language was steadily improving.

Linguistic confidence gave her more opportunities to befriend the diverse people around her. In addition to Paulette Bouvier, Nina became good friends with Joyce Jones, a divorced doctor's wife who had raised four children, now grownup and living on their own. Joyce was a liberated woman who enjoyed her empty-nest life. Like Nina, both Paulette and Joyce appreciated the theater, opera, and picnics at the Hollywood Bowl. They soon ended up spending a lot of time together.

Because the three of them all had birthdays in September, they started a tradition of celebrating every year in an extravagant way. It usually involved one of their favorite pursuits and always brought the ladies closer.

The first year they celebrated with a picnic lunch in the Angeles National Forest outside LA. Paulette knew a nice shaded area with picnic tables. She brought all the side dishes and utensils; Nina brought champagne; and Joyce brought a rotisserie chicken. Nina enjoyed being outdoors, away from the city life that was causing her so much strife.

During the celebration, as the ladies busied themselves setting up for their special day, Nina heard a buzzing sound that grew louder and louder. Looking around for the source, she saw movement in the chicken's vicinity.

"There're wasps all over the chicken!" Joyce screamed.

Paulette sprang into action. She tried to wave them off, but the wasps wouldn't budge.

Nina marveled at her courage, because she herself felt nothing but terror. She felt some wasps brush against her as they flew to the chicken and remembered a horror movie she'd seen in which gigantic insects attacked people. But her panic quickly gave way to common sense. This adventure was tinged with more comedy than horror.

"Do something before we get stung!" Joyce said.

Paulette took a long knife and tongs and pried off one of the chicken legs. She waved the leg around the whole chicken, trying to get the wasps' attention. It looked like she was casting a magic spell. Once she thought enough wasps were distracted and following the chicken leg, she flung it as far from the picnic spot as she could. The wasps flew into the air, circling Nina several times before following the leg.

Paulette started to laugh. She laughed even harder as she covered the rest of the chicken with a bag. "Nina, my dear, you may be divorced, but some things are still attracted to you."

Laughing, they toasted each other with champagne.

"Is the chicken still edible?" Joyce asked.

"No," Paulette and Nina said in unison.

———

Nina couldn't escape the turmoil of her family life. David had always wanted a younger sibling and when he heard that Lupe had become pregnant, he grew listless at home.

"I think I want to go live with Dad," he told Nina.

"Why would you do that?" Nina was stunned. "Why would you do that to me?"

"Mom, I don't love Dad more. Really. It's just that"—he chose his words carefully—"you made Dad move out, and then Vanessa left. I might as well go before you send me away too."

She glowered at him, trying to ignore how much his words hurt her. "And you want to be involved with the new baby? Is that it?"

"Yeah. That's why." David shrugged. "What's so wrong with that?"

The room blurred as Nina's eyes filled of tears.

"I knew you'd end up crying, Mom. I just knew it."

David seemed intent on living with his dad when his little baby brother or sister arrived. His wishes devastated Nina. The idea of losing her little boy, although he would live just a few blocks away and still see her often, wounded her to her core. No matter what he said, she saw his move as a sign that both her children favored Ernesto over herself.

The divorce settlement had established joint custody of the kids. Nina wanted to take matters into her own hands and sue Ernesto for full custody of David.

The court assigned a psychologist to talk to Nina.

Nina assumed a fully defensive posture when she met with the psychologist. She tucked her hands up under her arms and pulled her shoulders up near her ears. She felt the tension in her back, but there was little she could do about it.

The psychologist sat down on the floor and crossed his legs. "Do you feel comfortable?" he asked Nina.

She blinked at him. Was he really sitting on the floor?

"Please go ahead and get comfortable," the man said. "You should feel safe and cared for before we even begin to talk. Would you like to stretch out on the couch? Or sit in my chair?"

Nina got up and boldly sat in his chair. She felt better right away. Nina began to relax.

"Who do you think will suffer most if you bring a court action against your ex-husband regarding your son?" the psychologist asked.

"I don't look at it in terms of anybody being hurt. That's not the reason why I would do it."

"You might not think you're setting out to hurt anyone, but I can assure you someone will be hurt, and hurt very badly."

"I don't see how."

"Maybe you don't want to see." The psychologist silenced her objections with the next words he spoke. "Your son will be hurt the most by this."

"I don't see how," Nina said, feeling her resolve all through her tense body. "How can living with Ernesto and his pregnant, home wrecking girlfriend be in David's best interest?"

"Believe me, I have handled hundreds of these kinds of issues," the man said. "You're unfamiliar with this scenario, so I'm here to offer you my years of experience in these matters. Trust me, if you start any court battles, David will be the one to suffer most."

Nina felt her determination dissolve. She needed to put her son's emotional health before her own wishes. If he wanted to live with his father, she would let that happen. She didn't want to cause him further pain.

———————

Joyce grabbed Nina's covers and pulled them completely off the bed. "Get up, my friend," she said, dropping them on the floor.

Nina wakened thoroughly, blinking the sleep from her eyes. She'd heard Joyce and Paulette moving around her bedroom, but she hadn't expected them to assault her.

"Tsk," Paulette said. "Those pajamas could stand up and walk around on their own."

Nina was bleary and disoriented, trying to understand what was happening to her. She knew she'd let herself go a little, but Paulette's remark seemed far too harsh.

Before she could make her retort to Paulette, Joyce hoisted Nina to her feet with a surprisingly strong grip. "Don't worry. We're your best friends, and we're here to help."

Paulette stripped the bed before Nina even had time to blink and Joyce marched her double-time to the bathroom.

"I just want to sleep," Nina said.

"Nope. No more sleep." Joyce smiled despite her stern words. "First you shower, and then you eat."

"I'm not hungry, just tired."

Paulette stepped into the bathroom and turned on the shower. She stuck her arm under the water to test the heat. Nina watched her with little interest.

"Hon, you're depressed," Joyce said. "We understand why. You have every reason to be sad, but you have to get it together sometime."

Nina started to cry. Paulette and Joyce enveloped her in a huge hug.

"That's okay. Let it out," Paulette said as she rubbed her back. "We're right here."

———

In December of 1987, Ernesto and Lupe had a son named Nicholas.

Vanessa and David were excited to have a new little brother. Naturally, David called to tell her the news. She couldn't blame him. He wanted her to share in the moment with him. In many ways, it was very sweet, she thought, but it left a harsh ache in her chest. Nina couldn't genuinely share her children's joy, but she thought she needed to be happy for them. Ultimately, she just ended up feeling left out.

Chapter Eighteen

Much Lost, Little Gained

❧

N ina pushed her cart through the grocery store, sneaking another glance at the tall, shabbily-dressed man in the produce section. He was tapping melons, apparently checking them for ripeness. Had he been following her? Watching her, even? Nina thought he looked sinister.

Although she was a professional, independent woman, Nina didn't feel safe now that she was living alone. Her paranoia had begun to seep into all aspects of her life, causing her to eye even the most innocent-looking single men with suspicion. She could probably blame her South American upbringing for her worries, but although she often reminded herself that she was living in a culture where thousands of women lived alone, it didn't work. Instead of a husband or children, she had an empty four-bedroom house with a big backyard. It didn't matter if her alarm system was switched on; she never felt safe as she slept.

She told herself that her fears were unfounded, but it didn't change the fact that she lived alone. For Nina, living alone meant feeling afraid.

Nina swung her cart down the bread aisle. She paused at the end, peeking around a display of cinnamon rolls to look for the single man again.

He had vanished.

Nina's heart rate accelerated. The man had either finished his shopping or given up the pretense of selecting a melon. She felt sure she would see him right behind her when she turned around.

Her pager buzzed. Checking it, Nina saw the alarm company's number appear on the caller ID.

Nina didn't even know what had happened yet, but whatever it was, it seemed inevitable. She felt clear-headed but fatalistic as she abandoned her cart and hurried out of the store to find a public phone. She was lucky; several phone stalls stood just outside the entrance. She dialed the company's number, which she knew by heart.

A company representative answered right away. "Nina Rossi? I'm afraid an intrusion has occurred at your home."

Nina bit her lip. She'd gotten false alarms in the past, but the suspicious man had seemed like a bad omen and the news didn't surprise her. Still, she was afraid to ask for more information, and had to force herself to say, "Do you know what happened?"

"Somebody tried to break in through the kitchen door." The operator spoke with clinical efficiency. "The intruder fled the moment the alarm went off. The local police are at the scene checking things out."

"Thank you," Nina said faintly. As she hung up the phone, she realized that her car was parked just a few feet away from her. *I should just go home.* She didn't feel like shopping anymore anyway, not until she knew the extent of the damage. Hopefully a clerk would spot her abandoned cart before the perishable items in it were spoiled.

———❦———

On the drive home, Nina's mind whirled with worried thoughts. The operator had sounded too sure of the details for this to be a false alarm. Had he downplayed the situation? Was it worse than he'd described? She imagined her house torn apart, her belongings stolen or damaged, windows smashed...

She pulled up to the curb outside her house. The lights blazed in the windows, illuminating the early evening, and the doors stood open. Two policemen were standing outside the front door; a moment later, they were joined by two others who came tromping out of the house as though they owned it. Nina hoped they hadn't tracked dirt on her clean floors.

Then she laughed to herself. *Dirt is probably the least of my worries right now.*

She had thought she would feel safe with the police around, but instead she felt nervous and uneasy. Her home, the only thing left of her own, had been twice violated. She shuddered as she imagined a stranger in her house, going through her belongings. The burglar's intrusion and the police investigation seemed like equally distressing disruptions of her much-valued privacy.

Nina struggled to stop laughing as an officer approached the car. She didn't want to look like a crazy person, but it was hard. Everything seemed to be going wrong in her life. As she opened her car door, a general malaise overcame her.

"Ma'am, is this your house?"

"Yes, I own this house."

"Very good." The officer looked busy but respectable; Nina appreciated his manner. "You'll need to answer some general questions and fill out a bit of paperwork for us. It won't be much."

Nina kept telling herself that a break-in was not the end of the world. Her house had been damaged, but not extensively, and nothing had been taken. Most people would be able to deal with the situation in an adult way, even with relief. But Nina wanted to throw a grand temper tantrum. Why should she stoically accept the burglary? It shouldn't have happened in the first place.

The episode felt like the straw that broke the camel's back, but Nina somehow made it through the evening with dignity.

—ᴖᴖᴖ—

By the end of the month, Nina decided to move. She felt less secure than ever in her freshly violated home, and wanted to relocate to a condo with a stronger security system. Any opportunity to start over again would be welcome.

Vanessa helped Nina choose a new condo that had lots of light, motion detectors, and a street view. When she wandered over to inspect the condo's security system panel, a perplexed look came to her face.

"Mom, do you really need all these buttons and lights? It looks like something out of a weird sci-fi movie." Vanessa flipped through the manual that accompanied the system. "This must be at least two inches thick."

"You wouldn't be making smart remarks if the break-in had happened to you," Nina said. Even weeks afterward, she couldn't stifle the fear that came from knowing someone had been in her home.

"Well, I just want to warn you," Vanessa said. "Our neighbors have motion detector lights that go off all night long because of the animals in the area. It drives me crazy."

"It won't drive me crazy," Nina said. "I don't care if it's bright all night; I just want to get my sense of wellbeing back."

Her new condo seemed perfect. It had three levels and an attached double garage, and was located in a pleasant residential area near a beautiful shopping district. The master bedroom included a sitting room and a terrace balcony that faced the street. Several skylights illuminated the living room and bedroom, and both rooms had fireplaces as well. The dining room was elevated from the living room: it had a cute wrought iron fence around it and a built-in bar for entertaining. A breakfast room next to the kitchen had a balcony that opened to a family room where she could put her big-screen TV.

But the security system, with its twenty-four-hour a day direct link to the nearest police and fire station, was to Nina its most important feature.

—*∿*—

When Nina had decided to move again, she hadn't realized that packing would be so emotionally draining. Every memento she discovered reminded her that her life had changed immensely since her last move. She found her family's treasured possessions tucked away in closets, cupboards, and drawers, each item possessing an important emotional connection. The weight of the associated emotions threatened to overwhelm her as she worked.

She sorted through her children's' things without knowing what to do with them. She stumbled across Vanessa's old Cyndi Lauper albums and David's sets of Legos. She laughed when she came across an electric racecar track that Ernesto had given David one Christmas. Ernesto himself had ended up playing with it for several days before David got a chance.

Nina knew that many of the things she had found would seem extremely important to their respective owners if they saw them. Unfortunately for them, out of sight was out of mind. Nina couldn't waste time guessing what to keep and what not to keep. In the end, she packed away the personal childhood mementos that Vanessa and David were still too young to appreciate, but threw out most of their old toys and clothes.

Then, to her surprise, she found a shoebox with her own handwriting on it: "muy frágil e importante! Nunca tirar." The box clearly contained items from her first move to America. What could be so fragile and important that she'd commanded that it never be thrown away? *Obviously it wasn't too important if I never even opened it. Must have nothing in it worth displaying.*

Curious, Nina cut the tape to peer into the time capsule from her past. The box contained a few yellowed papers and some old photographs.

Nina wrinkled her nose as she sifted through the dusty contents, which smelled as ancient as they looked. She carefully slid the contents out of one of the envelopes and realized she was holding her test scores and admittance into high school. *It's amazing that I held onto this so long,* she thought, but she knew why as she remembered her pride and joy on the night she and Giovanna had shared their results. She smiled as she remembered sitting at her parents' dining room table, so full of anxious anticipation.

Turning over the papers, she discovered all her old elementary school class pictures buried underneath. She studied the faded faces and smiled at the friends so dear to her in her youth. She'd lost touch with many of them since those days.

In one of the photos she saw Héctor Torres's face in the back row. At her first thought of him, she felt her anger flare. A moment later, she realized that anger was merely a knee-jerk reaction. When she studied the faces collectively, she felt compassion for their shared experiences, growing up in a time of uncertainty and war. Héctor had tried to teach her to question what others had told her to accept as the truth. He had given her answers to questions that she hadn't even start asking for decades.

She slowly taped the box shut again, pondering. What could she do with these things? She had found many pieces of her past, but she no longer felt any connection to that past. Time, her move to America, and her many life experiences had all separated her from the memories she'd once held so precious.

Eventually she wrapped the box in garbage bags, took a shovel from the garage, and buried the box in the backyard. As the shovel rose and fell, Nina wondered if she'd ever regret not keeping the papers.

No, she decided. This was best. Maybe one day the box would be found by someone who had the heart to throw it away.

———∿∿∿———

After living her life in the Old World tradition, Nina found moving day both traumatic and enlightening at the same time. Her new home was very inviting, the first place she wouldn't have to share with anyone else. It seemed huge and empty, but it also felt friendly, welcoming, full of potential.

"I am completely independent," Nina said aloud, wonderingly, as she collapsed on her sofa at the end of the day. Boxes surrounded her. Every box contained only her own possessions, no one else's.

As custom dictated, Nina had lived with her parents until she got married. Then she'd lived with her husband, then her children. Now her house was completely her own.

I think I like this.

———∿∿∿———

A month later, Ernesto called, excited to tell Nina about a new opportunity for their business.

"There's a new *maquiladoras* program in Mexico," he said. "I'm going to move the business there, complete with all our equipment and machinery, but continue to run the business from California."

"Lupe gave you this idea, didn't she?" Nina said coldly, her tone far from matching his enthusiasm. Before he could reply to confirm or deny it, she asked, "What are the advantages?"

Ernesto was, as always, ready with an answer. "The printing paper will cost less and labor's a lot cheaper there, which will help reduce the cost of the finished product. We'll be able to beat our American competitors hands down."

"Would you be willing to do the same thing with my half of the business?" Nina asked.

"It's difficult enough to move a business, lock, stock, and barrel, to a new country when only one person is in charge," Ernesto said. "Because we're currently sharing the business, although I'm running both halves, the move will be more difficult."

The conversation left a bad taste in Nina's mouth. Worried about her future, she immediately contacted a business broker to sell her half of the printing plant.

"Nina, you're selling at a bad time. It's a buyer's market right now." The broker spoke to her as if she were a child.

She'd let Ernesto run her half of the business. Now her choice had come back to haunt her. She couldn't bear to stay connected to the business when decisions were being made—or even influenced— by Lupe. But the broker didn't need to know her personal reasons.

"I understand that," she said, "but the price they offered is still unrealistically low."

"Don't forget that they see the business being sold by a single woman and they can put two and two together. They assume you're in no position to run the business, so they plan to buy it cheap," the broker said.

After many tribulations, Nina sold her half of the business for a very low price. She felt relieved to have it off her hands, but the sale quickly put her immigration status into a new, unenviable category. During an interview at the Immigration and Naturalization Service, the INS requested a copy of her payroll as one of the requirements to get her E-2 visa renewed.

"I see your status has changed since you first applied," the INS officer said. "You were an employer when you first came here."

"Can't I apply under the 1986 amnesty law?" Nina asked.

He thought for a moment. "No, that's not possible. That law was for illegal immigrants. Since you're legal, it doesn't apply to you."

"So this is a case where playing by the rules doesn't pay off," Nina said. Her voice shook with frustration.

The INS officer nodded. "I'm afraid so. There's no way I can approve this visa now."

Nina left the INS office feeling alarmed and downhearted. When she got home, she immediately called Joyce and then Paulette. Crying into the phone, she told them the tale. The ever-sympathetic Joyce consoled Nina as best she could. Paulette, the most pragmatic of the three, started to suggest different solutions.

Even with the emotional support and practical help of her friends, Nina felt vulnerable. At any moment, she could be deported and separated from her children. For the first time since she had started living in America, she was disappointed with the immigration system.

—◦◦◦—

Six months later, Nina faced deportation. She still couldn't quite understand how it had happened. She'd followed all the rules, tried to keep track of all the small print. She went over the immigration laws for what felt like the hundredth time, looking for a way out of her personal nightmare.

"Hey, Mom," Vanessa said, strolling into the kitchen.

"Hello," Nina said. She shuffled the immigration papers to the side, slightly puzzled. Vanessa didn't usually stop by at this time.

Vanessa poured herself a cup of coffee and sat down at the table. "Thought I'd just drop in, see how you were doing."

"Is something wrong?" Nina asked.

"No," Vanessa said. As she sipped her coffee, a ring glimmered on her hand.

Nina leaned forward, staring. *It looks like—could it be an engagement ring?* She didn't want to believe her eyes.

"You've noticed!" Vanessa held out of her hand, wiggling her fingers. "Isn't it beautiful? I'm getting married."

"Oh, honey," Nina said. She hurried to Vanessa's side and took her hand. "This is a beautiful ring, but you have a lot of time before you get married."

"I thought you'd understand," Vanessa said, jerking her hand back. Her happy expression had crumpled; now she looked angry and upset.

Nina did understand. Vanessa wanted what Vanessa wanted. She'd always been that way.

"Have you talked with your father about this?"

"No. I decided to tell you first. I thought you'd be pleased."

"We should talk to your father," Nina said.

Vanessa dashed angry tears from her cheeks, setting her jaw. "I could have just gone to the courthouse and gotten married any time I wanted. I didn't have to tell you."

With a little probing, Nina learned that Vanessa had decided to marry her high school sweetheart. She was determined to go ahead with the marriage even without her mom's full support. Nina didn't want to turn a happy occasion into a messy fight, but she wanted to break Vanessa's stubborn determination before Vanessa got hurt. A talk with Ernesto might do the trick.

Nina took Vanessa to tell Ernesto the news. As she had anticipated, he shared her unease, fearing that Vanessa had made a hasty decision. However, after many family arguments, Vanessa remained adamant about getting married, and Ernesto and Nina agreed to let her continue with her plans.

Nina suggested that she and Ernesto both participate in the wedding. Ernesto agreed, and Vanessa was pleased with the idea. They also agreed to give Vanessa a small wedding reception. Nina couldn't remember the last time she and Ernesto had agreed on anything.

—◦◦◦—

On the day of Vanessa's wedding, Nina helped her slip into her beautiful, Victorian-style dress and arrange her hair. The preparations reminded Nina of how her own mother had helped her get ready on her wedding day.

"You're getting so old!" she said, smiling as she arranged Vanessa's veil.

Vanessa caught her hand and held it. "I can't even believe any of this is happening," she said.

Nina understood exactly why Giovanna had cried to see her looking beautiful and happy on the day she married Ernesto.

As Vanessa waited outside the church, her face radiated pure happiness. The sight of her joy convinced Nina to put aside the last of her reservations. She hoped there would be no terrorist attacks at *this* wedding. Although they did add a certain amount of excitement to the wedding, they ultimately proved to be a bad omen.

David entered the church first, accompanied by the young flower girl who smiled as she scattered rose petals down the aisle. He carried a small pillow with the wedding rings, looking startlingly grown up in his tux.

Ernesto sat with his new family. Estela and Miguel had traveled from Argentina to attend the wedding, and Eduardo and his family sat beside them. Among all her family members, Nina was the only one who had come to the wedding alone.

Nina could not believe how much both her children had grown. As she looked at the people around her, she felt as though time were running out. Although it seemed silly to panic, she couldn't repress the miserable thought, *What have I to show for my life?*

—◦◦◦—

Nina needed to face her destiny. She had no income, and what little money she had received from the sale of the business was running out fast. She had a mortgage to pay every month, condo expenses, and medical expenses. She decided to avoid spending money on unnecessary items, but it was not easy. She'd never had to live on a tight budget. She had always had wriggle room, even in the days when money had been a concern.

A few weeks earlier, Nina had asked her mom to take some of her paintings out of storage in Argentina and bring them to José. She thought he would be able to get a good price for them, because she knew the paintings were worth a good amount of money.

When her mom called, she seemed rushed and exasperated. It wasn't the reaction Nina had expected.

"The nerve! You wouldn't believe those people," Estela said. "How they treated me! And you!"

"What are you talking about?" Nina asked, trying to make sense of her mom's ranting. "Did you get any money?"

"I brought the paintings over like you asked, and José treated me like I didn't know they had any value!" Estela said. "He tried to buy them for a tiny fraction of what they were worth."

"Did you sell them?"

"It gets worse!" Estela said. "The moment I told them you needed the money because you'd gotten a divorce, both he and Lucia had a complete field day. They kept talking on and on about how 'wealthy, affluent Nina' was now a beggar. It was disgusting. I stormed out."

Nina was stunned by her old friends' behavior, but not actually surprised. Time and jealousy had only made them more and more resentful of her seeming successes. *It's so sad that we live in a world where people revel unashamed in someone else's misery.*

"So you didn't sell the paintings?" she asked.

"Not to them!" Estela said. "You're better off keeping them until a better option comes along."

"I don't know how many more options I have." Nina sighed. She admired her mother's principles, but she needed the money.

Finding a job was the next best solution, but the task was not an easy one. Nina didn't have a green card or a work permit, and every place she contacted asked for one or the other. When she finally got in touch with an immigration attorney, he quickly enlightened her.

"There are a limited amount of visas for professionals in your field," he said. "This comes down to a matter of securing one."

"Do you think I have a chance?"

"You should contact the Pharmacy Board to find out."

When she called the Board, it requested certificates and credentials from Argentina before she could apply.

Nina called her mom for more help.

"Mom? I need you to go to the university and ask for all my old paperwork," she said. "Then I need my certifications from the government board."

"Are you sure you need all that? It's going to take me forever and cost a fortune in taxes," Estela said.

"I'm sorry to have to ask you to do this, but I really need those papers," Nina said. She knew her mother wasn't young anymore, but if Estela wouldn't help her, her deportation seemed likely.

Estela sighed. "Fine, fine. Give me a list of everything you need, in great detail, and I will see what I can do."

Nina was touched that Estela would wait in the long lines and go from office to office to help her. It took three long months for Estela to gather all the required paperwork and send it to her daughter in America. On her end, Nina spent many hours in long procedures that cost her time as well as money.

When she finally mailed everything to the Pharmacy Board, Nina received a phone call from someone in the license office.

"We received all your paperwork," the clerk said. "You will need to take a test before we can give you a license."

"When is the test?"

"In three months."

Nina couldn't hold back a gasp at the news. "There's no way I could be ready in time," she said, recovering slightly. "Just learning the technical English alone could take a year."

"I'm sorry, but the state sets the test dates," the clerk said. "Rules are rules. We can't change them just for you."

"I don't want to change it because of some minor inconvenience. This is my life, and I want to excel at it."

Nina remembered all the late nights she had spent studying in her youth, when no test was too much to handle. She knew she could do the same with this test, but she needed extra time. She had to pass an exam based on all the subjects she had studied in pharmacy school more than twenty years ago. She hadn't practiced for ten years; she was no doubt behind on recent developments in the field. She also had to learn the technical vocabulary in English.

"Please. This is all I have left," Nina said. She waited—the clerk didn't respond.

"Please hold."

Nina was determined to fight hard if that were necessary. She loved her native country, but now she desperately wanted to live in America. She couldn't help but smile to herself as she noticed the irony. It seemed like everything she wanted most was always the hardest to get.

"All right," the clerk said. "I can push the date of the test back by nine months, but that's the absolute latest you can take it. Please remember, this is a one-time special case."

"Thank you so much!"

"Good luck," the clerk said.

—◈—

Nina started the long process of studying for her test, her sights set on the date nine months later. She knew if she didn't pass the exam, she would have to figure something else out, because there was no way she could leave America. She had so many reasons to stay now.

One night Vanessa phoned while Nina was studying. From the excitement in her daughter's voice, Nina quickly guessed the reason.

"I'm pregnant!" Vanessa said. "I'm going to have a baby around Thanksgiving."

Nina was not surprised. She had reservations about the timing. Her exam was scheduled for April of the next year, and she was disturbed that she would not have much time to spend with her grandson or granddaughter until the exam was over. *But what can I do?* she thought. *Life is relentless.*

The Salvattis wanted to be with Vanessa when the baby was born, so they traveled to LA at the end of October. Because Nina no longer owned a huge house, they stayed with Eduardo until just before Thanksgiving, when they accepted Vanessa's hospitality. Estela wanted to help as much as possible after her great-grandchild was born.

The Thanksgiving reunion was very cozy, with the whole family present. Vanessa was almost due. She made twice-baked potatoes for her in-laws since Nina and her mom did not know how. Nina and her mom cooked the turkey, and everybody enjoyed the family gathering.

—◦◦◦—

During this time, Miguel began to develop strange symptoms, including pain in his lower back and upper leg. Nina tried to juggle her time between her daughter's pregnancy, her studies, and her father's illness, but she felt herself wearing thin. At night she worried that her father might have cancer, but she tried to keep the thought locked away by daylight.

In some ways, it was easy not to think too far ahead. Nina's multitude of concerns kept her busy. She drove her dad and her mom to several doctors and specialists. They advised him to stay in America until his great-grandchild was born and then to immediately travel back to Argentina, where he had good health insurance. Whatever Miguel's illness, the prognosis was not good. The doctors predicted a long, difficult treatment process.

The baby arrived at the beginning of December. The whole family stood at the nursery admiring the beautiful infant that Vanessa had named Briana.

Following the doctor's advice, the Salvattis decided not to wait for Christmas, but reluctantly returned to Argentina right after the birth. Nina drove her parents to the airport. She hugged her father for a long time, too overwhelmed to say goodbye properly.

Her heart told her this was the last time she would see her father alive.

"Lupe did you a favor," Miguel said. "You should be forever grateful to her."

Nina stared at him in surprise, not knowing how to respond. Never in the world would she contemplate thanking Lupe.

"You don't see it now, but she took away the part of your marriage that wasn't working," Miguel continued. "You've been left with America, the best part, so go and make the most of it. If I had known more about the American system, I would have moved here after I got married, and you would have been born an American. Never doubt that you were meant to be here."

Nina hugged him harder. She knew her dad never liked leaving on a sad note.

"Anyway, when I die, I'm sending your mother up here." Miguel smiled. "She can fulfill my dream of living in America."

———◆◆◆———

Eduardo traveled to Argentina to be with Miguel in his last days. Unfortunately, Nina could not do likewise, because she didn't have the necessary visa. All she could do was offer him long telephone conversations, which were both painful and comforting. Her dad battled his cancer bravely but died a few months after Briana's birth.

Devastated by the loss of her father, Nina nonetheless found a reason to rejoice. Her father's promise would come true, Eduardo assured her. Her mom had started packing in preparation to move to America.

———◆◆◆———

When she took her pharmacy licensing exam, Nina thought about her dad. He'd faced death with a fearless demeanor. At the very least, she could face her test in the same way.

Waiting for the results was a different matter. After six weeks of anxiety, she got the letter from the board. Fearing its contents, she held the envelope in trembling hands before the courage at last arrived to open it. And then she saw the magic words: "Congratulations, you have passed."

Chapter Nineteen

Trying to Get It Right

❧

After she received her license, Nina's life began to smooth out and go as planned at last. She soon got a job at a hospital, which sponsored her for her green card. Her new routine had long working hours, but she was excited to return at long last to the profession she loved. On weekends, she visited her children and enjoyed occasional outings with Paulette and Joyce. She and her friends often celebrated their birthdays together, as well as attending a number of cultural functions: concerts, operas, art exhibitions.

We're like the Three Musketeers, Nina thought. *All for one and one for all.* Not only were the friends fiercely loyal to each other, but they cut a fashionable swath through their small corner of society. Partly thanks to them, Nina could feel America becoming home.

The day before her fiftieth birthday, Nina received a letter from the Immigration and Naturalization Service informing her that she needed to travel to Argentina to finish some paperwork. This was an important landmark, because Nina was the only one in the family without proper immigration papers: Eduardo and his family had obtained theirs through his business and Nina's children had obtained theirs through their father. Once Nina had completed the papers in Argentina, she would be able to receive a green card of her own.

The next day, Nina's children threw her a small party at a restaurant for friends and family. Paulette and Joyce, Eduardo and

Julia were all there, as well as several others. As they savored a delicious meal, they talked about the many twists and turns their lives had taken in recent years. Everyone was especially pleased that Nina would soon have a green card, and frequently hailed this development throughout the party.

A couple weeks later, Nina traveled to Buenos Aires. She immediately saw that the city had changed in the passing years. The harbor area had once held nothing but customs warehouses; these had been renovated in daringly artistic ways. Beautiful shopping centers rose around them; modern restaurants on the ground floors faced the river; the upper floors of tall buildings had been converted to ultra-modern lofts in different sleek designs. Despite the changes, the nineteenth-century brick exteriors had been carefully preserved, making the architectural innovations even more stylistically significant.

Nina admired the end results. They reminded her of the recent renovations done in Barcelona for the 1992 Olympic Games. She later learned that Santiago Calatrava, an elite Spanish architect, had designed a bridge over the river in Buenos Aires that imitated the new Barcelona style. The result was called Puente de la Mujer, the Woman's Bridge, and was a magnificent work of art that opened and closed to allow ships to pass.

Buenos Aires had finally become what Nina had always wanted Argentina to be, but she wished the wonderful changes had occurred sooner. Her hope for Argentina and her need to stay in America for her children pulled her in opposite directions. Caught between two countries, she didn't feel as though she could claim either one as her homeland. She felt like a nomad after traveling back and forth for so many years.

The days flew by. Nina met at the American Embassy several times to go over her paperwork. She also made a doctor's appointment that confirmed her complete health. Best of all, she spent every day visiting with family and friends, including Giovanna, whom she hadn't seen for years. Slender and graceful, Giovanna had become an imposing lawyer, but she greeted Nina with her familiar good cheer. The two spent several evenings catching up with each other's news.

All too soon, Nina's brief stay in Argentina came to an end. However, this time she would not be returning to America alone. Her mother had agreed to move to LA to live with her. She was getting too old to travel; Nina was glad she would have a chance to settle down at last.

"Did you manage to sell everything you're not bringing with you?" Nina asked Estela as they walked around the empty house for the last time.

"Yes, yes," Estela said. "My friends helped me take care of all those arrangements."

Even though Nina hadn't called this house home in years, every empty corner and wall made her long to return everything to its original place. She wished she could preserve her old house exactly the way she remembered.

This was the fourth time Nina had had to take a house apart. It wasn't getting any easier.

"Nestor at the post office called and said I had some magazines there that I need to get," Estela said. "Also, I have a prescription to pick up at the pharmacy and I need to say goodbye to a few friends."

"You were supposed to have done all that before I got here," Nina said, not sure if she were amused or exasperated.

She couldn't fault her mother for wanting to cover every possible base before she moved out of the country. Remembering how she'd felt forced into her first move, she knew she didn't want Estela to feel even a little rushed. After all, moving took a lot of work and preparation, but Estela had started weeks in advance. Things were pretty much under control.

"And there are a few boxes in your old room that we need to bring with us," Estela said.

Nina slipped away to her old bedroom, where she found a few scuffed boxes that contained innumerable mementos from her childhood. She'd already had to say goodbye to so many of her childhood memories; she hoped this was the last "very important, never throw away" set of boxes that she would encounter.

She steeled herself and sorted through them. Some items she could pack to bring home with her; unfortunately, other of the contents she would have to discard. The doll Evita had given her would be shipped to America in a box marked FRAGILE. Nina planned to display it in the guest bedroom above the sofa bed.

Finishing, she glanced at her mother. "Just one more thing to do, right?"

Estela nodded. "You know the way," she said.

————

Nina parked beside the cemetery that contained the family plot. She hesitated briefly before getting out of the car. This would be the first and last time she would visit her father's grave, and she wasn't quite sure what to do or say.

Before she could say anything at all, however, her mother gently took her hand and led her to the grave. Someone had put fresh flowers there. As Estela looked at the grave, she seemed at peace.

"He would be so happy about this," she said. "I do wish he could have come to America too."

Nina nodded. She missed her father very much, especially when she remembered the wisdom he had imparted to her. It had taken a while, but she had eventually came around to the way he felt about America. She wished she could tell him that.

"I wish he could be there to enjoy it with us too," Nina said.

"Well, we're not getting any younger here," Estela said after a moment. "Let's go."

—⟨∿∿⟩—

Nina soon adjusted to life with her mother in LA. The long flight from Argentina gave them a chance to finally relax together and put the events of the past few years in perspective. They gladly seized the opportunity to converse about the bitter and sweet vicissitudes of their lives. Once they reached LA, Nina immersed herself in her work at the nearby hospital and caught up with her friends. Her mother quickly settled into her duplex and seemed pleased with her move.

Several months later, one early morning in January, a strange rattling sound wakened Nina. The whole building trembled; walls and furniture vibrated. Terrified, Nina became aware of the racket of glasses falling and shattering, walls collapsing, metal screeching as it bent out of shape.

Nina pulled her pillow over her head, afraid that the ceiling might fall down on top of her. She had never experienced anything like this and didn't know what to do.

Through the noise, she shouted down the hall to her mother. "Mom, are you okay?"

"Yes, I'm fine."

Nina stayed in bed. *God, please keep me and my mother safe. Please, please keep us safe.*

The 6.7 earthquake lasted twenty seconds, but it seemed like many minutes. By the time everything stopped shaking and settled at last, all the lights had gone out, including the ones in the street. Nina fumbled for the light switch on her bedside lamp, but it didn't work. The flashlight she kept in her nightstand drawer was somewhere on the floor, lying among the scattered contents of every other drawer in the room. Nina couldn't find it. She could barely see at all.

"Hold tight! Just stay there until I come," Nina yelled. Her heart pounded and pounded.

Feeling along the walls with her hands and stepping carefully around the debris, she tried to reach the bathroom. All the drawers in the bathroom had also fallen to the floor, and the door was blocked. She followed the wall to Estela's room, grateful when the door opened and her mom peered out, unharmed but frightened.

They decided to go downstairs to the living room. Nina was afraid the staircase might collapse in the dark house, but the upper level felt too dangerous. They descended slowly, clinging to the bannister, and found the living room in the same state as the rest of the house.

Fortunately, they could see a little better there. The room had a large window facing the street and, with the aid of the moonlight, Nina could make out some of the tumbled furniture. It was a terrible sight, like something from a warzone. The armchairs lay upside down. Pictures were strewn at the foot of the walls. Nina's tall French curio had fallen on its face, destroying the souvenirs she had collected from her trips around the world. At least material things weren't as valuable to her anymore. She was just glad—and almost surprised—to be alive.

Proceeding to the kitchen, Nina discovered that it was in the worst shape of any room in the house. The refrigerator had tipped right over the counter and one door had swung open. The contents of every cupboard littered the floor. Jars, bowls, and plates had all smashed. Some of the cabinet doors had fallen off and the pipes were broken.

Nina was assessing the damage when a very strong aftershock hit. She grabbed her mother to steady her, and prayed silently as the whole house shook.

When it finally stopped, Nina and Estela stood motionless for several seconds, waiting for more.

"We should call Vanessa and David," Nina said.

Estela nodded.

Reaching the phone took several minutes, but Nina managed to pick her way through the wreckage to find it. When she lifted the receiver, she discovered the connection was dead.

"No luck," she told her mother. "I think we should get out of the house."

"You're right. It can't be safe in here."

But when Nina tried to open the front door, it wouldn't budge. She looked closely, squinting in the moonlight, and realized that the door had shifted in the hinges. Estela was watching her, so she tried to stay calm, but she began to wonder if they were trapped. *And the ceiling might cave at any moment. Another aftershock might do it.*

The curtains of the window nearest the street moved. Nina froze. What if someone were trying to break into the house? That was the last thing they needed.

"It's just the wind," Estela said. "The window's probably broken."

Nina left the door and crossed the room. Careful of the broken glass, she peeked through the window. She saw a flash of light: the beam of a flashlight. A face followed the light, and Nina recognized it as belonging to one of her next-door neighbor. She thought his name might be Sam Smith.

"Back away from the window, ladies," he said.

Nina backed away slowly and gestured for her mom to do the same. Sam pulled the window completely open, swung a leg over the windowsill, and came into the room. He had a scratch across his forehead.

"Are you two okay?" he asked.

"Yes," Nina said. "What brings you here?"

She didn't want to sound ungrateful, but she knew she still needed to be careful. She'd lived alone in LA long enough to realize that she needed to ask questions even of men whom she recognized.

Sam gave her an approving nod. "I know that you and your mother live by yourselves. I wanted to make sure that you two were okay after the quake. Is there anything I can do to help?"

Nina relaxed. "Thanks, Sam. We could use some help getting out."

Nina went through the window first, aided by Sam. Her mom followed, and Nina helped her from the outside. Sam came last. Other neighbors had started to make their way outside, wandering up and down the street in a daze as they tried to access the damage. Everybody was frantic to get in touch with loved ones, but it was impossible. No one could get a telephone to work.

Sam led Nina and Estela to his home and invited them in. Nina's gaze passed over her neighbor's furniture, some of which had stood serious damage. His Christmas tree remained standing—a comical, or possibly tragic, sight—and most of its ornaments remained intact. Evidently the tree's light weight had allowed it to remain erect through the chaos. It seemed like a picture of her own life. Nina kept asking herself how she'd survived the many hardships she'd experienced.

The devastation around them was even more striking by the light of day. None of the houses in the neighborhood had electricity, but they were able to receive limited news from Sam's battery-operated radio.

The initial reports were staggering. Dozens of people had died, apartment buildings had collapsed, interchanges had fallen onto the freeway, and traffic jammed the roads. The emergency broadcast service ran an announcement asking people to stay where they were.

"I have to get to Vanessa," Nina said. "I have to see with my own eyes that at least one of my children is okay."

"I'll come with you," Estela said.

They thanked Sam and hurried to Nina's car. Nina drove out

of the shattered neighborhood to the freeway, where it immediately became obvious that she wasn't the only one who needed to check on family and friends. Thousands of cars, nearly stationary, filled the road.

Nina's heart thudded in her chest. Everywhere she looked, chaos reigned. Estela prayed the whole time Nina drove, sometimes murmuring softly, sometimes speaking aloud.

It took two hours to drive only a few miles.

When they finally reached Vanessa's house, Vanessa flew to the car and hugged Nina and Estela very tightly.

"Are you all right?" she kept asking. "I'm so glad to see you!"

She bombarded them with questions and Nina asked many questions of her own. It quickly turned out that no damage had occurred where Vanessa lived, but everybody was scared.

A few minutes later, Ernesto also arrived to check on Vanessa. He reported that David and the rest of his family were fine. At the news, Nina finally felt able to breathe again. Even though she had always kept in close contact with her family, she now realized just how lucky she was to have them nearby.

———

The earthquake had completely shattered the smooth flow of Nina's life. For the next few days, she would have to put her most basic needs first.

"It's not going to be safe for you to go back to the house," she told her mother. "Eduardo lives far enough away that I think he'll be fine. Maybe you could stay with him?"

"But what about you?"

The thought was overwhelming. The damage caused in twenty seconds would take months to reverse. Nina had lost almost every memento and collectable that had meant anything to her. She knew already that almost all her furniture would need to be replaced; she would essentially have to start over again.

"According to the radio, the epicenter of the earthquake was only two miles from your house," Vanessa said. "We were so scared for you. You're really lucky to be all right."

Apparently Nina's frantic prayers had been answered. *Now I just need to* stay *all right,* she thought. Looters might still be a threat, and she would have a lot of cleaning up to do. Not only that, but who knew when her electricity and gas would be restored? Like her mother, she'd need somewhere to stay for a while.

Fortunately, Paulette came to the rescue the next day.

"I have a guesthouse in my backyard; you probably remember it," she said. "Why don't you stay there for a few weeks until your house is safe again? Don't worry about getting underfoot—I just wish I could help you more."

Even settled comfortably in Paulette's guesthouse, Nina felt as though she were living in a disaster zone. The local supermarket was disorganized, and some items were unexpectedly difficult to find. The most obvious shortage was water: tap water ran the risk of contamination, so the demand for bottled water had increased sharply. Still, with a little determination, Nina managed to find everything she needed.

The disaster showed her the goodness in the people she knew. Her coworkers at the hospital provided more help than she would have asked for; the ordeal of cleaning house and moving her belongings became more bearable with their support and friendship. Although wading through the wreckage of her house often made Nina feel depressed, some days the cleaning felt almost festive. Nina's friends, she realized, mattered more to her than any memento.

After a few weeks in Paulette's guesthouse, Nina moved to a small but pleasant apartment not far from her ruined townhouse. Her new location meant that she could easily oversee the remodeling now being done to her home. It also meant that Estela could live with her again. The apartment belonged to a complex with a swimming pool and gym, and Estela enjoyed getting to know several Spanish speakers who also rented apartments there.

"There's a lot to do here," she said one day. "I used to be alone while you spent all day working, but now I have friends and many activities to keep me busy."

"Would you like to stay here?" Nina asked.

Almost a year had passed, and her home was completely repaired and restored. Nina was excited to move back and enjoy the product of her many months of hard work, but she knew Estela would be sad to go. She'd spent more time in the apartment than in Nina's house, and it had become home for her in America.

"I would like to stay," Estela said.

"I know you'll be well cared for here," Nina said, smiling.

Looking back at the past year, she realized that everything had worked out better than she had ever expected.

Chapter Twenty

L'Amour

❧

Almost a year had passed since Nina had finished fixing her home. For a while, she'd been nervous when she went to bed, wondering if another earthquake would turn her life upside-down again. But those fears had soon faded. She was content with her friends, close to her family, satisfied with her work, and safe in her house. Life wasn't just going back to normal: it seemed to be getting better at last. Without even knowing why, Nina began to grow hopeful.

Paulette's son was to be married in the south of France. Nina decided not only to attend the wedding but to do so in style. She flew to Nice and rented a small car so that she could drive through the French countryside to Nimes, where the ceremony would take place. According to the guidebooks, the trip could be accomplished in only a few hours.

Those few hours, however, were some of the most delightful hours Nina had experienced. The region of Provence offered a beautiful, lush landscape to her eyes. Small, scenic roads took her past mountains and villages, rivers and valleys. Thousands of flowers of all varieties—grown to supply nearby perfume factories—filled the fields around her and flooded their surroundings with a fragile scent. Intoxicated by the beauty of it all, Nina felt her worries melt away.

The traditional French country wedding took place in an antique chapel in the middle of a little village. After the ceremony, the guests walked to an open-air restaurant where the chef had prepared a champagne reception. A band filled the air with their lively music. Waiters poured champagne from bottles so big they were held by two men. Dinner consisted of fourteen courses, each portion diminutive but delicious: figs infused with almond, thin slivers of perfectly cooked veal, delicately crafted ratatouille that seeped oil, lamb roasted with rosemary and thyme, soft bread and fine cheese. With each entree, a different type of wine was served.

Still thrilling from her journey, Nina plunged into the festivities with joy. She took the opportunity to meet new people and chat with Paulette's relations. Before she knew it, the sun had sunk below the horizon.

The newlyweds had left for their honeymoon, but the celebration continued into the next day with more music, wine, and food. As Nina sampled the exquisite dishes provided, she realized how confident she had become. Instead of feeling like the odd one out in the gathering, she felt independent and free.

After a good night's sleep, Nina jumped into her little car and headed out into the pastoral southern French countryside. As she drove, the very last of her tension slipped away. LA and its troubles seemed more distant than ever before.

The more she learned about the area of Avignon, the more interesting it became. During the Catholic schism in the fourteenth century, a number of popes had lived there in exile from Rome. The history of the city was replete with Machiavellian plots between the popes and the French court and its tales of political intrigue fascinated Nina. She had grown up in a country where such plots abounded.

She stopped at a café outside the city for breakfast and found it full of churchgoers, still wearing their Sunday best. The waitress approached with a pleasant, "*Bonjour.*"

"May I have a café latte and a croissant, please?"

"*Mais oui, madame.*"

"And could I have one of those cream pastries?" she said, pointing. She was in a vacation mood. She'd already been eating lots of rich food, and decided to throw caution to the winds and enjoy herself.

An hour later she found herself in front of Avignon Bridge. She remembered the song she had used to sing as a little girl and sang it softly to herself as she pulled into a small parking area.

"Sour le ponte d'Avignon
On y danse, on y danse."

When she jumped out of the car, camera in hand, an old woman approached her. She wore a colorful shawl, long dress, and red bandanna; her face was narrow and finely wrinkled.

"Bonjour, madame," she said. "Would you like to have your palm read?"

"No, thank you. I'm in a hurry."

Several other gypsies hurried toward her. Nina found herself surrounded by six of them, all chattering at the same time and offering souvenirs, fortune telling, and directions to antique shops and flea markets. The women were picturesque in their bright clothing, but for Nina, they were an overwhelming and alarming presence.

Nina took a deep breath, trying to fight her anxiety. When she'd been very young, various adults had told her that gypsies would take her away if she misbehaved. She wasn't a little girl anymore, but a grown woman enjoying her vacation in France. She had no reason to still be afraid.

"No, thank you," she said. "I don't need anything."

Nina fled to the bridge to take pictures. To her relief, the gypsies didn't follow her. She didn't realize that the women had used their onslaught of questions to distract her into leaving her car door unlocked. While Nina was taking pictures of the bridge, they were taking her overnight luggage from the trunk.

Nina didn't discover the theft until she reached Marseilles a few hours later and went to get her things. Her jaw dropped as she stared into her empty trunk. Her bag was gone. It had contained the dress clothes she had worn to the wedding, as well as a huge makeup case, and, more importantly, her plane ticket. *At least the rest of my luggage is in the hotel here,* she consoled herself, also relieved that she had left her passport in the hotel safe box.

When she tried to report the theft to the French police, she discovered that all the things she'd read and heard about the lackadaisical French attitude were completely true. She'd thought they were exaggerations meant for the popular imagination. But no—there she was at the police station, going from one office to the other, having her report stamped, and receiving a lecture about women traveling alone.

"These American girls are too independent," a policeman said. "See, madame, what happens? Next time, bring somebody with you."

I don't think there will be a next time, Nina thought, scowling. She didn't appreciate the lecture, especially after she'd had such a good time traveling on her own.

She wanted to run away but needed the police report in order to obtain a replacement of the plane ticket. After a whole day of bureaucratic nonsense, a man finally handed her the report. He looked like he was going to give her another lecture to accompany it, but Nina had no sooner taken the report than she had turned on her heel and left.

The replacement of the plane ticket was also complicated, although somewhat less frustrating, and she ended up with a new departure date. It gave her a few more days in France; she tried to put the unpleasant incident out of her mind so that she could enjoy the rest of her stay.

—⁕—

Nina had a layover in Paris before she caught the flight home. It was almost funny how thoroughly a few airports could suck the joy right out of traveling. After the short domestic flight and several hours spent walking from one terminal to another in De Gaulle Airport, she was exhausted. She boarded the American Airlines plane bound for LA and collapsed into her seat, too tired to feel relieved.

The next thing she knew, a flight attendant had wakened her and was offering her a chicken or fish entrée for dinner. As she struggled to waken enough to reply coherently, Nina noticed that the man beside her was slim and remarkably attractive. She chuckled. At least on this flight she wouldn't have to worry about sharing the armrest with an overweight Ukrainian businessman and his briefcase. That made a nice change.

Seeing that she was now properly awake, Nina's seatmate turned to give her a direct and friendly look. "So where did you travel in France?"

Unaccustomed to conversations with strangers, Nina peeked at him slantwise in hesitation. Evidently he had no problem striking up a conversation with a fellow passenger; his large dark eyes were filled with expectant interest.

"But I forget my manners," he said. "My name's Marco. I'm returning to LA from a business trip."

"I'm Nina. I was at a wedding in Provence."

Marco smiled. "That's my very favorite region in France."

"Yes, it was breathtaking, so beautiful." Nina's words tumbled out of her mouth. She felt nervous and excited.

"Have you been to France before?" he asked.

"A few times," she said, sitting up straighter. Marco was a handsome man with a charming and engaging manner. *Is he just being polite or is he truly interested?* She hadn't played the attraction game in a long time and felt as though she were on foreign ground.

"And do you usually travel alone?"

Nina hesitated. "I, uh… no, I don't. Travel. I don't travel alone."

"I see," he said. His warm brown eyes urged Nina to spill her secrets.

"I'm divorced," she blurted. A second later, she wondered if she'd made a mistake, sounded too blunt. She didn't want to drive him off.

"I'm sorry. I, too, am a fellow traveler."

Nina felt disappointment course through her body. He'd seemed so nice; she'd thought they were clicking. "Yes, we're on the same airplane."

Marco touched Nina on her shoulder and flashed her a grin, the epitome of compassion and friendliness. "No, pretty lady. I only meant that I'm divorced too."

"Oh." Nina blushed, placing her hand on the base of her throat. The "pretty lady" comment had ruffled her more than it should have, but she was pleased. "Sorry. I'm so embarrassed."

"Why?" His grin morphed into a big smile. "It's a common condition these days. Just a sign of the times."

"I suppose you're right," Nina said, smiling back. "What's your business?"

"Cosmetics."

Nina's expression lit up as she remembered how she'd wanted to join the glamour industry. But she also became cautious. She'd heard about gigolos and phonies; a man like Marco seemed too good to be true. She asked Marco about his work and he responded with infectious enthusiasm. Although she remained on her guard, she had to admit the conversation lifted her spirits.

Soon the conversation moved on to their respective lives and families. They discovered they had much in common: not only were they both divorced, but they both had two children whom they loved very much. They lived in LA—not far from each other, it turned out. In fact, Marco had lived in LA all his life, and spoke

English, Italian, and Spanish well. He loved to travel and had seen many parts of the world.

Nina found it easy to become comfortable with him. In no time, his sharp sense of humor had her laughing.

When the seatbelt light came on again, Nina blinked up at it in surprise. The twelve-hour flight had seemed ridiculously short, and she knew exactly who she had to thank. Marco had kept her amused for the entire journey. With Marco, she was able to be herself—more herself that she usually was. She couldn't remember having so much fun or feeling so special in a long time.

After the airplane landed, Marco stood up to get their luggage out of the overhead compartment.

"Nina," he said, "this has been really enjoyable. I was wondering, would you like to go out to dinner with me?"

Nina hesitated. The encounter had been so perfect, but she didn't want to get involved in anything that might hurt her later. *Maybe I should just stop here and keep a happy memory.*

"Please?" Marco said.

Nina looked at him. He was still fresh and confident after the long journey, and his smile, his face, his good manners won her over completely.

"Yes," she said. "I would really like that."

———

After they parted, buyer's remorse set in. Nina trudged through the airport to find the rest of her luggage, wondering. Had she done the right thing in accepting a dinner date from a total stranger just because they'd had some fun conversation on a long, boring flight? She felt young and naïve again, worried about making wrong choices and being deceived by a charmer.

Her mom was eager to hear about Nina's adventures in France, but Nina ended up talking about Marco instead. As she voiced her doubts, she realized her mother was smiling at her fondly.

"My dear, you can't stop living or loving out of fear of being hurt," Estela said.

"I guess."

"And remember, it's better to have loved and lost than…"

"Yes, I know," Nina said.

As she got ready for her dinner date, Nina had to smile to herself. This felt like being young all over again, but with a twist. She was a mature woman who had learned a lot from her life, yet she could still get butterflies in her stomach. Far from making her more nervous, the butterflies added to her anticipation. She hadn't had an attack of nerves in a while. She hoped Marco was worth it.

Nina went to her date armed with her life lessons. She didn't want to be paranoid, but she did want to be careful. She was getting too old to make mistakes.

When they met in the restaurant, Marco's smile reassured her completely. He was genuinely pleased to see her again, and his conversation was even more witty and carefree than before.

Nina trusted her instincts. When she listened to them, they told her the difference between a phony person and an honest person. Marco was honest. The more she was with him, the more she realized that she never felt anything but good about him. He could make her laugh until her sides ached, yet she trusted him to never use his charm to take advantage of her. There was no phony pretense or braggadocio about him. Throughout their dinner together, he made no attempt, however small, to control or manipulate her.

Nina felt her guard relax. She didn't need it. She felt safe; she felt appreciated. *This is amazing.*

Their conversations about the struggles of single parenthood went beyond empathetic; they were *simpatico* on the matter. But Marco's sense of humor surprised her: he saw the absurdities in circumstances

Nina regarded as grim, not mirthful. He could make her laugh at her own troubles. After that first shock, she realized how wonderful it was not to take her hardships so seriously. She felt as though she had conquered them more thoroughly than ever before.

Marco was truly special. *Or maybe he's just a nice man,* she thought, *and I haven't had much experience with men, nice or otherwise.* She didn't count being married as having "experience with men"—that had been more like a battle of wills.

—*∿∿*—

Nina started dating Marco on a regular basis, and quickly introduced him to her mom and kids. To her delight, they were as fond of Marco as she was. He was a good man, honest and compassionate, and he placed an important emphasis on family. Marco enjoyed being with her family, and Nina felt like she had always belonged in Marco's family: his two children were as charming and friendly as their father. Things felt right.

Far from isolating her, Nina's relationship with Marco extended her connections. The two shared a large group of friends. A true Angelino, Marco liked the glitzy Hollywood life and was always dragging Nina to parties, charities, and other social functions. Nina had missed the social life of Argentina when she moved to America; even her outings with Joyce and Paulette hadn't quite filled the gap. At last she felt like she was catching up; Marco's energy was boundless.

She soon discovered how much Marco enjoyed taking cruises and frequent vacations. From the beginning, he was eager to bring Nina along.

"Remember," she said, smiling, "I do have a job."

"You do," he said, "and I want to support you in that. Still, remember to enjoy life too. There's so much out there."

Marco accommodated his life to Nina's routine without complaint.

Her job started feeling like a career instead of a necessity. As she became more confident in her work, she grew more at ease and more outgoing in her love life. Unlike bored or overburdened married couples, she and Marco were free to explore, to revel, to enjoy.

Nina ended up going on a couple cruises with Marco: one to the Mediterranean and one to the Baltic sea. As she strolled along the deck in deep conversation with Marco, Nina felt full of peace and joy. The beautiful voyage seemed emblematic of their relationship: together they were traveling far, discovering a new world. Nina had never imagined she could enjoy a man's company so much. Every time she looked at Marco, she felt lucky beyond belief.

One night at dinner, Nina sighed with pure happiness. "It's so wonderful to feel trouble-free and not stressed. It's like I could fly."

Marco, in a way she had learned was typical of him, didn't automatically agree.

"Let's face it, Nina. When we are young and struggling with life's problems, we can't be carefree. With an empty nest and new partners, of course everything can be wonderful… in the beginning. The trick is to keep it that way."

Before he could sound too serious, he took her hand and grinned. Nina knew he was completely sincere when he said, "Darling, you are the wind beneath my wings."

Thrilled by this level of honesty, Nina realized it had bonded her to him even more.

—⁓—

Popular songs, especially those of Nina's youth, promised that "love is better the second time around," but Nina was still hesitant about the subject of marriage. Like every divorced person, she feared making a mistake, even though the conventional wisdom and her mother's advice suggested that the risk would be worth it. Nina knew she could never marry a man her children disliked, but David and Vanessa both adored Marco. It seemed promising.

Still, Nina couldn't help but watch Marco intently, waiting for him to do something wrong. Marco bore up well under her caution. Instead of withdrawing from her, he remained outgoing and fun, as confident and inviting as ever.

"I don't want to rush into any decision, no matter how right it seems," Nina told Estela. "People with families and assets have to think out a second marriage very carefully."

"I see." Estela looked ever-so-slightly amused. "The carefree abandon of youth has passed?"

"It has."

"But you've got experience now," Estela said. "Your youth may be over, but that doesn't mean you have to make yourself suffer."

Nina had to admit that she had missed a full and rewarding social life, and the one Marco gave her reminded her of Argentina. That nostalgic connection was a good one, she knew—politics and economics aside.

As she looked back on her first two years with Marco, Nina saw that they had been remarkably fulfilling in every regard. She knew she was ready to commit fully to Marco, and he told her, in no uncertain terms, that he felt the same way.

Although Nina would enter this second marriage with less naiveté than the first, her joy was just as great and her wisdom much greater. As she prepared for the simple wedding ceremony that would be attended by family and close friends, Nina saw that she looked as stunning as she had all those years before. Only one change mattered: her eyes were bright with new understanding.

—◦∿◦—

Nina felt like she had finally emerged from a long, dark tunnel.

Chapter Twenty-One

Shattered Happiness

California sunshine filled the kitchen with a warm glow. Nina sat at the kitchen table, absorbed in the Sunday *LA Times*. She normally enjoyed the little pleasures in life, like reading the newspaper on a leisurely Sunday morning with a cup of coffee at her side. The bulk of her normally light breakfast still lay on the table, untouched. One article had her full interest.

Marco shuffled in, but Nina kept staring at the paper.

He stopped. "Nina, you haven't eaten your breakfast. What's wrong?"

Nina didn't answer. It took some prompting before she said, "I'm all right, sweetheart. It's just I've read something in the paper that's really disturbing."

"And that is?" he asked as he sat opposite her.

She still seemed reluctant to talk and tried to change the subject, "Would you like some breakfast?"

"I would rather you told me what's upsetting you so much."

After gathering her thoughts, she said, "It's about Argentina in the late '70s and early '80s."

"Oh," he said. "The bad times."

"For a country full of bad times, those times were the worst. Thousands and thousands of people disappeared. It says here in the article most of the people who disappeared were tortured and killed.

Even those proven innocent weren't returned because they would have told the world what happened to them." Nina took a deep breath and continued. "I remember people, mostly mothers, forming large groups in the plazas and marching with signs, protesting their missing children. It was a terrible thing to see. All they wanted to know was what had happened to their loved ones. Even those who believed they were already dead wanted their remains, so they could at least give them a proper burial and have a grave to visit."

Her eyes were glossy with tears, and her hands trembled imperceptibly. Every time she remembered the dark times in the '70s that had devastated her country, she felt a strong compulsion to obliterate the events from her memory. Unfortunately she couldn't.

Nina knew Marco sympathized with her but didn't know what to say. He was not able to fully understand her feelings about the matter. Although he was a kind person, he was pragmatic. He would attribute her strong emotions to the fact she'd been forced to relinquish what she saw as her part in her country's history. He often said Nina had "the Argentine drama." These intense feelings were the same depths of passion that had given birth to dramatic tango lyrics.

"This article says they're beginning to gather evidence concerning what happened to the thousands of pregnant women who disappeared during the Dirty War, as well as what happened to their children."

Now her husband seemed curious. "What evidence?"

When Nina paused, his face grew grim. "Don't tell me they were…"

"No, no, they weren't killed. I guess even the government wasn't that barbaric."

"Then what happened to them?"

"The infants were either sold or given to any member of the regime who wanted a child or paid enough money."

Marco shook his head in disbelief.

"And the worst of it was the secrecy. Many of the recipients of the children had no interest in who they were or where they came from. I remember those days. Everything was so secret and hush-hush. Nobody dared ask questions about anything."

Marco reached over and took her hand. "From the way you look, it's like you're taking this personally."

"I… I am."

She stopped, and Marco squeezed her hand for reassurance. "What?"

"I'm concerned about David."

Marco looked puzzled. "What about him?"

"I'm afraid someone might think… You see, David was adopted at that time. I couldn't conceive a sibling for Vanessa, so Ernesto and I adopted instead."

"But there's no reason for anyone to think David is the son of a disappeared political prisoner, right? Who would think that?"

"I don't know." In the silent that followed, Nina stared down at the article, chewing her lip. "I know for a fact he's not. But this is unsettling. I have to tell David about this article right away."

Before Marco could answer, she was dialing the phone.

David had grown into a responsible and considerate young man. He was a good son to Nina, very close to his sister, and extremely fond of Marco. He maintained strong family ties with his relatives in Argentina and in America even now that he was a medical student at the University of California, Los Angeles. He was grateful for everything Nina had done for him, and she in turn was very proud of him. She couldn't bear to think that the article might catch him off-guard.

"David, have you read the *LA Times* Metro Section today?"

"No, Mom."

"It's about Argentina back in the '70s."

"Ancient history, Mom. Why would I be interested? Besides, I'm up to my neck in my studies. Midterms are coming up."

"I need to tell you about this. I…"

"Mom. You know I was only two when we left Argentina. How could I know or remember anything?"

"This concerns you," Nina said. Her throat was dry.

"Okay, Mom. What's it about?"

"The late '70s, the Dirty War."

"Yes? What is it?"

"You know, during that time a lot of pregnant women were arrested by the government." Nina spoke softly. "Lots of the women never emerged from the jails and prisons alive."

"Yeah, I suppose so."

"That meant there were lots of infants available, either on the black market or through official channels."

"What's that got to do with us?"

"I just need to assure you about something." Again, she hesitated. "I just want to assure you that even though you too were born during that period, you don't belong to that group of people."

"Sure. Don't worry about it."

"Everything I've told you about your birth is true. I want you to know that. Your biological mother is alive and still lives in Argentina. I have her address and phone number."

David's voice grew softer. "I know, Mom," he said patiently. "There's nothing for you to worry about."

"And if you want to visit her, I will help you. I'll contact her and arrange a visit."

"I understand, Mom. But don't worry about it. I'm not interested." She could hear David smiling as he reassured her. "You and Dad have been my parents since I can remember, and that's good enough for me."

Nina hung up, feeling slightly better. As she reflected, she began to realize people feel differently about their heritage at different times in their lives. David might feel indifferent now, but one day, he might feel an irresistible urge to meet and know his birth parents and his blood relatives. He might one day want to know where he came from.

Nina honored David's wishes and didn't bring the subject up again.

That night when they were ready to go to sleep she told Marco the whole story of David's birth, leaving nothing out. She remembered all the little details attached to the special moment. Marco listened very carefully. After Nina finished, he hugged her tightly and told her he admired the way she had managed the situation for all those years. Once more, Nina cried for all the events that had occurred in Argentina.

The newspaper article was relegated to last place in Nina's mind. The many routine daily tasks in the family took priority.

Vanessa had decided to go to college now that Briana was in elementary school, giving her the time and the motivation to study. She attended community college for two years before she was ready to transfer to California State University, Northridge, to complete her English degree. Vanessa worked hard and was dedicated to school and her studies. Nina and Marco were very proud of her.

In August of 2001, several years after obtaining her green card, Nina applied for American citizenship. Soon after, she was sworn into citizenship in a touching naturalization ceremony. As she recited the Oath of Allegiance, she recalled the bumpy road behind her. She was grateful to God that she was now an American citizen, with all the rights and obligations that came with it.

Just a few days after her passport arrived in the mail, Nina experienced her first shock as an American. Very early one morning, she had started brewing coffee when Vanessa called. Vanessa usually got up early to go to school, but it was unusual for her to call so early. The first thought that crossed Nina's mind was something might be wrong with her little granddaughter.

"Oh, God, Mom. It's so horrible. I don't understand what's going on," Vanessa said. She was sobbing, and Nina could barely make out what she was saying.

"What's wrong? Is Briana okay?" Nina asked. Vanessa sounded so upset that Nina started crying as well, even though she didn't know why. She was sure that something awful had happened to Briana.

"Someone hit the building," was all Nina could make out.

"Someone drove into your building?" Nina was confused, and Vanessa was too incoherent to clarify anything.

"Turn on your TV!" Vanessa screamed.

Nina dropped the phone and ran to the television in the family room. She was looking for the news station, expecting to see something about a drunk driver running into Vanessa's building, but she quickly realized every television station was broadcasting the same thing.

Two airplanes had flown into the World Trade Center towers in New York City.

At the sound of Nina's cry, Marco charged out of the bedroom, still stumbling from sleep.

"What? What? What?" He sat beside Nina and watched the television with her, not understanding what he was seeing.

They sat in silence while the horrifying images repeated over and over: buildings falling, people jumping to their deaths, the wounded fleeing amid clouds of smoke. America was under attack.

"It feels like the violence from Argentina followed me," Nina said.

Marco put his arms around her.

"Why would anyone do this to America?" Nina asked. "I can't believe anyone would be so audacious."

Over the next few weeks, like most Americans, Nina put miniature American flags and other patriotic symbols in her yard and around her home; she donated to the Red Cross and prayed for the families affected by the catastrophe.

Nina's American friends were shocked and didn't know how to react to the terrorist attack. For Nina, however, the attacks brought back a familiar pain that she had never wanted to feel again.

Chapter Twenty-Two

Ghosts from the Past

M arco and Nina were lying on the beach at Waikiki; the sun
dappled over the sparkling blue expanse of the Pacific. The
towering dome of Diamond Head loomed in the distance. Behind
them the soft breezes rustled the coconut palms, the idyllic setting
for their own private Shangri-La.

They spent the morning reading, taking long walks on the
beach, and swimming in the sea, frolicking in the foaming surf. At
lunchtime they started the lazy walk toward the hotel.

As they got ready for lunch in the hotel room, Nina's cell phone
rang. She saw it was David. Nina was excited to share her vacation
stories with him, but the tension in David's voice suggested it would
be a serious call.

"Hi, Mom."

"Hello, David."

"Mom, do you have a minute?" His tone and question were well-
known preludes to troubling situations.

"Yes, I do." Nina's heart rate accelerated. She gestured to Marco
that their leisurely lunch would have to wait.

"Mom, my father wants to talk to you."

Nina's heart sank. "Okay, put him on."

Ernesto was very direct. "Nina, an attorney from Argentina

named Martín came over to the house asking for David, so I gave him David's cell."

"Yes?"

"He said he had a very important matter to discuss and asked if they could meet at a coffee shop alone."

"Yes?" she said, her voice urgent.

"Anyway, they met over a cup of coffee. The attorney had a laptop with him, and he went to a website named for Angela Brando, a woman who disappeared during the '70s. He went on to say he was representing the human rights association called Las Abuelas de Plaza de Mayo—the Grandmothers of May Plaza, the next generation of the Madres of Plaza de Mayo. They haven't been able to locate many lost children and are now looking for their grandchildren who might have been born in prison."

"Oh?" Nina experienced full-blown trauma.

"Martín showed David a picture of Angela and a story about her disappearance," Ernesto said. "He told David that Angela was Martín's aunt and David's birth mother, and insisted that he and David are cousins and that David was supposed to be called Pedro."

"What? That's absurd!" Nina said, her voice quivering.

"It might be absurd, but it's made David uneasy," Ernesto said. "According to Martín, Angela lived in our old neighborhood and her baby was due in mid-September. I guess that was enough of a coincidence to convince David that he's this woman's child. Martín told him that he was born in a jail cell and sold to us."

"Who do these people think they are, telling him such blatant lies? How is he feeling now?"

"When he got back, he said he felt like he's living some bad dream. He's just waiting to wake up. He told the attorney he needs time to digest this information, and arranged to contact him again tomorrow."

"How could he possibly believe this guy?" Nina's voice shook. "What do we do now?"

"I told him to call you and we'd talk about it together. He's right here with me now, really shaken up."

Nina's fear morphed into anger. *The nerve of that attorney, barging into people's lives to disrupt them. What possible good could this information do for anyone involved?* "Put David on the phone, please."

"Hi, Mom." Nina thought David sounded slightly cautious. "This attorney wants me to have a DNA test."

"Why?" Nina asked. "What's the point?"

"I don't know exactly. It's not that I don't trust the story you told me, but I'm confused and I'd just like to be sure. So I agreed."

Her voice softened. "I understand. We'll get to the bottom of this. Call me when you're done talking to him tomorrow."

—*∕∕∕*—

Nina didn't want her anger to ruin the rest of her and Marco's vacation, but the damage was done. They changed flights and headed back to LA the next day.

After they arrived, David told Nina he'd agreed to have a DNA test.

"What will that accomplish?"

"It will clear you and dad of any wrongdoing."

"Whatever made Martín think you're this woman's son?" Nina asked. "What evidence does he have for his accusations?"

"He's not accusing me of anything," David reassured her.

"He's accusing me!"

"Apparently the Abuelas keep files on everyone they think might be one of their grandchildren," David said. "I made him promise to send me my file before I consented to the DNA. He said it's not normally their policy to give out that information, but he'd send it right away when he gets back to Argentina."

Several days later, David received an email from Martín with an attachment. Even though he spoke fluent Spanish, he found that reading the Argentine Spanish was difficult. He printed out the information and brought it so Nina could help translate.

When David and Nina sat at her kitchen table, she was amazed at the size of the stack of papers David brought.

"What's all that?" she asked.

"Martín said they're anonymous letters and phone call transcripts the Abuelas have collected over the years."

Nina picked up the top paper and began to read it. "From July 17, 1985! You were seven." She composed herself and kept reading. "'On July 14, 1985, I learned the details of an adoption of a baby in 1977 or 1978. The father's name is Ernesto Rossi. Rossi is the last name of a general incriminated in the military's crimes who is a relative of Ernesto Rossi. In the year 1977 or 1978, the Rossi family appeared with a boy they said was adopted. This calls attention because the couple never talked about planning to adopt.

"'At the end of the repression, Ernesto Rossi and his wife Nina Salvatti opened a pharmacy. They opened three more pharmacies during 1980 and 1981. Until that time, they had lived from their work, but now they began to show off their assets and money. At the end of 1981, they took the boy and moved to the USA using these mysteriously acquired assets. They then opened a printing factory there.

"'They returned to Argentina in December of 1983, saying they didn't want to raise their kids in a society corrupted by drugs. Throughout 1984, they continued to be ostentatious with their fortune.

"'When the trial of the military juntas began, they learned about the crimes that were coming to light. They moved back to the USA a few months later, which seemed suspicious. Nina's mother currently lives in Caballito at the corner of Yerbal and Espinosa and is known in the area as Telly.'"

Nina was shocked. Lucia used to call her mother Telly. *Could Lucia have written and sent this letter?*

Nina looked up at David. They stared at each other. Nina didn't know where to begin to defend herself. She scanned the letter again.

"We were not related to anyone in the military," she said. "I never talked about more children because it's no one else's business. We worked very hard to build all our businesses. And no one outside of the family knows your grandmother as Telly."

David interrupted. "Mom, you don't have to read these if they are too upsetting. It's no big deal."

"This is obviously from a family member or a close family friend. These aren't details a mere stranger would know."

"You don't have to translate more of this if it's going to make you upset."

Rage built inside Nina as her mind frantically searched for clues in the letters as to who would say such things against her.

She picked up the next letter and read it out loud. "Previous to the adoption of a boy, the couple had a biological daughter. This makes the circumstances of the adoption more suspicious. The address in the USA for the boy's uncle, the mother's brother, is 7526 Flower Ave # 12, Tarzana, California, USA, 91356. Good luck! God bless you!'"

"How did they know Uncle Eduardo's address?" David asked.

"I don't know," Nina said. "I suppose your grandmother wrote a lot of letters to friends and family back home. She must have used his address as her return address."

Shaking her head, Nina picked up another piece of paper. "'October 23, 1985. Ernesto Rossi is married to a pharmacist, with whom he invested military money in pharmacies in the south area. The parents of the wife are Miguel Salvatti and Telly Salvatti. They run a small business. The Rossis left the country, but returned to Argentina in April or May of 1981. They left again in 1983 after obtaining more military money. They have a biological daughter. During the "Process," they suddenly appeared with a boy. They named him David, and they claimed he was adopted. They had a nanny for David and a lot of money. No one seemed to know where it came from.'"

Nina grabbed the entire stack of papers and flipped through them. "They all say the same thing. Listen to this." She began reading various sentences from each of the papers. "'In 1977 or 1978, Ernesto Rossi and Nina Salvatti bought a baby boy they named Daniel from a clandestine hospital.' They didn't even get your name right! 'Seems the couple is divorced and the minor is living with the father. A captain gave the baby to a family friend, who gave the baby to the Rossis.'"

The last sentence Nina read gave her pause. "They couldn't mean Marta, could they?"

"The woman who set up my adoption?" David asked.

"Yes. She was a secretary at a government office. She had nothing to do with the military. I saw her talking with your birth mother at a coffee shop. We were all there the night you were born. She knows you weren't given to me by some military officer."

"So you saw my birth?"

"We weren't in the delivery room, but we saw you in the nursery when you were minutes old," Nina said.

David tried to take the papers from her.

Nina jerked them back. "No! I will translate every last one of these for you."

"Mom, it's not important. Why read so many lies?"

"Listen to this. 'When investigations started, the whole family left the country in a hurry. Eduardo Salvatti moved to the USA with military money in April of 1982. In the airport, he looked desperate.'" From another letter, she read, "'The adopted boy now goes to UCLA.' You just started going there a few months ago!"

Nina's nervous laugh sounded too loud to her, but she couldn't stifle it.

"Mom, please. I don't believe any of what these say."

"Don't you understand? Close family and friends betrayed my trust. These letters are dated all the way from 1985 to just a few months ago."

One letter caught Nina's attention, because it was signed by someone she recognized. "'I personally know the mother, Nina Salvatti, a pharmacist, has a girl named Vanessa (legitimate daughter) and a boy, David Rossi. They are both registered as legitimate children, but the boy's birth certificate has been faked. They live in USA, and the couple is divorced. In September 1978, all of a sudden, they had another baby. Between '82 and '83, they left abruptly after the military trials started, and later they came back to stay a short period to get more money.' Signed, Jorge Varela."

"Who's that?" David asked as he put his arm around his mother.

Nina's hatred prevented her from explaining. All she could do was cry.

The number of reports denouncing Nina and Ernesto and accusing them of crimes was completely overwhelming. Nina never could have imagined such vicious, unfounded accusations.

Trying to think of an explanation for the inexplicable, Nina could only remember how jealous and vindictive Argentines could be. The culture encouraged revenge. Witch-hunting had been practiced since the Middle Ages, and was certainly honed to a fine art by the time the Argentine military decided to kill pregnant mothers. The Abuelas' actions seemed like the beginning of a new witch-hunt, now headed by previous victims.

Nina accepted the paranoia faced by people in Argentina during the Dirty War, but it was another thing to be able to accept the accusations and poison directed at her when she knew she was innocent.

The letters talked about Nina and Ernesto being involved with the military and given money and eventually the "gift" of a child. They never specified what the couple had done to be awarded the baby. Nina knew she and Ernesto had left the country because Ernesto was disgusted with the way the military had been running the country. In these letters, they were being accused of accepting handouts from the same military. Nina was disgusted. Although lines from the letters ran through her head over and over, she couldn't fully grasp how outrageous the accusations were.

It took a few weeks for David to return his blood sample to Martín. The blood sample had to be taken in a special laboratory the United States government provided for the Abuelas within the Argentine Consulate. David was told it was impossible for the sample to be falsified that way.

David called Nina when he returned home after giving blood.

"I still can't believe this is happening to me," he said. "It seems like a movie or a bad dream."

"I know, dear." Nina couldn't even imagine how he felt. "It will all be over soon, and they'll realize what we've known your whole life."

"There was a girl about my age in the waiting room with me," David said. "We avoided talking to each other; we didn't even make eye contact! What they're asking us to do seems so shameful. Even if we are stolen children, that's not our fault. We're victims."

"I know, but someone led them to believe your father and I are the enemy," Nina said.

For Nina the most disturbing part of the whole sordid affair was that only the people close to her and Ernesto could have supplied the accusations. Many details that had been exposed had only ever been disclosed to close friends and family members. Instead of honoring their relationship, those people had provided a pack of lies in order to hurt Nina and Ernesto. It made Nina feel ill to be so betrayed.

While she knew the accusations weren't true, Nina couldn't tell what David believed. To think that anyone, complete strangers or family, could think she was capable of such horrors was incredibly hurtful. Except for one name mentioned, all the accusations were from anonymous sources. Jorge Varela's address from a popular resort where the Varelas had a vacation home was the only address mentioned. The whole affair left her with feelings of distrust and suspicion and a definite paranoia about her friends and associates.

It took Nina a while before she could even mention the ordeal to Marco, Eduardo, and finally with Estela. As she anticipated, they too were flabbergasted and enraged. Their response encouraged Nina. In the far corners of her mind, she knew she could find a way to end the awful injustice.

Chapter Twenty-Three

Taking Stock of Everyone

❧

Nina decided to put her analytical mind to work to solve the mystery. She sorted through the information contained in the letters, trying to figure out who would want to betray her and her family and, most importantly, why. Unfortunately, her blood boiled with rage whenever she thought about it, making it harder for her to see things logically. Vanessa phoned, and the two decided to discuss it at dinner as soon as possible.

At dinner, Vanessa reminisced about her memories of David. As a little girl, she had been as closely involved with her little brother as any mother.

With a rare smile, Nina said, "I remember how you used your little brother; you needed to be with him as an excuse for skipping your homework."

"But, Mom, it wasn't about skipping my homework. I really liked being like a mother back then. I loved David and everything about caring for him too."

Nina sipped some coffee, drifting down memory lane too. "I remember the little scam you had going with Mr. Rivera, the piano teacher, and Fernanda, the nanny."

Vanessa grinned. "Wasn't I a little brat?"

"Yes. You were never ready for your lesson, so you'd have

Fernanda fix your piano teacher a coffee while you tried to prepare in your bedroom. He always forgave you for not being ready."

With a far-off look, Vanessa said, "He was the best. And Fernanda was always so thoughtful. Do you remember that she wrote down everything David and I ever did? She said we would be grateful later in life when we forgot what we were like as children."

"Her diary must have been ten thousand pages long," Nina said.

"She never told on me when I went into your closet to try on your clothes."

"One day, you chose the new gown I was going to wear to a gala that night. You were admiring yourself in the mirror when I came in, and in your dash to hide in the closet, you stepped on the hem and ripped the dress."

"It wasn't a complete loss, Mom."

"No. The remnants made a very nice cocktail dress," Nina said. Thinking of Fernanda, she wondered aloud, "You don't think she wrote down her thoughts about the family and sent them to the Abuelas, do you?"

"She didn't give us anything she wrote." Vanessa shrugged. "I know she said they'd help me remember my childhood, but I remember it all anyway. I remember when you and Dad told me I was going to have a new brother in four months. That was a happy day for me."

"What you didn't know was the inefficient mess the Argentine bureaucracy was, and how they messed up most aspects of the adoption process. David's birth mother was not one of the disappeared, so his was a regular adoption. Considering the circumstances then, we weren't able to do it strictly according to the letter of the law. But he wasn't smuggled goods from a prison. The Abuelas are suspicious of David today because they went looking for irregular birth certificates. In his case that was necessary in order for us to get him at all."

"That's probably what brought his adoption to somebody's attention," Vanessa said. "Think about it. Those irregularities must have been a red flag to someone. Eventually someone got hold of the information and distorted it in order to hurt you."

Of course this revelation didn't help calm the angry waters of Nina's soul. Someone she knew—presumably a friend or relative—wished her so much ill will that he or she would concoct and spread blatant lies.

When Vanessa saw the anger building in her mother, she tried to calm her down before the evening was ruined. "We don't know anything for certain. It could have been just one person who wrote all the letters, not everyone you've ever met."

"No matter how many people wrote to the Abuelas, the hate in the letters is the same," Nina said.

"The chance of finding out exactly who wrote those things about you is almost impossible. What can you do about it now? David believes you."

"The Abuelas will just keep hounding us until I can prove without a doubt that what I'm saying is true."

"How will you do that?" Vanessa asked.

"I'll locate David's birth mother."

After that dinner, Nina began calling anyone who would talk to her two or three times a day, seeking answers. Nina could tell that Marco was becoming more and more concerned. He thought her search had gone beyond the point of disappointment and family intrigue, toward an obsession. *Maybe he's right,* she thought. Either way, Nina knew she had to be vindicated.

Ernesto wrote a letter to the Abuelas on behalf of Nina and himself, explaining the circumstances of David's adoption. He tried to explain the tenor of the times and the chaos and confusion that reigned during the Dirty War.

He wrote that David's mother was not one of those carted off by the authorities to have their babies in jail to be put up for adoption, either on the black market or to influential citizens. David had not been adopted according to the strict letter of the law, which hadn't even been possible in those days, but his adoption certainly had nothing to do with the terrible practices of the Argentine military and authorities involving the children of those who disappeared.

—⁓—

A few weeks later, David was notified that his DNA did not match any the Abuelas organization had on file. Unwilling to let him or the family off the hook, they advised him that they might require his future cooperation.

Nina was shocked. How could a so-called "human rights" organization try to dig up facts that simply weren't there? In her mind, the Abuelas' accusations were the lowest level of speculation, hurting entire families. She and Ernesto had done nothing more illegal than sign an adoption paper with an incorrect name, and only for the sake of expediency. They'd done nothing to merit this persecution.

It seemed so ironic that the activists who had lost family members during the height of the government's witch-hunting were now witch-hunting themselves. Nina couldn't accept it. *Don't they see the hypocrisy in trying to lay blame on anyone they can?* They were being grossly insensitive to other affected Argentines. The women killed in the jails weren't the only victims of the Dirty War, but the Abuelas seemed to have forgotten that.

—⁓—

Nina thought it would be easier to clear her name if she went back to where it all started. A few months later she flew back to

Argentina. During the long flight, sleep eluded her. David's file with the accusation letters was in her overnight bag, stowed away in the overhead luggage compartment. She was tempted to pull it down and reread it for the umpteenth time, but she resisted the urge in order to avoid disturbing fellow passengers.

After dinner and the onboard movie, the passengers began to socialize and relax. Nina noticed a woman in a red sweater across the aisle, a bald man whose head stuck out above the front seat headrest, and a young student with glasses and spiky hair carrying a backpack and a laptop. She imagined the lives they were living. Who were they visiting? Above all, she wondered if any of them had had to deal with the same kind of ordeal that she was experiencing.

It was hard for Nina not to consider which of the different people in her life might have written to the Abuelas. Jorge Varela had known Nina since she was a little girl. She had no idea what would prompt him to think she was capable of buying a baby. In her eyes, his connection to bribing military officials was more suspicious than anything Nina had ever done in her entire life. Her distant family members had always seemed jealous that she moved to America, but she didn't know how far their vindictiveness might have gone. The last Nina heard about Fernanda, the children's nanny, she had met a rich man through the newspaper, married him, and was living happily in America with two children of her own.

Nina wondered if an old business associate or friend she hadn't spoken to in years might have held a grudge. She thought about all her former business partners at the pharmacy, but they had all seemed so happy for her and Ernesto. Marta had set up the adoption all those years ago, but Nina hadn't spoken to her since the first time the Rossis moved to America. She had shared in one of the happiest moments of Nina's life, and then she had seemed to vanish. Nina hadn't directly talked to José and Lucia in years. The last contact Nina had was when Estela told her Lucia had called looking for

Ernesto's address in America because she wanted to send him a birthday card. Ernesto had told Nina that he had never received a card from Lucia.

Upon landing, Nina again experienced the warm déjà vu feeling she always felt upon returning to her homeland. It wasn't until she'd passed through customs that the genuine feeling of homecoming swept over her, moving her to her very core.

Argentina was the land of the tango. She heard the music in every taxi, store, restaurant, and hotel lobby, attesting to the country's love of the dance. Buenos Aires, with its elegant French style townhouses and the Recoleta, the great nineteenth-century French-style building, seemed so European to her, so cosmopolitan, a city where young people socialized and intellectualized until the break of dawn. The parks of Palermo resembled the parks in the Bois de Boulogne in Paris. Few in Buenos Aires started dinner before nine in the evening, and the theaters didn't let out until after one in the morning. Some patrons dined after the theater, and the streets of the district were busy until first light. It gave Nina pleasure to rediscover that Buenos Aires was always busy and alive.

But this time Nina's stay in her beloved homeland was fraught with suspicion, making her feel even more like a stranger. She wondered whether every friend and relative was the traitor, the one who had caused her infamy. She told everyone what had happened, not with the glee of a gossiper but rather with the thoughtful, inquisitive demeanor of a detective as she tried to ascertain who might be guilty.

When Nina gathered with some of her family members, a distant cousin tried to comfort her. "What's happening to you is just outrageous! How is Daniel handling all this?"

"David is fine… He's really taking it well."

Nina stopped herself. One of the letters referred to David as Daniel. She continued talking and accepted her family's concern, but she found herself on guard. She knew many of her family members envied her move to America, but she couldn't believe anyone would stoop to the level of lying about her and David to an organization like the Abuelas.

—⟫⟫—

At the beginning of a workday morning, Nina walked into the head director's office of the Abuelas. The woman sitting behind the desk barely looked thirty, far too young to remember the events of the Dirty War, even if she'd lived through them. She glanced up from her papers and stared at Nina over her horned-rimmed glasses. "Can I help you?"

Nina seriously doubted the woman could help her. *How the hell would she know what things were like back then?* "I'd like to speak to the director."

"Uh huh. About what?"

Nina cleared her throat. "An adoption."

The girl shook her head. Disgust rolled off her in waves. "Let me guess. You stole a child and now you want to keep it."

"No, nothing like that. I've already adopted a child. Legitimately."

"Right." Her voice dripped with barely suppressed sarcasm.

Nina knew she should just walk away, but she felt compelled to explain herself. She needed to convince this skeptical young woman that she spoke nothing but the truth. "I adopted a young boy because his mom couldn't keep him. She needed my help."

"And you have the proper adoption papers, I suppose?"

Nina hesitated, staring at the girl's stony face. "Well, no. You see, we went to the doctor and he…"

"Oh, I see." The girl looked utterly unsympathetic. "You don't have legitimate adoption papers. That's clear enough."

Tears tugged at the corners of Nina's eyes. "It just… it would have taken time."

"So, basically, what you did was illegal."

"No!" Nina shouted.

"Don't raise your voice to me," the woman said.

Nina couldn't hold the tears back any longer. Horrified and angry, she felt them trickle down her face.

The girl sneered. "Save your tears. I've seen them before. I don't suppose you ever thought about the tears of the mother whose child you stole?"

Nina continued to sob. She wanted to shout back at this girl, make her see the truth, but pain and frustration kept the words from forming inside her head. All she could do was cry. Without another word, Nina rushed from the office.

———————

That night Nina had dinner with Giovanna, in whom she had the utmost trust. Such people were very few and far between in her present life. Giovanna had made dinner reservations at Las Lilas, located in Puerto Madero, a recently renovated area by the river full of restaurants, where people could dine al fresco.

As they sipped cocktails at their table listening to the river lap at the banks, the two women discussed the situation.

"The way the letters talk about me, I was afraid I'd be stopped at customs and thrown in jail," Nina said.

"If you had something to do with this, they would have nabbed you at the airport," Giovanna said.

As a high-powered lawyer, Giovanna had a lot of contacts, a necessity in Argentina. She had worked with several prominent television personalities in the past, which gave Nina an idea.

"I want to go on TV," she said. "I want to tell my side of the story.

The people of Argentina must know that what the Abuelas are doing now is just as bad as what the military did to their children."

"Nina, I don't need to remind you that this is not America. People don't have the privilege of free speech, on television or in print. Think of all the ups and downs of Argentinean political life, where middle class people always get the short end of the stick. Today's reality might not be tomorrow's reality. You really should count yourself lucky you got out in time and just let it go," Giovanna said.

"Can you help me somehow?" Nina asked. Giovanna's lack of enthusiasm frustrated her. Surely her friend should care more about helping to clear her name. "Could you get David's birth mother to give her DNA so I can prove to the Abuelas they have no claim to David?"

"Now that David's not a child anymore, he would have to make the request for his birth mother's DNA."

"So unless I get him even more involved, there's no way to prove what I say is true?" Nina felt discouraged as she felt her possibilities narrow. She looked desperately to her friend for help. "Please, anything you can do for me would mean the world to me. Here are some hair samples from David."

Giovanna took the plastic bag with David's hair in it and put it in her purse. She regarded her friend with a worried look. "I'll look into it, but don't get your hopes up. I'll call you if I can do anything."

For the rest of the evening, they avoided the topic, but it was all Nina could think about.

As Nina said goodbye to Giovanna, she heard a familiar laugh at the front of the restaurant. She couldn't believe her eyes when she recognized José and Lucia.

"Lucia?" Nina asked.

"Oh, my! Nina, I didn't know you still came back to Argentina. I hear you have it pretty good in America." Lucia hugged Nina.

Nina noticed José's suit had a frayed hem around the jacket, and Lucia's dress was faded and worn in places. Nina knew once their tattered clothes became obvious to everyone, they wouldn't try to get into such nice restaurants. She started to feel sorry for them before remembering how they had gloated over her own misfortune after her divorce.

"So what are you doing here?" Lucia inquired.

Nina normally didn't share her personal details outside of close friends and family, but she felt compelled to tell Lucia about the Abuelas's accusatory letters.

"My son David received some letters accusing me of illegally adopting him after his birth mother was murdered in the Dirty War," Nina said. "Someone just showed up at my son's house and told him that. Can you believe it?"

"It's shocking," José murmured.

"It looks like someone I knew and trusted accused me of this," Nina said. "Who would say such awful things about me to strangers?"

"It wasn't me!" Lucia said. José glanced at her nervously.

Her defensive response made Nina curious. "Nobody said it was you."

"Well, you just said that it was someone you knew and trusted. And I'm just saying that I would never do something like that to you."

"Oh, look, our table's ready," José interrupted.

"Sorry we couldn't catch up more. Call me. Maybe we can get together while you are still here," Lucia said. She and José both hurried off before Nina could respond.

Chapter Twenty-Four

Lessons Learned

The next morning, Nina decided to explore the neighborhood where she had grown up. Although a number of changes met her eyes, it was easy for her to look past them to her memories of the place. She had strolled down these streets many times before. Her memories burst with the moments she'd shared here with her mother and her best friend: all the Septembers they'd spent shopping for birthday presents, the days she and Giovanna had walked to their tutor's home with their minds full of their future plans, that special night she had spent on a first date with Ernesto.

She smiled when she came across the small market where her mother had bought so many birthday party supplies. Every time she turned a year older, that was magic—wasn't that what her mother had said? It was true. Every year had bound Nina's life closer to each building and corner. The familiar smells and sounds were as closely connected to her as the memories they evoked.

She wandered down one street after another until her feet began to ache, drawing her out of her pleasant reminiscences. Looking around, she spotted a familiar café: the little shop where David's birth mother had agreed to let Nina and Ernesto raise her baby. That event had been real and true, no matter what the Abuelas said. It seemed fitting that her ramblings should have brought her here.

Stepping into the café, Nina saw it was much as she remembered.

The paint had been freshened up, while the tiles had grown more faded, but the espresso coffee machine still occupied its prominent place behind the white marble counter. A variety of croissants and pastries lay in a tempting display underneath. A younger couple talked animatedly in a corner, their cups of tea cooling before them, and an elderly man read a newspaper near the window.

As Nina ordered a cup of coffee, she tried not to stare at the table where Laura, her mother, and Marta had agreed upon the terms of David's adoption more than two decades before.

A middle-aged woman was sitting there now. The years hung heavily on her face and shoulders. She scowled at the young couple and tensed if anyone passed too closely, but Nina saw a longing for companionship in her eyes. Nina understood that.

The waiter approached the woman's table, bending to ask if he could refill or freshen her coffee. The woman smiled as she looked up to reply and the waiter chatted with her as he poured more coffee.

This comfortable exchange and easy smile seemed so different from the woman's usual behavior that Nina suspected she was a regular patron at the café, someone known and liked by the staff. She wore sturdy shoes and carried a good-sized bag, so she probably lived in the neighborhood. Her presence at the table where Laura and her mother had once spoken to Marta seemed to Nina to be a good omen for her investigations.

Nina knew the bits and pieces of Laura's life story that she'd been able to accumulate over the years from her mother and a few of Laura's neighbors. She'd always kept Laura's address and phone number for David in case he ever wanted to contact her. Now she remembered that this was Laura's neighborhood. That seemed like a good sign too.

Deciding it was now or never, Nina wandered in the woman's direction with her cup of coffee in hand. On her way to a window table, she bumped against her chair.

"Oh, I'm so sorry," she said.

The woman smiled. "It's nothing."

"I love this coffee shop," Nina said. A little of her drink had spilled on the table. She started to mop it up with her handkerchief.

"Yes, it's very nice," the woman said.

"I came here a lot when I was younger," Nina said. "Have you lived in this neighborhood a long time?"

"Oh, yes," the woman said, "ever since I was a young girl."

"Funny we've never met before then," Nina said. "My name is Nina."

"Mine's Carmen. I've never seen you—at least, that I can recall."

"I live in California these days. I'm only back in Argentina for a short time," Nina said. "Not long enough."

When Carmen smiled, Nina rallied the rest of her courage. "Do you mind if I join you?"

"Not at all." Carmen pushed back the chair beside her. "I'd love the company."

Nina settled down at the table. Her brief return to Argentina gave her the perfect excuse to ask questions about the people in the neighborhood; excited to have someone to talk with, Carmen was only too glad to catch her up on local news. Gradually it became evident that she knew Laura and her mother quite well.

"At least, I know Laura as well as she *can* be known," Carmen said. "She stays in the same house, never talks to anyone, follows the rules her mother laid down in her childhood. It's very sad."

"Her mother is so controlling even now that her daughter is grown up?" Nina asked.

Carmen shook her head. "Laura's mother passed away ten years ago. She died of cancer."

"How terrible!" Nina said.

"And Laura lived her whole life with this woman; she never

married, never had children. Now she cleans offices at night for very little money."

It seemed that no one knew Laura had ever had a child. Marta had assured Nina that Laura's pregnancy had been hidden from the world; apparently Marta had been completely right. Nina respected her secret and didn't mention anything about it. She only thought to herself that Laura's story was sadder than Carmen even knew: to all intents and purposes, her life had ended the moment she got pregnant with David.

After a good half-hour, Nina's cellphone rang. Glancing down, Nina saw that it was Giovanna. She excused herself as gracefully as possible, exchanged goodbyes with Carmen, and stepped out into the street to answer.

"Giovanna! Do you have any good news for me?"

"I do indeed," Giovanna said. "When can we get together?"

"As soon as possible. Tonight?"

"Sure. I'm free for dinner," Giovanna said.

As she and Giovanna agreed upon a time and place, Nina felt her excitement grow. Her string of bad news seemed to have finally reached an end. Perhaps Giovanna had found a way to sue the Abuelas. Maybe she'd persuaded Laura to agree to a DNA test. *Whatever it is, if Giovanna thinks it's good news, I'm sure it won't let me down,* Nina thought.

That evening, Nina reached the restaurant first. She sat stiffly at the table, tapping her fingers against its dark wood as she sipped her water.

Giovanna arrived five minutes later, smiling widely and holding a large envelope.

"Lovely to see you so soon, Nina," she said, slipping into the seat across from her.

Nina leaned forward, resisting the urge to snatch the envelope from her hand. "What is it? What's your news?"

"You, my friend, have good luck on your side," Giovanna said. "Just a few days ago, I talked to the lawyer who handled the death of Laura's mother. It turned out that she left something for David in her will."

Nina stared. "Really? But why didn't he receive it ten years ago when she died?"

"It wasn't a letter or heirloom. Nothing so ordinary as that," Giovanna said. "She left him her DNA in case he ever wanted to find her or his mother."

"It's a miracle." Nina slumped back in her chair, awash in her relief.

"Rather a sad one," Giovanna said. "The lawyer indicated that Laura's still in denial about David, but apparently her mother hoped he would find them in her lifetime."

"So now what?"

"I submitted a request on your behalf." Giovanna tapped the envelope, but kept it on her lap. "These are the results."

"Thank you so much," Nina said. "I don't know how I can repay—"

"I think you need to consider David in all this," Giovanna said.

Nina jerked back. "What do you mean?" she asked. "This is as much for him as it is for me. He needs to know for certain where he comes from. And once he knows, the Abuelas will have to leave us alone."

"The lawyer insisted that Laura doesn't want to meet David," Giovanna said. "She wants to forget the past, forget she ever had a son."

"It's sad, yes…"

"From what you've told me, David believes you. He doesn't want evidence. He doesn't need to be convinced." Giovanna frowned. "If you share this information with him, he may be inspired to try to meet her. A number of people could be hurt."

Nina shook her head. She didn't want to hear this. *This is the best way to clear my name. Maybe the only way.* "David is grown," she said. "He can handle it."

"Can he? Are you willing to risk his happiness?"

Giovanna had a point, but Nina didn't feel like conceding it. Not yet. She set her jaw. *Damn you. I'm so close to resolving all this.*

Giovanna sighed unhappily. "Nina, you need to understand… Even with these results, the Abuelas can still demand more DNA from David in the future."

"How? How can they do that?"

"Easy," Giovanna said. "They'll claim that these results are fake."

Nina stared. "No, they wouldn't."

"Think about it. They're accusing you of faking a birth certificate. How hard would it be for them to convince a judge that you also bribed a doctor to fake DNA results for you? The Abuelas have the courts wrapped around their fingers."

"They can't accuse me forever."

"You have a loving son and a happy marriage," Giovanna said. "You live in a stable country. Go home, Nina. Count your blessings."

Giovanna slid the envelope across the table to Nina. Nina took it, feeling the last of her excitement evaporate.

"You'll never see justice in Argentina," Giovanna said.

———

Nina left the restaurant and started walking. It was a soft Buenos Aires night, and the familiar streets were full of people patronizing the restaurants, upscale boutiques, and antique shops. She walked down the long Avenida Alvear, admiring the demi-palaces built in the French architectural style so favored by President Marcelo T. de Alvear, a well-known Francophile now seventy years dead.

She and Giovanna had ordered their meal and eaten it without any further mention of the Abuelas or the DNA. The envelope on Nina's lap had grown less weighty as she and her friend had reminisced about childhood memories, laughing at events they'd thought they'd long forgotten. She remembered the other envelope of her childhood: the one containing her important exam results. That had turned out all right too.

The sky darkened. The air smelled like rain. Nina hurried along, drawing her coat tightly around herself.

As she passed an antique shop, she spotted a picture of Evita in an elaborate gilt frame. Evita wore a white camellia in her lapel and smiled serenely into the distance. Nina had owned that very same picture, only hers had been dedicated specially to her. She'd lost it long ago when Jorge Varela had taken her most treasured childhood possession away from her. Now he was trying to take her son.

Nina stared at the picture and Evita stared back, calm and brave as ever. *Let it go.* There had been injustice in Nina's life, but injustice had haunted Evita too. *Let it go.* She couldn't let Jorge Varela drag her down. She could be stronger than that.

By the time she reached the Palacio Duhau hotel, Nina was cold all the way through. She sat near the fireplace in her suite with the results of the DNA test resting so lightly in her lap.

What did this mean to her family? Very little, she admitted to herself. Her family already believed her. They hadn't demanded proof, because they didn't need it. David was her son; he loved her as his mother. And she was so proud of him: he had grown into a fine young man. It didn't matter whether Nina had these results or not. Her life wouldn't be any different either way.

The Abuelas were greedy for proof against their suspects, even proof in the form of anonymous letters. They wouldn't stop accusing and harassing everyone they received evidence against. They certainly weren't going to stop just because Nina wished it. The paranoia the military used against their daughters now fueled the hunt for the many missing grandchildren. The same paranoia drove Nina's own anger against the Abuelas.

Nina looked around the luxurious hotel suite, filled with beautiful art and furniture. One phone call would bring room service running to supply her with anything she desired, all easily paid for. Back in America, a loving husband waited for her. She had a good house in a good location. Better yet, she had two children who accepted and loved her. She even had a grandchild now.

Nina knew she was fortunate, especially when she thought about the many people she knew who were suffering. The ones she suspected of writing letters against her were suffering most of all. Jorge Varela had suffered several heart attacks in recent years; his wife had arthritis so severe that she'd had several hip surgeries and now walked with a limp. José and Lucia's financial troubles had grown so dire that Lucia had contacted Nina to ask for money. A distant family member had been in a car accident and needed extended rehabilitation. Another had divorced and could no longer afford to visit his children.

Any or all of these people might have set out to hurt Nina, but now they themselves were hurting. They couldn't cause Nina pain unless she let them.

Nina turned the envelope over in her hands. She already knew the results. She didn't need to look at them. The people whose opinions mattered in her life knew the results as well. Their belief in Nina didn't depend on a piece of paper. Nothing could change it.

Nina smiled. She'd thought these results would bring her security. Now she realized that she'd always been safe. She had nothing to prove.

Nina walked over to the fireplace and tossed the envelope into the fire. It was so light, so insubstantial. It curled like a dry leaf in the flames and quickly burned to nothing as she watched.

Suddenly invigorated, Nina hurried to her luggage, gathered the accusatory letters in handfuls, and flung them into the fire as well. They too were insubstantial—nothing but the shadows of bitterness and anger. Mere hatred was powerless to hurt her. None of her enemies could control her anymore.

———

Nina watched the letters burn until nothing remained of them but ash. Her anxiety had lifted; her euphoria had died down. Now she felt what had lain underneath it all: her love for her family. They were all she wanted. They would come with her into a golden future.

The bright red embers faded slowly. Gazing at them, Nina knew she could never return to Argentina. Her heart had found another home.